MW01378647

THE SOLDIER'S ANGUISH

The Soldier's Anguish

Pete Biehl

The Soldier's Anguish – First hardcover edition December 2024

Cover Art by Joseph Gruber

Map made with Inkarnate

www.petebiehl.com

For Mercedes,
Always my number one fan!

Books by Pete Biehl

The Rawl Wielder Trilogy
The Path of the Rawl Wielder
The Throne of Thornata
The Hoyt War

The Imperial Soldier Trilogy
The Soldier's Burden
The Soldier's Anguish

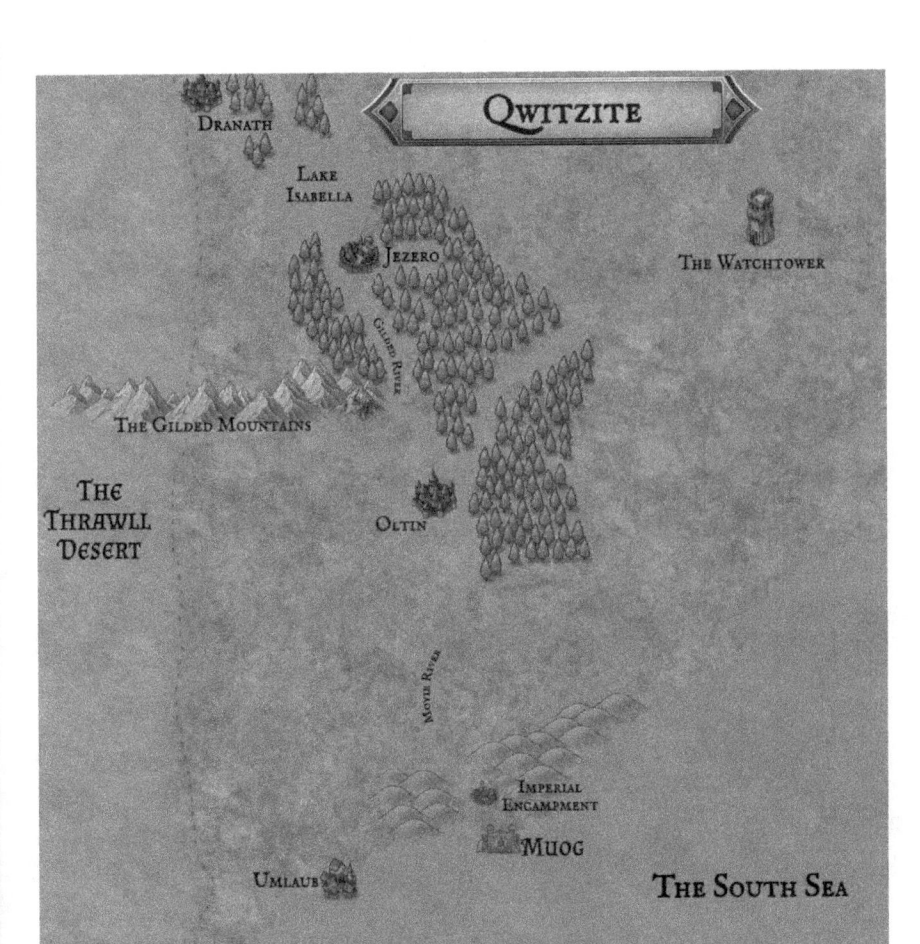

Chapter One

The thoughts running through Captain Thaddeus Dunstan's mind were nearly as dark as the starless night sky above him as he continued his search in vain. For the past two nights, he had crept out into the neutral territory separating the Imperial Army encampment and the dwarven capital city of Muog. From dusk to dawn, he had paced back and forth, desperately searching for any trace of the concealed tunnels the dwarves had been using to launch their relentless attacks against the Imperial camp. He turned over every stone, dug through the base of every bush of sagebrush, and raked his fingers endlessly through any patch of dirt that appeared to be even slightly miscolored. Thus far, his search had borne him no fruit, and with each passing hour, his spirits sunk deeper and deeper into the depths of despair. As the hours passed, he had become increasingly reckless in his efforts, taking fewer precautions to conceal his presence. If he was caught in the act, he could expect to be relieved of duty and likely thrown into the stockade, but he didn't care. Those captured men were depending on him, even if they didn't know it. He was their sole hope of freedom and of escaping Muog with their lives.

The previous day had passed with no word from the dwarven city, but the silence brought Dunstan little comfort. Initially, the lack of executions occurring on Muog's walls had brought him hope. He had thought it possible that the captured Imperial soldiers had managed to escape Muog, but there was still no sign of them in the camp. He didn't know what was causing the delay in the executions Odpor had promised, but until he saw evidence otherwise, he had no choice but to assume the soldiers were still captives within Muog. He would continue to search until there was a definitive sign they had escaped or the dwarves had killed all of them. Thaddeus Dunstan would never give up on those men, his orders be damned.

His disgust with the utter disregard Supreme General Cadmus Twilcox showed toward the captured soldiers intensified with each hour of his futile search. The Imperial Army he had joined as a much younger man would never have left thirteen men to die with no attempt at a rescue, or so Dunstan chose to believe. Twilcox had been content to send General Alexander Sylvester to negotiate for their release, negotiations which had been unsuccessful thus far.

Of course they've been unsuccessful; Twilcox has been unwilling to negotiate in good faith. The dwarves will never release those men without Twilcox making meaningful concessions. The negotiations have been approved for optics, nothing more.

At least Sylvester had courage enough to enter the dwarven city and try to negotiate the soldiers' release. Dunstan respected the man for that. But the dwarf chieftain, Odpor, did not have the reputation of a man who would be willing to make concessions under any circumstance. If the Imperial Army did not withdraw from Qwitzite, Dunstan suspected that Odpor would make good on his threat to kill every last one of the thirteen captured soldiers.

Twelve now, he reminded himself. Odpor had already done so once, and there was no reason to suspect he would not do so again. Furthermore, Dunstan believed Odpor would enjoy every second of doing it, relishing the waves of despair he was sending through the Imperial camp with each death.

Frustrated by Imperial High Command's lack of action, Dunstan had decided to take matters into his own hands. Determined to attempt a rescue on his own, he had set about trying to find a way into Muog by himself. The dwarven capital city was surrounded by walls that reached two hundred feet into the air, and Dunstan knew he stood no chance of getting close to those walls without being spotted by the sentries above, let alone up and over them. So instead, he had set about searching for a way beneath them. He knew tunnels existed; they were common knowledge within the encampment. The dwarves had used them to devastating effect in their many guerilla-style assaults against the Imperials. Unfortunately, the dwarves had proven to be as equally skilled at concealing the tunnels as they were at utilizing them.

Standing alone in the middle of the barren plain, Dunstan knew how unlikely it was for him to find one of the tunnels. It was not as though the Imperial Army had made no effort to locate them before. The best scouts and trackers the Imperial Army had to offer had spent months scouring the neutral territory and the surroundings of the encampment repeatedly to no avail. The dwarves were known as the best miners and craftsmen in the Empire, and if they didn't want their tunnels found, they knew how to ensure they weren't. Dunstan had no particular experience in such fields, but he still could not sit back and do nothing but wait for his men to die.

Forcing his drooping eyelids open, he continued his search. He had hardly slept in days but would not be deterred. If he was doomed to fail those men, it would not be due to a lack of effort.

As the night wore on, Dunstan couldn't help but sink deeper into his despair. Each search that came up empty left him with a hollow, empty feeling in his stomach. But he would not give up—not as the rest of the army seemed content to do. He had to keep fighting for those men; he was all they had. Thaddeus Dunstan had made his share of mistakes throughout his lengthy military career, but giving up on his men had never been one of them.

Dunstan was no fool. He understood perfectly well that even if he found one of the hidden passageways into Muog, his chances of freeing the captive soldiers were minuscule at best. He knew virtually nothing about the layout of the dwarven city, and he had no idea where to begin looking. All of this was in addition to the fact that he would visibly stand out inside the walls of Muog, for he was clearly no dwarf. He would be spotted easily from a distance and probably end up dying alongside the captured soldiers. It didn't matter to him. Somebody had to at least try to do something.

"Captain Dunstan?"

The voice came as a shock to Thad Dunstan, who spun toward the source, his hand immediately snapping to the pommel of his sword. If someone had noticed him slipping off into the neutral territory without proper authorization, he would almost certainly spend the rest of his life rotting away in a stockade. With his prior offenses in Thornata, nobody would be much interested in his explanations or good intentions.

Squinting through the darkness for the source of the voice, he was shocked to find not an Imperial soldier but a dwarf standing before him, heavily armored and carrying a large mace on his back. He drew his sword, taking a few careful steps away from the dwarf before assuming a defensive posture. He could ill afford to get into a prolonged fight with this dwarf. The sound of clashing weapons was bound to draw unwanted attention from the nearby camp. He would have to finish his foe quickly if he wanted to have the opportunity to continue his search.

"Please, Captain Dunstan, lower your weapon. I assure you I mean you no harm. I have come to seek your assistance. If you are willing to hear me out, I can lead you to your captured soldiers. You are Captain Thad Dunstan, are you not?" The dwarf threw his arms out wide, making no move to reach for the mace.

Did this dwarf believe him to be stupid? Did he think that merely knowing Dunstan's name would be enough to earn his trust? He remained in his defensive posture and made no move to sheathe his sword. It was hard to make out the dwarf's features in the dark, impossible to examine his facial expression. All he could make out was the red hue of what appeared to be closely cropped hair and a beard. As far as he could tell, the dwarf was alone, but there was always the chance that more were lurking nearby. Better to let his attacker come to him rather than stepping into a potential trap.

"Captain Dunstan, I understand your mistrust. But we are wasting time, and your men do not have much of it to spare. My name is Radig. I helped your men escape from a prison in Muog, but Odpor's men found us before I could get them out of the city. Odpor will not want to take any chances this time. I am certain all your remaining men will be executed at dawn, which is only a few short hours away. You must trust me if you want to have any hope of saving them. That is why you are out here by yourself, is it not? I cannot think of any other reason an Imperial captain would be wandering around the neutral territory in the dead of night."

"Why should I believe you? Why would you set my men free in the first place? You are spinning quite the tale, Radig, assuming that is, in fact, your name," Dunstan said, still not trusting a word of it. This had to be some elaborate trap. Why would a dwarf want to help him rescue his men?

"Not all dwarves are beholden to Odpor's dreams of secession, Captain Dunstan. Some of us understand withdrawing from the Empire is not a positive thing for all of the people of Qwitzite. How would such a move benefit the common people? All it has brought us thus far is war and death. We do not wish to see most of our brothers and sisters suffer for the sake of stroking Odpor's stubborn pride. Qwitzite will burn for his desire to see himself as a king. But this is not the time nor the place for a political discussion. We need to hurry; you do not have many men left to save. You will not have any if we do not get moving at once."

"What do you mean by that? There should still be a dozen men.

There was no execution yesterday. Odpor would not have killed more without announcing it. He clearly loves to put on a show."

"There was no execution because I set your men free before it could take place. But their absence was discovered before I could lead them safely out of Muog. So, I took them to the headquarters of the Resistance. But Odpor's men found us before we could plot an escape. We came under attack a few hours ago. Many of your men were killed in the struggle. I managed to escape through a secret passage once I could see the battle was lost. I saw them taking four of your men out of the headquarters, along with one Resistance dwarf. I overheard their leader, a rather sadistic dwarf named Krillzoc, gloating about executing them at dawn. We only have a few hours left, Captain Dunstan. I sought you out because I cannot hope to free them by myself, and I have nowhere else to turn."

Some of Radig's story almost made sense. It was a valid explanation for why there had been no execution the morning before. He had never heard of this Dwarven Resistance Radig claimed to represent, though admittedly, Imperial intelligence from inside Muog was limited at best. But even if this tale of a Dwarven Resistance was true, why had they placed themselves at risk to save the lives of Imperial soldiers? It seemed like a ridiculous risk to take, one that could jeopardize everything they were fighting to achieve. Why did Radig need his help? Why could he not turn to fellow Resistance dwarves if he was so desperate to free the soldiers?

"I have questions. How do you know my name? Let's start with that, Radig."

"I overheard your men talking about you a few hours ago. Private Tor believes you to be an honorable and trustworthy man; he said as much to Sergeant Stark. His word is all I have to go on, but it is a chance I am willing to take. I need help, so I slipped into your encampment and found your tent. Toward the northern end of the captains' row, is it not? The security of your encampment leaves much to be desired. When you were not there, I made to return to Muog to attempt this rescue on my own, but

I spotted you in the distance. I did not know your identity for certain, but I surmised that no other captain would be out here in the neutral territory in the middle of the night. Am I correct to assume you are searching for tunnels into Muog? You will never find them without my help, though you must know this."

"Why me? Why do you need my help? Why not ask your fellow Resistance dwarves to help you? You make it sound as though this Dwarven Resistance is a sizeable force. Why would you risk your life by sneaking into an Imperial Army camp to look for me? You must realize if you had been wrong about my identity, you would likely be dead already."

"It is simple, Captain Dunstan. I do not know how Krillzoc discovered our headquarters. We have been based in the same location for close to a year. I can only assume some of my fellow Resistance fighters have been discovered and tortured into giving up the location. It is possible that more Resistance dwarves inside Muog are being watched and that Odpor suspects I will do precisely what you suggest. There is no way for me to know which of my fellow dwarves I can trust. You are a potential ally, one who I know is not being watched. You are the only one I can trust will not betray me to Odpor. I know exactly where your loyalties lie. We need each other."

Radig was saying all the right things, but the matter still didn't sit right with Dunstan. It still felt like a trap. A dwarf appearing in the middle of the night and offering to help him save his men? It was too good to be true. Still, what would be the purpose of such a plot? He was only an Imperial captain, and not a well-regarded one by any means. If the dwarves were trying to ensnare a high-value captive, they could do far better. Only a few minutes earlier, he would have loved for a mysterious stranger to appear from thin air and offer him a solution. Now that it was happening, he was deeply mistrustful. Was he willing to place his trust in the hands of this dwarf who had appeared out of nowhere?

"Why do you care about my men, Radig? Why would you risk your life to free them before and then again now? What is in this for you?"

"I set your men free the first time for a simple reason: I wanted to make Odpor look incompetent in the eyes of his people. The more dwarves who see how inept his leadership truly is, the more will flock to our cause of overthrowing him. Now, as I have said, a Resistance dwarf has also been captured. I will not abandon one of my fellow fighters. We are wasting time, Captain Dunstan. If you will not assist me, I must take my leave. I will return to Muog and try this rescue on my own. I will most likely die in the attempt, but at least I will die with a clear conscience, knowing I did all I could. If you can return to your tent and fall asleep knowing you passed up this opportunity, maybe that is what you should do. If not, you need to come with me now. What will it be?"

"What's your plan? I want to know exactly what you are proposing we should do."

"We will slip back into Muog via the tunnel I used to get into your camp. I have already eliminated the sentries. If we hurry, their bodies will not have been discovered yet. I do not know where Odpor's men have taken your men to await execution. Odpor has almost certainly not returned them to the main prison complex; he will take no chances of me freeing them again. But I do know they will be executed on top of the outer wall for your whole camp to see. Odpor will not miss an opportunity to make such a statement. He has always loved his theatrics, and that predictability works to our benefit. We will lie in wait nearby and ambush the guards while the prisoners are being transported. A direct assault is far from ideal, but it is the best chance we will get. There is no time to plan anything more elaborate."

"You plan to do this with just the two of us? How many guards will be transporting them?" Dunstan was skeptical.

"After their last escape, I imagine at least a dozen, if not more. There will be countless others nearby, ready to rush to their aid. I never claimed to have an easy solution, Captain Dunstan. It is entirely possible that we will fail and the pair of us will die in the attempt; I have never pretended otherwise. If we are lucky, your men or my fellow Resistance dwarf may be able to get ahold of weapons in the confusion and help us fight off the guards."

"You're being quite optimistic about our chances as far as I can tell, Radig. But let's be generous and assume we succeed. We kill the guards and free all of the prisoners. Then what? As soon as we make our move, the city will be locked down, just as you say it was after the first time you freed them. You weren't able to hide them last time. What makes you think things will be any different this time around?"

Radig paused this time, his head hanging low. Dunstan could still not make out much of his facial expression in the dark but thought the gesture might be a sign of shame.

Radig sighed deeply. "I made a critical error, Captain Dunstan. I told too many of my fellow Resistance fighters of my plans. I took your men to our main headquarters, a place every Resistance dwarf was aware of. I was overconfident. Several of my friends are now dead because of it, and another will be at dawn if we do not act, along with the rest of your men. I have learned from my mistakes and do not wish to see more of my fellows die. Nobody knows I have come here. Nobody within the Resistance even knows I survived the attack on our headquarters. There will be nobody for Krillzoc to torture our whereabouts out of this time. I understand your need for assurances, but I have given you all I can. We are running out of time. Dawn will be upon us in about three hours, and our trek through Muog must be slow and cautious. As you can imagine, you will be difficult to conceal in a city of dwarves. We need to be in place before morning comes and there are dwarves out in the streets. What do you say, Captain Dunstan? Will you come with me or not? Decide now. There is no more time to waste."

Ever since he'd begun his military career at the age of eighteen, Thaddeus Dunstan had prided himself on always doing what he believed to be right. His actions had not always been in line with what Imperial High Command considered to be appropriate, but he regretted none of them, even the business in Thornata. If Radig was lying, he would be dead within hours. But it didn't feel right. For some reason he could not quite place, he trusted the dwarf. Such an elaborate plot to capture a single officer didn't make sense. He had always trusted his instincts in the past. Doing so had gotten him into trouble on numerous occasions but had also helped to keep his conscience clean.

There was no promise of success with the plan Radig was proposing, and he understood this. It was just as likely that he would end up being thrown from the wall himself as it was that they would succeed. Still, did he have a choice? If he turned his back on this opportunity and watched those men go off the side of the wall the next morning, it would haunt him until his dying day. He had lived a long life. Those young men deserved a chance to see another day. If that meant he had to risk his few remaining years to give them that chance, then so be it.

"Very well, Radig. Let's do this. Let's get them out of there."

Chapter Two

T he pain was the first sensation to return to Private Darian Tor as he began to regain consciousness. It was a dull throbbing pain originating in the side of his head and radiating throughout the entirety of his upper body. Even the simple act of forcing his eyes to open caused the pain to intensify, and he had to blink through tears to take in his surroundings. What he saw triggered a flood of memories, none of them pleasant. Within seconds, he found himself wishing he could drift back into the void of unconsciousness.

The dwarf Kalayo was the first one he saw, sitting with her back against a brick wall. She didn't meet his eyes as he looked at her. She merely continued staring stoically off into space, apparently lost in her own thoughts. Max Preston was seated a few feet to her right. He also didn't notice that Darian had awakened, his eyes cast downward toward the floor, his shoulders slumped in apparent defeat. Darian became aware of a set of feet pacing anxiously behind him and assumed it must be Berj Jenson, who had never been one to take anything sitting down. He couldn't see Darnold Dans from where he was lying, but it was Darnold who finally noticed him stirring.

"Darian! You're awake. You've had us all worried. We were beginning to think you might never come around. Don't try to move too much; just take it slow. You took one hell of a hit to the head, just in case you can't remember."

Yes, it was the last thing he could remember. Krillzoc had taken great pleasure in delivering that blow. His cruel sneer was still burned into Darian's mind. But it was what Krillzoc had done before striking him that was bringing uncontrollable tears to Darian's eyes, tears he was already trying desperately to conceal from his friends. The images of the life fading from Axel's body as Krillzoc's sword plunged through his chest, and then his lifeless body collapsing like a straw doll being tossed to the ground. Axel had surrendered to Krillzoc in a last desperate attempt to keep them alive and had paid for it with his own life. Darian's oldest, best friend, gone in an instant for no reason at all.

"Oh, good. He's awake. I'm sure he wouldn't want to miss whatever is in store for us next," came the shockingly bitter voice of Berj Jenson from behind him. Darian had never heard the eternal optimist sound so defeated.

"Where are we?" Darian asked, finding that even the simple act of speaking intensified his pain. To his own ears, his voice sounded foreign, as though a stranger were using his mouth to speak.

"Beats me," Darnold said. "Another prison, but not the one we already escaped. I guess they didn't want to test their luck twice. As far as we know, we're all that's left. The other soldiers, Radig, the rest of the Resistance dwarves—they're all gone. Krillzoc gloated about everyone else being dead as they dragged us out of there. I wouldn't trust his word about most things, but he does seem to genuinely enjoy death and suffering. And if there were more prisoners, I assume they would be held with us. Your pulse has been faint. We weren't sure if you would ever wake up."

"Well, here I am. I'm a little surprised myself. I wouldn't think Krillzoc would be too happy with me after I tried so hard to kill him. Once he had me beaten, I figured I was as good as dead."

"Quite the opposite. He seemed downright delighted when he discovered you survived the blow," Berj said. "I think he's happy to have the chance to publicly kill as many of us as possible. After all, it's far more fun for him if we die while being publicly humiliated in front of our entire encampment, isn't it?"

"You don't know that, Berj. General Sylvester might still be able to negotiate our release. Don't give up yet," Max Preston said, speaking up for the first time. His words were optimistic, but his tone of voice did not match them, and his gaze never left the floor at his feet.

Darian forced himself up into a sitting position, the effort nearly causing him to lose consciousness again. Darnold placed a steadying hand on his shoulder, keeping him from slumping back to the ground. The room spun for several long seconds before finally coming into focus once more. It was a room similar to the previous cell they had been held in but much smaller. There had been more of them last time. Their captors had executed one soldier, Private Lester, shortly after their capture. The others must have died in the battle in the Resistance's headquarters, along with Radig and his comrades. It was all coming back to him now, the sight of bodies in Imperial garb strewn across the floor. They were all that was left, four of the thirteen who had left the Imperial encampment, plus Kalayo.

Darian noted a lit torch in the corner of the cell, an irregularity in Muog from his experience. The light, something so simple and that might have once filled him with hope, caused a sensation of dread to wash over him. The torch was no act of kindness by their captors—he knew better than that. Krillzoc must've wanted them to see the utter hopelessness of their situation. There was a single door made of thick iron, and it appeared entirely impenetrable. Apart from that, the room was unremarkable and delivered little hope to Darian. He tried to find his feet but was immediately met with shock waves of pain radiating through his legs, a cruel reminder of the wounds he had taken during the battle.

The single iron door swung open without warning, immediately filling the room with a sense of foreboding. Krillzoc strolled into the cell as though he had not a care in the world, flanked by three heavily armed dwarven fighters. He shot a wink at Darian as he strode into the cell, smirking the same merciless smile he had flashed as he murdered Axel Stark. For a fleeting moment, Darian wondered if he could get his hands around the hated dwarf's throat. He knew he would die in the attempt, that it would accomplish nothing, but at the moment, he did not much care. If he were able to find his legs, he probably would have acted, no matter how foolish such an act would have been.

"Ah, I am glad to find you all awake and alert. It is nice that you have a chance to spend this quality time in the company of friends. I hope you savor every second of it, because to be perfectly clear, you do not have many remaining," Krillzoc announced.

"What do you want, Krillzoc?" Kalayo asked. It was the first time she had spoken; in her silence, Darian had nearly forgotten she was with them.

"You have some nerve opening your mouth to me, you filthy traitor. You should be counting your blessings right now. If we had not already tortured all the information we needed about your pathetic excuse of a resistance out of your friends, you would be having a much more unpleasant evening. The quick death you will soon receive is far better than you deserve. Fear not, Kalayo; you will soon join dear Radig in the great beyond. Chieftain Odpor asked me to inform you that all of you are scheduled to be executed at dawn. You will be hanged from the walls in view of your Imperial encampment to serve as a reminder of what happens when your kind dare to enter our city. This traitor will swing beside you. Still, I feel you should always look for the bright side. I am sure the vultures will be grateful for your sacrifice. They have had precious little to nibble on since I shoved that last piece of Imperial scum off the wall."

Krillzoc was trying to make them angry, and it was working. Undoubtedly, he wanted one of them to attack, to give him an excuse to torture them one last time. Darian refused to meet his eyes, knowing if he did he was likely to launch himself at the dwarf despite the horrible pain in his head and legs. He would not give Krillzoc the satisfaction of knowing his taunts were working.

"Well, I will take my leave, my friends. I have a lot of work tonight, nooses to measure and such. It is an art form, you know. You cannot make the rope too long; otherwise, your necks will snap, and you will die instantly. We cannot have that, can we? After all, we have to put on a show for your fellow soldiers; they have had precious little to amuse them of late. Of course, if I were to make them really long, you may even be decapitated by the force of the fall; that has happened once or twice. It is a rather horrific sight, though a good one for your fellow soldiers to witness. But Chieftain Odpor wants to leave you swinging for the vultures for a few days. If I get the nooses measured just right, you will thrash and twitch for quite a while after you drop. It should send quite a message to the Imperial Army, don't you agree? Oh, listen to me rambling on about my duties. I must be boring you all. I must be going, but fear not. I will be back to collect you in just a few hours!"

With that, Krillzoc was gone, the iron door clattering shut behind him. Darian remembered how real his own mortality had felt that day Krillzoc had led them up onto the wall for one of them to die. It was a more intense feeling than he had ever felt in the heat of battle. At least in a fight there was no time to dwell on the possibility that your end could be only seconds away. Now he knew it to be so, that in just a few hours, he would be dead, dangling by his neck from the end of a rope, his body food for the vultures.

"Don't listen to Krillzoc. We're still alive. As long as there is life, there is hope. Maybe we can get ahold of one of their weapons while they are transporting us," Darnold said, trying his best to lift their spirits.

"Don't kid yourself, Darnold. Our best chance to get away was back in those headquarters. We should have kept fighting. I don't know what Axel was thinking, surrendering. He must have realized what would happen if we gave up. How could he have been so stupid?" Berj exclaimed.

Darian was hardly aware that the strength had finally returned to his legs. The insult had barely left Berj's mouth, and Darian was on his feet. Berj's eyes widened in surprise at the sight of him climbing to his feet. The expression of shock only intensified when Darian punched him in the face. Berj stumbled backward from the blow, and Darian staggered after him, hitting him again. Berj swung back wildly, struggling to regain his balance, but missed. Darian crashed into him, dragging him to the stone floor, his fists hammering downward repeatedly. Several shots missed the mark, his hands crashing painfully into the stone floor instead, but he paid the pain no mind. It would be gone soon enough.

Darian didn't know how many times he managed to punch Berj before Darnold and Preston grabbed ahold of him, dragging him back across the cell. In his rage, he felt that no number would be high enough for the insult Berj had uttered toward Axel. Berj surged back to his feet, roaring in fury, one eye already swelling shut and blood dripping from his nose. He flew toward Darian, who was still struggling to free himself from Darnold and Preston. Kalayo met him halfway across the cell, diving into his legs, catching him just below the knees, and driving him back into the ground.

Berj cried out in anger, once again trying to climb to his feet. But Kalayo had other ideas, somehow scrambling behind him faster than the blink of an eye. Before Berj knew what was happening, she had one forearm pressed firmly to his throat, her hands clasping each other, with her other arm pressing hard into Berj's back. Every time Berj struggled to move, he only pushed himself tighter into her choke hold.

"Will you stop struggling, you blabbering idiot?" she hissed. "You had that beating coming to you, so get over it. Next time, keep your stupid mouth shut. Can you two get him under control already?"

"Darian, calm down; it's over. We can't fight one another, not now.

We have to stick together," Preston was saying into his ear.

Darian did not much feel like calming down but was forced to accept that his body could not keep fighting. The surge of energy was fading fast, his arms and legs going limp. A moist feeling on his leg told him at least one of his wounds had reopened during the scuffle, and he finally allowed himself to relax. Darnold and Preston cautiously released him but did not move far, clearly concerned he may decide to launch himself at Berj again. He would have loved to, but he had no more strength to spend. Across the small room, Berj seemed to accept that he would not be escaping Kalayo's choke hold, just as his face began to turn a deep shade of purple.

"Axel did what he did because he thought it would give us the best chance of surviving, Berj," Darian spat, venom dripping from every word. "If we do somehow survive this, don't you ever let me hear you disrespect him like that again. I swear I'll rip your tongue out of your fat mouth if I do."

Berj looked for a moment as though he would love to throw back a snappy retort, but as Kalayo tightened her grip again, he seemed incapable of speaking. Seemingly realizing he couldn't escape, he relaxed. He slumped over, and Kalayo cautiously released him. The stubborn young soldier stared at the ground in silence for a minute. When his head came up, every one of his companions was shocked to find tears streaming down his face. They had never seen Berj cry, even after the brutal torture Krillzoc had subjected them to during their last captivity.

"I'm so sorry, Darian. You're right, Kalayo; I did have that coming to me. I'm such an ass. Axel was a hero, and he had more of a spine than any of us could ever dream of having. I'm scared, you guys. I don't want to die here. I lashed out at Axel because I wish he were here with us. He would have a plan, something we could at least try to get out of this hopeless mess. I can't stand this, sitting here with no hope, waiting to choke to death at the end of a damn rope while the whole camp gawks at us. We spent all those months with that miserable old bastard Harter Arsch, and he never taught us anything to prepare us for this. It's not fair; why did they even send us on this mission?"

Even in his anger, it was disconcerting for Darian to see Berj, usually so confident, break down like this. He had always been the rock among their foursome, and nothing could ever get Berj down.

Maybe there truly is no hope for us, Darian thought. *Perhaps we should just sit back and await the inevitable.* But that didn't feel right. Axel Stark had died trying to give them their best chance of survival. To willingly wait for the final blow to fall felt like an insult to the memory of his dearest friend. He would not give in—not until the very last breath left his body.

"It's okay, Berj. I understand what you're feeling; I think we all do. I'm sorry, I shouldn't have hit you," Darian said. While he still felt deep inside that Berj had deserved what he had gotten, he knew he needed to bring his friends together. If they were to have any hope at all, they needed to unite. Even if the dawn brought their death, better for them to face it united.

"No, Kalayo was right. I deserved it. Nice choke hold, by the way. If we live another day, can you teach me how to do that?"

The dwarven woman simply rolled her eyes and turned away from him with a snort.

"So, what should we do?" Darnold asked. "I assume we're all in agreement that we should not accept our fate lying down."

"Maybe we can rush them when they open the cell door. If we can get ahold of one sword, we have a chance to get more. Most likely, they'll kill us all right here in this cell. But if not, maybe we can fight our way out of wherever we are," Preston suggested. "At least we can die in a fight, not as a prop for Odpor to use to terrorize the rest of the army."

"I do not believe that would be a wise decision," Kalayo said.

The four soldiers turned to her. Darian was surprised she had spoken up. She had said relatively little to them in the brief time they had known one another. If anything, she had seemed irritated when Radig brought them back to the Resistance's headquarters, though she had shown them no open hostility, unlike some of the others. But now she was caught up in this mess with them. Kalayo knew more about what they were up against than any of them. Hopefully she would have valuable input.

"Then what do you suggest we do, Kalayo? You know more about this city and our enemies than all of us combined," Darian said.

She did not answer right away. Instead, she rose and moved over to the iron door, pressing her ear against it. She stood silently for a long moment, listening, though what she hoped to hear, they could not guess. Seemingly satisfied by what she'd heard, she turned back to them.

"I needed to be certain there were no guards within earshot. There are not. If they could hear us, I would be able to hear them," she explained, her voice low.

"Well, that's nice, but what exactly are we worried about them overhearing?" Berj asked. "So far, we have come up with nothing that's likely to be all that dangerous for them. If we are going to die in a final act of defiance, I'm all for it, but let's just call it what it is. They're sure to expect us to try something."

"Everyone in that safe house who is not sitting here was killed in the battle last night. Except for one."

"What do you mean? I was conscious the whole time; only the people in this cell were still alive in that building," Darnold pointed out. "Maybe a few of the others were still just clinging to life, but it wouldn't have taken long for them to bleed out. No on appeared to be treatable, and I doubt Krillzoc would have expended the effort anyway."

"Radig was not killed in the battle. I searched for his body very carefully before they took us out of the house. It was a mess and hard to make out everybody amid the bloodshed, but he was not there. I am sure of it. I would have seen his red hair among the bodies."

Darian thought back to the battle, struggling to remember through the throbbing ache in his head. Before he had charged at Krillzoc in a frenzy, he was confident that only Berj, Darnold, Preston, and Kalayo were still standing. If Radig were not dead, would he not have been standing alongside the rest of them? Even if the resourceful dwarf were somehow still alive, could he be of any help to them now? He had broken them out of one prison, but Odpor was aware of that treachery now. He would not be able to get close to them again.

"If Radig isn't dead, then where is he?" Preston asked.

"I can only assume once he saw the battle was a lost cause, he escaped through one of our alternate entrances. Amid the chaos, Krillzoc would not have noticed; his focus was on recapturing you Imperials. I was observing him closely when he was in here. When he mentioned Radig being dead, his face twitched, and there was a change in his tone. I think he was lying."

"Wait, escaping was an option? Why didn't we do that when Krillzoc started smashing down the door in the first place?" Berj demanded furiously.

"It was not an option for you. Remember that our buildings were not designed with your larger statures in mind. You would never have been able to escape through one of our escape tunnels. They are tight even for us, and you barely fit through the main door. I do not doubt that Radig is alive and searching for a way to free us as we speak," Kalayo explained.

"How can you be so sure? Even if he did escape, what makes you think he will come for us? I'm sure you Resistance dwarves are loyal, but do you really think he will risk his skin against such impossible odds to try to save you? He might be hiding and counting his blessings to still have his life. I couldn't blame him if he was," Berj said.

"Radig is not simply a fellow Resistance dwarf. He is my husband. He will not abandon me, even if that would be the smart choice to make. He will try to rescue us, even if he dies doing so."

Darian was unsure what explanation he had been expecting, but it wasn't that. Radig had not revealed the nature of his relationship with

Kalayo. But he also had not told them much of anything else about himself either. But even if he did try to save them, what could he possibly hope to accomplish on his own? He had proven resourceful in freeing them from their last prison, but this seemed to be a much taller order.

"Fair enough, though it would have been nice to know that earlier," Berj said. "But even if he tries, do you think he has a chance?"

"Radig has been deep undercover, serving in Odpor's inner circle. He knows more about their movements and methods than anyone. If anyone has a chance to help us, it is Radig."

"So, I think I see where you're going with this, and I don't much like it. Are you suggesting we allow them to take us out of here for execution and hope you are right?" Darnold asked. "What if you aren't? What if we get out there and there is no help coming after all?"

"We will have the same chances of getting ahold of one of their weapons out there as we would in here—that is to say, not very high. Radig could come with more Resistance dwarves, enough to kill the guards and set us free. Think it through carefully, Imperial soldiers. I have no more desire to die at the end of a noose than you do. But we have a chance, small though it may be. Do not be so quick to throw your lives away in this cell when there is a better option."

Darian and his friends exchanged glances. It was clear none of them wanted to be the first to speak. It was tempting to accept Kalayo's suggestion. The idea that somebody could be coming to save them was an enticing one, and Darian longed to believe it. The thought that a suicidal rush at the guards was not their only hope was encouraging. They would need help. He was still feeling the effects of his wounds from the night before, and the rest of them probably were as well. But what if Kalayo was wrong about this? What if Radig was dead after all? What if they'd captured him after he'd fled the headquarters? There was so much information they did not have, information they needed to make this decision.

"It's a tempting thought, but I don't know," Darnold said, turning to his comrades. "What do the rest of you think?"

"Can I ask something, Kalayo?" Berj asked. "And to be clear, I'm not being a jerk here, so please don't strangle me again. But if Radig is your husband, why did he make a run for it and leave you behind?"

Kalayo didn't answer right away. It was something Darian had wondered as well. At the least, one would think Radig would have tried to take his wife with him on his escape. It was one thing to leave the rest of them behind. He had already broken them free of one prison; he owed them nothing. But his own wife?

"You might not understand, but I will try to explain. We vowed long ago that we would do whatever is necessary to overthrow Odpor. We are both willing to give our lives for this cause, and we have been united in this for years. But Radig is so important. He is a leader, the only one the Resistance has here in Muog. You saw it for yourselves, the way some of our companions behaved in the safe house. They are good people, but there is not a leader among them, someone willing to make difficult choices. I made him promise me that if we ever found ourselves in a situation like last night and he had the opportunity to save himself, he would. I admit I do not know much about Imperials and your customs. But when a dwarf makes such a promise to their life partner, it must be kept, even when it goes against everything they want to do."

It was unthinkable to Darian, but he had to remind himself that these were dwarves. They were a different people who lived in their own way, according to their own customs. In the end, who was he to judge them? If Radig did end up saving them again, they would all be jumping for joy at the fact that he had abandoned them.

"I think we should listen to Kalayo," Darian said. "Axel died because he wanted to give us a chance. We shouldn't throw our lives away on something we all know won't work. Most of us can barely stand, let alone fight. We need help. Ever since we started this cursed mission, we've been reacting to one horrible circumstance after another. Maybe it's time we have a little faith that things will go right for us, just this once. If it doesn't, at least we won't have to worry about being let down anymore."

He didn't even know exactly how he had arrived at this conclusion. He understood there were no guarantees, no matter which option they chose. But Darian felt as though his entire term in the Imperial Army had been nothing but an endless struggle, and he was feeling the fatigue of that struggle now more than ever. His decision was made. Now all that remained was to persuade his friends that he was right.

Chapter Three

C aptain Thaddeus Dunstan held his breath repeatedly as he crept across the neutral territory, following closely behind the dwarf Radig. If caught out here without authorization an hour earlier, it would likely have meant the rest of his life in a military stockade. Now, accompanied by an enemy combatant, he would find himself at the end of a noose for treason before night could fall again.

They did not utter a word as they walked; Radig had made it clear they would be passing perilously close to the edge of the Imperial encampment. One wrong move when too close to a sentry would be the death of him, as well as the soldiers he sought to rescue.

Despite the silence, his mind was racing. He was still trying to make sense of what he had agreed to do. Going alone into Muog with a dwarf he had just met was an utterly ridiculous proposition. A few hours earlier he would have scoffed at any man who would suggest he might do such a thing. Yet here he was, trying to keep his eyes on Radig's back. Why was he doing this? Yes, he was determined to save the remaining captive soldiers, but that was not enough of an answer to soothe the lingering doubts hovering in the back of his mind.

Did he possess a death wish he was unaware of on a conscious level?

No, that didn't feel right.

If Twilcox weren't such a timid coward, I wouldn't need to do this on my own. A real commander would have mounted a proper rescue attempt days ago.

In his heart, Dunstan knew that to be the true reason for his decision. His frustration with the incompetence and indifference of Imperial High Command had finally reached its boiling point. Was that frustration making him reckless? It was a possibility, but in the end, his motivations were irrelevant. Those men imprisoned in Muog were all that mattered.

Radig led him along the edge of the Imperial encampment, coming to a stop less than a hundred yards from the nearest cluster of tents. *Their tunnels come this close to our camp, and we still couldn't find them. I don't know if that says more about their intelligence or our lack of it.* The dwarf motioned for him to keep watch on their surroundings, which Dunstan did, his eyes scanning for any sign of Imperial soldiers. It would only be a matter of time before a patrol swept through this area; Radig needed to hurry. The patrols weren't being sent out often, a concession by command that they were mostly ineffective against the guerilla-style attacks by the dwarves. Still, scarce though they may be, patrols were still passing through at least every hour. He glanced back every few seconds to see what Radig was doing.

The dwarf was digging hastily in the sand with his fingers. After a few furious minutes, he seemed to achieve what he wanted and frantically began motioning for Dunstan to join him. Dunstan watched in amazement as Radig's fingers worked their way into imperceptible grooves within the earth. How did he know exactly where to place his fingers? Once he seemed satisfied with the position of his hands, Radig squeezed, and a stone handle appeared to form right in his hand. Radig lifted, and a stone door rose slightly out of the ground, revealing the tunnel entrance below. *We never had a hope of finding these on our own.*

Radig nodded for Dunstan to enter first. He did so, dropping down into the tunnel, his hand clasped on the hilt of his sword. If this was a trap, this dark tunnel would be the perfect place to spring it. Radig followed after him a split second later, pulling the hatch down behind him. Dunstan stepped forward, smacking his head on the stone tunnel ceiling in the process. He stumbled backward, trying to suppress his yelp of pain, rubbing his head furiously.

"Just give me one second, Captain Dunstan," Radig whispered. "I know you cannot see in here."

They stood in silence for a long moment until, finally, a faint light began to radiate from Radig's hand. He opened his palm to reveal a rock, the light emanating from its surface. Dunstan had never seen such a stone before, but he was glad his companion had it. The light was faint, but it was better than fumbling his way along the tunnel in total darkness. The first things he spotted were the dead bodies of two dwarves lying a few feet away from the tunnel entrance. The dwarves had not yet discovered the guards Radig had killed on his way to the Imperial camp.

"I need to put these on you," Radig said.

Dunstan turned to find the dwarf holding a pair of iron shackles. This was not part of their agreement, and Dunstan's hand immediately returned to the hilt of his sword. If Radig thought he would willingly be double-crossed, he was sorely mistaken. He was already inside the tunnel. If he had to kill Radig and try to do this alone, so be it.

"This is the first time you are mentioning this part of your plan, Radig," he hissed. "What kind of a fool do you take me for?"

"You would never have agreed to come if I had mentioned it sooner, Captain Dunstan. Listen to me, please. What if new guards come to replace these two? If we are walking down this tunnel together, we are as good as dead, both of us. If you wear the shackles, I may be able to convince them you found the tunnel on your own and I am taking you to Odpor. I will release you as soon as we are free of the tunnel, but this is a necessary precaution. Think logically. If I meant to betray you, would I have announced myself out loud when we first met? I would have attacked you before you had any idea I was there."

It made sense, but it did not make Dunstan feel any better as Radig secured the shackles to each wrist. The dwarf also relieved him of his sword, vowing to return it before they exited the tunnel. With Radig leading the way, they began to shuffle down the tunnel, moving slowly due to Dunstan's need to crouch to avoid the low ceiling.

"Won't somebody notice the hole you just dug to reveal this tunnel?"

"Have faith in dwarven ingenuity, Captain Dunstan. Those doorways are designed to funnel the earth right back into them. That entryway will be completely covered within two minutes. Nobody who does not know exactly how to spot such an entry will ever notice it. Why do you think your scouts have not spotted it despite it being so close to your camp?"

"Why are you so invested in this, Radig?" Dunstan asked. "There are plenty of ways to make Odpor look ineffective without risking your skin for my men, especially after what happened last time. I can't imagine anyone who does what you have done has a pleasant fate awaiting them if they are caught. I've seen a glimpse of what Odpor does to his enemies."

"I did not foresee these complications when I originally set your men free. I assumed I would be able to free them while maintaining my cover. They were meant to be safely back in your camp, and I would have returned to my duty before anybody realized they had escaped. Unfortunately, I was wrong. Now it is a course of action I am committed to completing. Besides, I told you, they have a Resistance dwarf they will also execute."

"I understand the need to stand by your fellows, but risking so much for one fighter? I realize I am not one to comment on this, considering where I'm standing as we speak, but it seems like quite a risk to take."

"It is not any fighter. It is my wife," Radig replied, his voice as hard as steel. "Unlike you Imperials, dwarven women fight for causes we believe in strongly enough to go to war. We do not force them to sit by and timidly wait for their fate to come to them. This is something I never understood about you Imperials. Why would you prevent half of your people from fighting for a just cause? It does not make sense."

"I'm sorry, Radig. It's not like I'm the one who sets those policies. A captain in the Imperial Army has fairly little authority in the grand scheme of things. For what it's worth, I agree with you. We will set her free. We will set them all free. Just to clarify, you do have some idea of what we are going to do after that, right?"

"Yes, of course I do. After everything that has happened tonight, I am not taking any chances. We will be going to a safe house known only to me. I set it up over a year ago in case Kalayo and I needed to go into hiding, to a place even the rest of the Resistance does not know about. I told nobody else of its existence. It was always a possibility that Odpor would find out I am working with the Resistance. I had hoped we would never need to use it, but here we are. We will be safe there until we can slip out of Muog undetected. That is enough talk for now, Captain Dunstan. We are getting close to the end of the tunnel."

Dunstan looked up, smacking his head on the low ceiling once again as he did so. Cursing himself under his breath, he stumbled onward. He had heard rumors of the dwarves allowing women to join their military, but this was the first time he had received confirmation. Since its inception, such a thing had been forbidden in the Imperial Army. It was a lead most of the provinces had followed. It was an archaic rule, one he found asinine. The contents of a person's heart had a far more decisive impact on the type of warrior than what could be found below their waist.

Memories of the Hoyt War in Thornata swirled through his head, particularly of the young woman named Alsea. That girl had as much fight in her than any man he had ever met, and far more than the weak-minded fools currently commanding the Imperial Army. She had slain a treasonous

Thornatan general in single combat, along with countless Hoyt fighters in that final battle in Oreanna. For the second time in the past few days, he wondered what had become of her and Adel, the Rawl wielder. When he had parted ways with them in Verizia, they had intended to charter passage south to the Ogra Mountains in the province of Gryttar. They had wanted to stamp out ogre slave dealers in the name of their valiant friend Ola. While Dunstan bore no love for slavers, he hoped the young couple had not bitten off more than they could chew. He had heard nothing of them since the day they had said their goodbyes. What he would not give to have the pair of them by his side on this night.

"We are about to exit the tunnel. Hold still and let me unshackle you. You can have your sword back as well," Radig said, his voice barely a whisper. "You see, Captain Dunstan? I am a dwarf of my word. I will go out first and make sure the coast is clear. If you hear a struggle, come out ready to kill whoever is standing in our way, and please do not keep me waiting too long."

Dunstan extended his arms, and Radig released him from the shackles. True to his word, the dwarf also returned his sword. The silence of the tunnel had briefly filled Dunstan with a false sense of calm, but now the city of Muog was only steps away, and the gravity of what he had gotten himself into was fully setting in. Had they noticed he was missing from the Imperial encampment yet? When they did notice his absence, what would they think? Would they assume he had been captured, or would there be whispers of treason?

You should have asked yourself these questions an hour ago, you fool. Not that you need to ask them at all. With your history, you know exactly what they will think. There's no helping it now; just get this done and worry about the consequences later.

He had come too far to turn back now. He watched as Radig's fingers worked an intricate pattern over the stone wall before them, a small doorway appearing to his touch. He slipped through, gone for a moment that felt like an eternity. Dunstan held his breath, waiting for a shout or the crash of weapons colliding, but none came. Radig reappeared a second later, beckoning for him to follow. He placed a finger over his lips. The message was clear enough. There was to be no talking from this point onward, and Dunstan was all too happy to oblige.

Radig stepped back out through the doorway, and Dunstan followed, forced into an awkward bowlegged stance to wiggle his way through the dwarf-sized opening. As he emerged into the fresh night air, the first thing to catch his attention was the brightness of the sky. The sun would fully rise within the hour, and his men's time would run out. They had to move fast. Radig had better know what he was doing. He was placing more trust in this dwarf he had just met than he had placed in any other man in his entire life.

At least if this was a horrible mistake, I won't live to regret it for very long.

To his credit, Radig did not waste any time. Motioning for Dunstan to follow, he stepped out from the cover of the tunnel entrance. Dunstan followed, his eyes darting from left to right as he did. The desperation of their circumstances aside, he could not help but admire the dwarven capital city's stunning architecture. The dwarves had long been lauded for their masonry, but seeing it firsthand was an entirely different experience than listening to the tales of others. Still, he knew he had to keep his focus on the task at hand.

Radig led him through a series of narrow streets and alleyways, sometimes forced to slow down so that Dunstan could squeeze his way through sideways. The dwarves had evidently not anticipated many Imperial visitors to their fair city, or perhaps they had purposely meant to discourage such visits.

It's brilliant. Even if we ever managed to breach their gates and get our army into this city, they would butcher us in these tiny streets and alleyways. Imperial High Command has no idea what they are in store for if they ever try to attack.

The route Radig led him along was winding and disjointed, and Dunstan found himself lost within minutes. If anything happened to Radig in the battle to come, hope would be lost for all of them. He would never be able to remember all these twists and turns, nor would he be able to open the entrance to the tunnel. He understood Radig must be taking this particular route to avoid detection but was still somewhat resentful. All of their hopes of survival rested solely on Radig, and they were about to wade into dangerous business. It was a position no Imperial soldier ever wanted to find himself in, with his future resting in the hands of another.

As more light crept into the sky, Dunstan realized their route seemed to mostly run parallel to one of Muog's massive inner walls. As their reports had indicated, the dwarves were shielded by not one but two impenetrable walls. He wondered how Radig planned to reach the outer wall unnoticed, for that was surely where Odpor intended to execute his men. No sooner had the thought crossed his mind than Radig wordlessly provided an answer.

Crouching low in the street, Radig closed his hands around a piece of stone, lifting it to reveal a sewer entrance. Once more, Dunstan was amazed at the ingenuity of the dwarves. The sewer entrance had blended in perfectly with the rest of the street. Had Radig not known precisely where to find it, it would have gone unnoticed.

We could learn so much from these people. Most of the cities I have been to in the other provinces can scarcely mask the stench of their sewers, let alone conceal their entrances.

Radig motioned for him to jump down first, an order he hurried to follow. His doubts about Radig's motives were fading more as the sun crept closer to showing itself on the horizon. Time was running out, and there was no time to dwell on the questions swirling through his mind. If Radig was betraying him, it was too late to do anything about it now.

Just like the tunnel they had used to enter the city, the sewer was far too low for him to walk through properly. Radig dropped to his side a moment later, pulling the sewer entrance closed behind him. Once again, the strange stone appeared in Radig's hand to light the way. They would have to traverse a narrow walkway alongside a gently moving stream of rather foul-smelling water. Dunstan took a deep breath, which was no pleasant experience, and began to step forward, but Radig placed a hand on his arm, holding him back.

"Not much farther now, Captain Dunstan," he whispered. "Just a short walk through this sewer, and we will be in the courtyard between the outer and inner walls. That is where we will be at the highest risk, and we will need to move fast to avoid being seen from above. Once we are out of this sewer, move immediately to the right. Several wooden crates are stacked near a stone staircase leading up to the wall. Get into one of the crates and close the lid behind you."

"That's your plan? This is the best you have come up with? How do you know they will bring the captives to this particular staircase?" Dunstan hissed, immediately seeing several holes in Radig's strategy.

"Because this is the staircase that leads to the top of the main gates, right in the center of the wall. It provides the best view for the men in your camp. Odpor cares a great deal about theatrics and optics, more than he would ever openly admit. You may have sensed this from his earlier performances. This is where they will be; you can count on it."

"What if they see us running for the crates?"

"In that case, our fight starts a little earlier than we anticipated, Captain Dunstan. The guards on the wall are more focused on watching the neutral territory; they will not be looking down into the courtyard, or so we can hope. There is no scenario in which this operation goes off smoothly. We will have to get our hands dirty one way or another. You understood this when you agreed to come with me. Once you are in the crate, stay silent. When I attack, I will make myself heard. Please do not wait too long to join me; I will be badly outnumbered. Once we have

Kalayo and your men, I have one last diversion to allow us to escape. Stay close and listen to my commands, and I will lead the way to safety."

So much that can go wrong and so little that can go right, Dunstan thought. But he was far past the point of no return. As a man who preferred to have every avenue covered when strategizing, he despised this plan, but it was the only one he had. Those young men depended on him; he was their only hope. Thaddeus Dunstan had always wanted to do what was right, and it had gotten him into deep trouble five years earlier in Thornata. But the risk of discipline meant nothing to him now. The only thing that mattered was being able to look at himself and not feel disgusted by what he saw. He nodded his consent, and they continued onward.

Just as Radig had promised, their trek through the sewer was brief. They had only walked around two hundred feet along the causeway when the dwarf brought them to a halt.

"This is it, Captain Dunstan."

"Just call me Thad. The moment I'm discovered missing, I'll probably be stripped of my rank anyway. I know we aren't exactly friends, Radig, but we're the closest thing we each have at the moment."

"As you wish, Thad. Good luck to us both. I look forward to talking to you again after this is over, but if one or both of us should fall, you have my thanks for undertaking this mission with me."

Without waiting for a reply, Radig reached up and opened a similar doorway to the one they had used to enter the sewer. Dunstan leaped up, dragging himself out of the hole as quickly as he could. He began running to the right, just as Radig had instructed. He ran, waiting all the while for a shout to tell him he had been discovered. The cry never came, and the crates were in front of him within seconds; Radig had planned their route well. Heaving the lid from one large crate, he threw himself in, pulling the lid closed behind him. Now all that remained was the intolerable waiting.

Chapter Four

I t felt as though no time had passed before the cell door swung open again. There was Krillzoc, the ever-present malicious grin stretched across his face. In fact, Darian thought he appeared more gleeful than he ever had before.

A contingent of six guards filed into the cell after him, immediately closing the door behind them. The unmistakable scrape of a latch sliding into place outside followed.

They aren't taking any chance of us escaping this time, Darian thought. *Hopefully we catch them off guard by waiting.*

To his surprise, he was not as frightened as he had been the first time Krillzoc had come to lead them up to the wall. It was strange considering this time he knew they were taking him to execute him. *Maybe that blow to the head has dulled your wits,* he told himself, but he didn't think that was the case. Perhaps it was the fact that he knew they would be fighting back at some point before they reached the wall that was helping him stay calm. If he was going to die today, he would die doing everything in his power to escape. He would not stand meekly by, awaiting the inevitable. There was no promise of success, but with any luck, he would at least take Krillzoc with him.

"Good morning, traitor and gentlemen. Time flies when one is having fun. It has been such a pleasure for me to host all of you as our guests. I do hope you have enjoyed our hospitality. Dawn will be upon us soon; I have come to collect you for the big event. Listen carefully, for I will not repeat myself. You will be shackled together at the ankles, but fear not, we do not have far to walk. I will not even bother to hood you this time. After all, I do not think we have to worry about you taking details of our city back to your encampment. Enjoy this last breath of fresh air. I expect you will all want to thank me when we reach the wall. In fact, I look forward to it."

Krillzoc's arrogance, which would have once enraged Darian, brought him a faint sense of satisfaction. Odpor's psychotic enforcer was so sure of himself, so certain that nothing could possibly go wrong. Live or die, Darian would be delighted to see that look of confidence finally wiped off Krillzoc's smug face, hopefully when he shoved something sharp into it. *This is for you, Axel. If I have another chance at him, I won't waste it, I promise.* He rose to his feet, falling quietly into line between Berj and Preston.

"I must confess, I am a little disappointed at how docile you all are this morning," Krillzoc remarked as the soldiers and Kalayo fell wordlessly into line. "Especially you, Kalayo. I am disappointed to see a dwarf, even a traitorous rat like you, go so meekly to her demise. Do not get me wrong, I have always known you Imperials are cowards at heart, but I was hoping for just a little bit of a struggle, at least. I suppose you follow the lead of your dearly departed sergeant. Take comfort, for you will be reunited with him soon."

A vein was throbbing in Darian's forehead, and it was taking every ounce of self-control he possessed to keep himself from launching at Krillzoc right then and there. It was what the cruel dwarf wanted; he knew that, knew he could not play into Krillzoc's hand. But the insult against Axel tested his reserve. They had to be patient; their best hope of escape would come outside. All of the soldiers kept their cool, none of them rising to Krillzoc's taunts. To Darian's surprise, it was the stoic Kalayo who spoke up.

"Very clever, Krillzoc. Tell me, do you tell these little jokes to Odpor? I am sure you would make a delightful jester for him. If he does not have you dressing up as a clown to deliver them, he is wasting your true talents. Or are your services limited solely to licking his boots?"

One of the guards moved toward Kalayo as if to strike her but halted immediately at a gesture from Krillzoc. Darian thought he had seen the smile fade from Krillzoc's face for the briefest of moments, and then there it was again, firmly in place as always. He stepped up to Kalayo, his face inches from hers. If she was the least bit intimidated by this gesture, she didn't show it, meeting his gaze unwaveringly with a faint smile on her face.

"I suppose you want me to dishonor myself by striking a woman. That is your goal, right, traitor? If I lead you through the city with a fresh bruise on your face, there would be whispers and questions about my honor. Your fellow commoners do love to gossip among themselves, do they not? I will not give you the satisfaction. Watching you twitch and gasp as the life fades from your body at the end of a rope will be all the satisfaction I require from you. My only regret is that your spineless coward of a husband perished before he had the opportunity to swing beside you."

"As you wish, Krillzoc. I understand you would not want anybody to question your honorable nature. After all, I am sure none of the people in this city already know you for the snake you are. If that is what you need to believe to make yourself feel better, it is not my place to deny it. I wish you many years of happiness in your delusion."

Turning away from Kalayo, Krillzoc made his way down the line of soldiers, inspecting their ankle restraints one by one. As he turned his malicious gaze on Darian, the young soldier gave a moment's thought to making a grab for his sword right then and there. The hilt was right there, within easy reach. *I could get it free and shove it into his gut before he could stop me.* Once again, he fought down the primal urge that was screaming at him to act rashly. His friends still had a slim chance of survival, and they needed him to keep his head.

Once satisfied that all the prisoners were adequately restrained, Krillzoc tapped the cell door in a series of knocks. The latch slid back, and the door swung open. The guards led them from their final prison, one after another. Once outside the cell, Darian could see they were in a dimly lit stone corridor, apparently underground. Their guards led them through the labyrinthian maze of passageways. It was even more complex than the prison Radig had freed them from what felt like a lifetime ago.

After several long minutes of weaving their way through the identical corridors, they came to a set of stairs leading up. They stepped out into the open air to find the sun's first light was just beginning to show itself in the sky. As soon as they stepped out of the prison facility, more guards fell into line beside them. Glancing out of the corner of his eyes, Darian estimated their number to be at least two dozen. Odpor was not taking any chances. *It just means there are more of them for you to kill*, he told himself, trying his best to make himself believe it.

Looking straight ahead, he found they had been imprisoned in a facility not far from the city's walls. It made sense; Odpor would want them transported to their place of death as quickly as possible. Darian took a deep breath, knowing that if Radig was somehow out here, waiting to try to set them free, his window would be narrow. With this many guards, they would have to find a way to get weapons; it was the only thing that might turn the odds in their favor. Krillzoc had unwittingly done them a favor by not hooding them or shackling their hands. He no doubt wanted to observe the fear on their faces as they walked, but his twisted desire may prove to be his undoing. For the first time, Darian stole a glance at the chains around their ankles. They were thick, but not exceptionally so. A hard strike or two from a heavy weapon should be enough to sever them, or so he could hope. Now all they had to do was get their hands on that weapon.

Curious faces began to emerge from their homes as the prisoners shuffled their way through the streets of Muog. A few shouted curses or insults at them, and on a few occasions, pieces of fruit were hurled, though none found their mark. Despite Radig's claims the previous night, the Resistance did not appear to be prevalent in Muog. Not a single voice spoke out in support of the condemned. Either the Resistance wasn't there, or they were unwilling to speak out against Odpor publicly.

They reached a gate leading through Muog's inner wall, and Darian's entire body tensed. It was soon coming, the moment when they would have no choice but to act, with or without help from Radig. Once again, his eyes darted furtively to the guards around them. They were keeping a safe distance, but he might be able to grab a sword if he was quick enough. Berj Jenson was closest to one of the guards, giving Darian a slight sense of comfort. He was still bitter toward Berj for his earlier comments about Axel, but there was no denying a simple truth: if any of them possessed the reckless, empty-headed courage needed to do what must be done in the face of certain death, it was Berj Jenson. Already, Darian could see Berj's head continually turning slightly in the guard's direction, never for more than a second. He was gauging the distance, preparing to make his move.

Once through the inner wall, Darian could see a set of stone stairs off to their right, leading up to the top of the outer wall. *This is it. When we get to the foot of that staircase, it's time. Maybe their guard will be down by then; they will be expecting us to try something sooner. Perhaps they'll assume we're going to accept our fate meekly,*Darian thought, doing his best to ignore the throbbing pain radiating throughout his legs.

Krillzoc led the way, Kalayo behind him, followed by Berj, Darian, and Preston, with Darnold at the rear of the procession. Odpor's enforcer seemed tense in his stride, though Darian could not see his face. His hand was resting firmly on the pommel of his sword, the sword that had cut the life from Darian's oldest friend, and his head was in constant motion, shifting from side to side.

Krillzoc was within fifty feet of the foot of the stairs when Darian decided it was time. He glanced to his right and left, trying to determine which guard was closer. Deciding he would go for the man to the left, he tugged slightly on the ankle restraints with his left leg, signaling Berj and Preston what he was about to do. He waited a split second for the responding tugs as his friends alerted Kalayo and Darnold. He was just beginning to make his move to the left when all hell broke loose around them.

Radig appeared first, charging toward them, brandishing a heavy mace and bellowing incoherently. Krillzoc ripped his sword clear of its scabbard, crying out for his men to respond to the attack. Kalayo lunged forward, dragging Berj along with her, crashing into Krillzoc and sending him tumbling to the ground. It was a valiant effort, but the sight of it still filled Darian with dismay.

Radig is alone; nobody came to fight with him. We don't stand a chance.

No sooner had the thought flashed through his mind then he spotted what appeared to be the shining star sigil of the Imperial Army.

There was Captain Dunstan, inexplicably charging toward them, sword in hand. Unlike Radig, he was not shouting, his face a mask of concentration as he closed in on their right flank. The guard to Darian's right was reaching for the heavy axe belted to his waist, his eyes locked on the charging Imperial captain. Realizing there would be no better opportunity, Darian lurched to his right, the shackles giving just enough for him to reach his target.

He swung his fist as hard as possible, connecting with the back of the dwarf's head. It was not an ideal target, the impact causing shock waves of pain to radiate through his hand and lower arm, but it was effective. The dwarf was caught off guard, his grip on the axe loosening just enough for

Darian's other hand to rip it from his grasp. Knowing he had only seconds before the rest of the guards realized what was happening, Darian hacked downward at the chains connecting him to Berj Jenson. To his relief, the chains gave way with only two hard strikes. Two more swings freed him from Preston, and at last he was free to engage his enemies.

He went first for the previous owner of the axe. One clean swing to the gut as the dwarf reached for another weapon was enough to neutralize him as a threat. He tore the sword from the dwarf's belt, turning and tossing the axe to Max Preston so he could free himself and Darnold Dans from each other. Berj and Kalayo were already separated, fighting alongside Radig, who must have gotten to them and severed their chains. Captain Dunstan drew close to Darian, cutting his way through the dwarven guards with exceptional skill. Darian still had no idea how the captain had managed to come to their aid but was immensely relieved that he had.

Hopefully that's a story he will have the opportunity to tell us.

***

Thad Dunstan was overjoyed to see his men still breathing, but he was far from relieved. He had dispatched the first two guards who had met his initial charge in short order, but the remainder of the resistance was proving to be formidable. The dwarves were showing themselves to be every bit the skilled warriors the soldiers in camp had claimed. The third guard met him head-on, brandishing a heavy war hammer. At once, Dunstan could see that despite the dwarf's smaller stature, he was unlikely to be able to effectively parry any blow from such a weapon. He sidestepped the first swing, expecting the miss to leave the dwarven warrior off-balance and vulnerable to a swift counterattack. This assumption proved wrong, as the guard was exceptionally skilled at wielding the unwieldy weapon, bringing it immediately back into an attacking position.

Dunstan attacked, his sword slashing out at the dwarf's neck, but the dwarf ducked beneath the blow, swinging the hammer once more. Dunstan barely managed to avoid it this time, slipping out of its deadly path at the last possible second, the breeze from the swing racing across his face. The dwarf did not let up, obviously realizing he had Dunstan in a compromised position. He swung over and over, never leaving himself vulnerable, and each time Dunstan escaped with his life by mere inches. Dunstan spotted the opening just as he thought he was done for, the dwarf's hammer coming down in a wicked downward strike. Once again, he barely evaded the attack, the heavy weapon smashing into the cobblestones beneath their feet. Knowing he was not likely to have a better opportunity, Dunstan countered again, his sword slashing at the dwarf's right arm.

To his relief, the blade found its mark, opening a deep gash on his foe's arm as he moved to raise his weapon again, the hammer tumbling from his fingers. Dunstan never hesitated, stepping close to his opponent and thrusting his sword deep into his neck. The dwarf fell backward, an expression of shock etched across his face. Within seconds, another warrior was there to take his place, this one wielding a pair of swords. Dunstan parried one strike, then a second, and then a third before finding a gap in his new foe's guard, opening a devastating wound along the side of the dwarf's head. Before that dwarf hit the ground, yet another had lunged forward to take his place. Dunstan's arms ached from the prolonged strain of battle, and there was no end in sight.

I was too old for this ten years ago, he thought sarcastically, knowing he could not give in to his weariness if he wanted his men to escape Muog with their lives.

***

On the opposite end of the formation, Berj Jenson was feeling every sensation except for fatigue. Radig had broken him free from Kalayo, and the female dwarf had tossed him a sword she had snatched from the corpse of one of their fallen guards. Now he was attacking every guard in sight in a frenzy, unleashing every bit of anger that had built up over days of captivity and abuse. The pain of his wounds from the previous night's battle were a distant memory, the thrill of this new fight pushing everything else aside. As he hacked his way through one foe after another, he silently vowed to himself that either every one of these guards would die, or he would. He knew he was receiving wounds in return, but in his rage, the pain didn't even register in his mind. *Screw it, I'll worry about the pain later*, he told himself as he charged headlong into yet another pair of foes.

The first dwarf took a hard but clumsy swipe at his head with an axe. Berj ducked under the blow, slamming into the dwarf with his shoulder and knocking him to the ground. The second dwarf sprung to his defense, but three vicious swings of Berj's sword left him bleeding out on the cobblestones. His comrade fared no better, Berj kicking out and connecting hard with his face as the dwarf struggled to find his feet. Before he could regain his bearings, Berj struck a fatal blow, his sword sinking into the dwarf's torso.

***

Darnold Dans was angry as well, but he knew he had to keep his rage under control if he was going to survive this battle. The days in captivity had caused his muscles to begin to atrophy, but he fought through the pain that screamed through them, knowing his friends needed him. All his friends had been injured worse than he was in the battle the night before. He had to be a rock for them to lean on if they were to fight their way free of this madness.

Two dwarven guards closed in on him at once but could not breach his superb defenses. He managed to hold both of them off long enough for Max Preston to approach unnoticed from behind and cut one of them down. Darnold managed to slip into the guard of the other and drive his stolen sword home, deep into his opponent's gut.

"Thanks, Preston!" he cried, spinning to find another guard closing in on him from the side.

***

Max Preston did not take any time to pause; Darnold could handle himself. He had to keep his focus on the battle raging on all sides. He had managed to defend himself thus far with the axe Darian had thrown him in the opening seconds. It was a weapon he was unfamiliar with, but he had managed to use it to keep himself alive.

His first foe had opened a fresh cut on his left leg, but the wound did not feel too deep and had not yet begun to hamper his mobility. Another guard was crashing in on him from the right. He sidestepped the first swing of the dwarf's sword, bringing the axe around to counter. The dwarf moved just in time to avoid taking the blow to the head, but it still slammed into his shoulder with crushing force. The guard fell to one knee, and Preston finished him with one well-placed strike to the skull. He tossed the axe aside and snatched up the dwarf's sword, relieved to have a familiar-feeling weapon in hand at last.

A dwarf was closing in on Berj Jenson from behind, his mace raised high, preparing to deliver a killing blow to the unsuspecting soldier. Preston sprung forward, slashing out desperately with his sword as soon as he was within range. It was a glancing blow, opening only a minor cut on the back of the dwarf's leg, but it was enough to save Berj. The dwarf wheeled on him, his mace lashing out wildly. Preston scrambled backward, trying to stay out of the range of the devastatingly powerful weapon. Before the dwarf could swing again, the tip of Berj's sword emerged from his throat in an explosion of blood, Berj catching the distracted guard from behind.

"Watch yourself, Maxwell! How many times do I have to save

you?"

Preston couldn't help but chuckle despite his flash of irritation at Berj using his full name. There was no opportunity to shout back a retort. Another guard was already advancing on him, and he raised the stolen sword to meet the charge. The dwarf never came close, Darian Tor intercepting him while he was still a dozen feet away, hacking the dwarf's hand off at the wrist before moving on the confront another foe, leaving Preston to finish the dwarf with a swift thrust to the neck.

***

Darian Tor fought as though a maddened demon had possessed his body, throwing himself into foe after foe with reckless abandon. He was no longer thinking about finding an escape; he was no longer thinking about anything at all. All he knew was that he finally had a weapon in his hand and could finally extract some small amount of revenge against those who had killed his best friend. He pressed through the chaos, so consumed by his anger that he almost didn't recognize the hated face of Krillzoc only feet away from him. He didn't hesitate, launching himself at Odpor's chief enforcer, desperate to kill the man he hated more than he had ever thought possible.

If Krillzoc was intimidated by Darian's furious charge, he did not show it. His sword snapped up to deflect Darian's wild initial swing, the hated smirk splitting his face as the blow clattered harmlessly away. The smirk only enraged Darian further; he could see nothing but the vision of that same smirk flashing at him as that sword plunged through Axel's heart. He struck again and again, his rage intensifying as Krillzoc effort-lessly parried each attack. Twice Krillzoc's blade slipped past his lackluster defenses and opened deep cuts—one on his left arm, one above his hip. Darian fought on, refusing to fall first, determined that Krillzoc would die before he did. He would not allow himself to be bested by this madman again. He was doing his best to ignore the injuries, but the blood loss began to take its toll on his body quickly. His vision was starting to blur, and though he was putting the same effort into his swings, they didn't seem to carry the same force. He would not be able to maintain the attack—or even defend himself, for that matter—for much longer.

It was Radig who saved him, the dwarf appearing out of a crush of battling bodies, driving his shoulder into Krillzoc's back with splintering force. Krillzoc stumbled forward; he hadn't seen the attack coming. Recognizing his opportunity, Darian hurried forward, desperate to put an end to Odpor's enforcer once and for all. Radig blocked his path, one strong hand clasping Darian's shoulder and forcing him backward as several of Krillzoc's men rushed to his defense. Darian fought back, outraged, but found he lacked the strength to fight his way free of Radig's grip. Old wounds and new were sapping his strength faster by the second.

"We have to get out of here now, or we are never getting out of here at all!" Radig shouted at him.

It was true, Darian realized. Reinforcements were starting to arrive from the wall above. The battle, which had seemed so fierce, so drawn out, could only have lasted a few minutes at most. The guards who had brought them here were mostly dead, but Odpor had no shortage of warriors to send to kill them. If they lingered here much longer, they would be completely overrun. Forcing his hatred for Krillzoc to the back of his mind, Darian allowed the calm, collected soldier to take over control once more.

"Where do we go, Radig? I assume you have a plan?"

"Of course I do, but we need to move right now. Get behind me, and get the attention of your friends; we do not have long. We have to group together."

Darian assumed a position directly behind Radig. Kalayo appeared a second later, taking a spot behind Darian. They worked their way around the perimeter of the still-raging battle, calling out to each Imperial soldier as they did, fending off attacks from all sides. Within a minute, all four captive soldiers, plus Captain Dunstan, were moving along with the dwarves in a tight formation, desperately fending off attackers from all sides.

Radig better have something amazing up his sleeve to get us out of this one, Darian thought, fighting off his injuries and exhaustion with every breath.

"Everyone, put your hand on someone else. Close your eyes now!" Radig shouted.

Darian obeyed without question. Radig had gotten them this far, and it was no use to question him now. Clasping Max Preston's shoulder with his left hand, he clenched his eyes tight. *If only Harter Arsch could see me now, closing my eyes in the midst of a battle.* He did not know what happened, only that a loud crack rang out, rising over the cries of the dwarves pursuing them. There was a flash of light, one bright enough that he could see it through his tightly closed eyelids. Within seconds, there were cries of pain and clattering metal sounding out all around them.

"We do not have long. Move, move, move!" Radig shouted.

Darian opened his eyes, a shocking sight awaiting him. Dozens of dwarven warriors were writhing on the ground in agony, their hands clasped over their faces. A strange haze hung in the air as if an intense fire had just been burning. Remembering that dwarves possessed far superior vision, Darian thought he understood what Radig had done to disrupt their pursuit. But there was no time to admire their rescuer's handiwork now. Radig was already moving again, urging them to hurry and follow. Vowing never to find himself in captivity again, Darian Tor ran, finally a free man once more.

Chapter Five

When Chieftain Odpor was in a foul mood, every dwarf in his general vicinity could sense it before a single word left his lips. He had always liked it that way, never wanting the dwarves beneath him to feel complacent. Those who were able usually sought out excuses to take themselves far from their volatile leader's eyesight in such instances. Odpor had a reputation of making unpleasant examples out of those whose only crime was being in his presence at the wrong moment. If the rumors flying throughout the city of Muog were true, every moment could be the wrong moment. It was as though a dark cloud hung in the air over his home, and he could sense even his most faithful servants were fearful of being caught in the imminent storm.

Odpor's thoughts were every bit as dark as his servants feared as he impatiently awaited Krillzoc's arrival. Twice in the span of two days, his most trusted servant had failed him. His enforcer had always been a rock, steadfast and able to produce results when no other dwarf could. But now the Imperials had escaped from under his nose for the second time in two days, and Odpor's faith was waning. Krillzoc had been his enforcer and most loyal servant for almost ten years, but a changing of the guard may have been in order. Krillzoc had served him well until the past two days, but these blunders were of a magnitude that Odpor simply could not overlook. If he returned from his hunt empty-handed, Odpor would have little choice. Krillzoc's failures could set the timeline for Qwitzite's secession from the Empire back by months, if not years. Already, the names of potential replacements were dancing through his mind.

"Chieftain Odpor, Krillzoc is approaching. He should arrive within a few minutes, my lord," one of his guards announced before turning and leaving the room as quickly as his feet could carry him.

I hope you have not failed me, my old friend, Odpor thought grimly to himself. He had not risen to his current position by allowing his emotions to rule his decisions, but where Krillzoc was concerned, it was more complicated than with others. Krillzoc had been among his most ardent supporters in the early days of his rule. He had ascended to the rank of chieftain upon the death of his father, one of Qwitzite's most beloved rulers in recent memory. However, most of the dwarves correctly believed that Odpor would be a far different ruler from his father. There were not many dwarves in those days who had embraced the idea. From the beginning, there had been whispers about overthrowing him.

Odpor had never viewed his father's reign as favorably as the commoners. A weak, simpleminded fool, his father had always been content to live under the rule of the Empire. He had been all too happy to live out his days as their servant, paying their taxes and licking the Emperor's boots whenever it was demanded of him. While his years as ruler had been peaceful, the dwarves had failed to prosper in the way Odpor felt they should. Qwitzite produced more wealth for the Empire than any other two provinces combined, and what did they have to show for it? They received nothing from Valdovas in return except for disdain and high taxes. The time was long past due to show the Imperials that the dwarves were their own people.

There had been whispers even in his youth that Odpor was not fit to take his father's place—whispers that Krillzoc had stepped up to assist him with silencing. His loyalty and effectiveness had earned him his position as Odpor's top enforcer, a role he had always shown great aptitude for performing. A man with a talent for committing violence and no moral qualms about it was just what Odpor needed. Thanks to Krillzoc, one by one, those who had dared to speak out against him had been silenced.

Now the whispers were back, though they had already gone too far this time. The Resistance was a disease that needed to be eradicated from Qwitzite, but thus far, Krillzoc had not shown the ability to do so. He had found the missing Imperial soldiers within a day of their first escape with his effective interrogative techniques, yet mere hours later, they had slipped through his grasp once more. How could he have allowed them to escape as he was leading them to their demise?

I owe you a lot, dear friend, but you cannot live forever on your past accomplishments. If you have lost your razor-sharp edge, I will require a new weapon to wield against my enemies.

"If I give the order to take Krillzoc into custody, I want it done as respectfully as possible," he ordered the four guards standing in the corners of his throne room. "If he resists, you are authorized to use whatever force is necessary to detain him, but I would prefer he be taken alive. Take him to the cell beneath this house and see that he is guarded around the clock. He is not to be harmed in any way once he is a prisoner. He will be fed well and given any comfort he requests, within reason. His years of loyalty and service to our people have earned him a certain amount of respect. Is this understood?"

"Yes, sir," his guards replied in unison.

A few moments later, Krillzoc entered the room, making his way around the reflection pool in the center, stepping in front of Odpor's seat and sinking into a deep bow. Odpor already knew his enforcer did not bring welcome news; the pair would typically never bother with such formalities. He regretted more than ever his ill-fated decision to make a deal with that snake, General Sylvester. The bargain had paid him no benefits, and it was about to cost him his most faithful servant. But there were few other options. He could not publicly allow such failures to pass unpunished. He had a reputation to uphold, one of a leader who would not forgive incompetence. If Krillzoc accepted this, he may be able to live out his days in exile outside of Muog rather than in a cell. It might be the best he would be able to offer his old friend.

"Chieftain, there is still no sign of Radig, Kalayo, or any of the Imperials. Every available resource is continuing to search for them in every corner of the city. I have already questioned several known Resistance dwarves, but it seems Radig told none of them of his plans. He must have realized how we managed to find them last time. Forgive me; I am afraid I need more time to continue my hunt."

"I see. Krillzoc, you have served me faithfully for nearly ten years, since the day I first sat upon this throne. You have been a companion and friend for much longer. I am grateful beyond measure for this service. I will speak to you truthfully now, for your loyalty has earned you as much. I must confess I am beginning to lack faith in your ability to do what I have asked of you, regardless of how much time I give you. How much time can I possibly afford you? I need results, not excuses. With every passing hour, my position appears weaker to our people. If you are not able to deliver what I need, I have no choice but to turn to another."

Krillzoc dropped to one knee, his eyes staring down at the floor. Odpor knew this moment must be equally hard on him. He had invested years of his life into everything Odpor was trying to accomplish. Odpor was sympathetic, but strong rulers could not show weakness, even under the most trying of times. Ultimately, every one of his servants was expendable by necessity, even Krillzoc.

"Chieftain, may I speak frankly?"

"I would expect nothing less of you, Krillzoc."

"I have failed you; it is true. It brings me the deepest sense of shame I have felt in my entire life. In the end, if you are going to punish me, I have earned it. I will accept any penalty you deem fit without protest. But I would respectfully remind you that I advised you against striking this bargain with the Imperial general from the beginning. We would not be in this predicament if you had heeded my advice. We should have killed every last one of those soldiers the second they dared set foot inside our walls. Thirteen corpses should have dangled from our walls the following morning for every one of the soldiers in their camp to see. But you are our chieftain, and I will always follow you faithfully, even when I consider you to be acting in error."

Odpor could see some of his guards tensing up; they suspected the order would come soon. Truthfully, he would never have allowed any other man to even finish that statement. But Krillzoc was not any other servant, and the fact of the matter was, he was right. Not that it would save him—it couldn't, not if Odpor wanted to maintain his image of strength.

"Very well, Krillzoc. You clearly feel you know better than I do. Sitting in your position, it is an easy claim to make, but I will humor you nonetheless. What do you suggest my next move should be?"

"No, Chieftain Odpor, you are more of a leader than I could ever aspire to be. But even the greatest of leaders is far from infallible. We need to find the Imperials, but that is no longer our greatest concern. We must find Radig at all costs. He poises the far greater threat to us. He knows too much about how we work. If he shares what he knows of our defenses and capabilities with the Imperials, and they make it back to their camp, it could prove disastrous for us. We must not allow it to happen under any circumstances."

It was true; everyone in the room understood it. His deal with General Sylvester was no longer at the forefront of Odpor's mind. Radig was the real threat, the traitorous weasel who had worked his way into a position close to Krillzoc and Odpor. He knew far too much. If he made it back to the Resistance or helped the Imperials reach their camp, the damage he could do was difficult to imagine. *How could we have let a*

Resistance dwarf climb so high within our ranks?

"I hear you telling me about various problems, but I do not hear you offering any solutions, Krillzoc."

"They cannot hide forever, nor will they try. Radig did not rescue them from execution so they could crawl into a hole and hide until they die. Sooner or later, they will have to make a move to get out of Muog; there is little they can accomplish here without help. Please leave me in command of this hunt. Radig made a critical error by setting the Imperials free. He likely did so as a means of freeing his traitor of a wife, but he would have been better served to allow her to swing beside them. He has encumbered himself with these Imperial soldiers, who will be of minimal assistance to him inside our walls. He has given us a gift, even if he does not realize it. This is our chance to destroy the Resistance. Radig will attempt to either return them to their camp or back to whatever hole the rest of the Resistance is hiding in. We have long suspected they may be using Jezero as a base of operations. This is the perfect opportunity to prove it. We just have to bide our time and wait for him to show himself. When he does, we follow him."

"You are assuming they are still in Muog. This seems a bold assumption from where I sit. How can you be sure that he has not already spirited them out of the city?"

"Because we locked down every tunnel leading out of Muog within twenty minutes of their escape. There was not enough time. Trust me, Chieftain Odpor; they are still here."

"I have trusted you. I have trusted you more than I have ever trusted anyone else, and look where it has gotten me. My trust is eroding, and you have nobody to blame for that but yourself, Krillzoc."

For the first time in years, Odpor could see some of the confidence fading from Krillzoc's face. The bravado was always there, even when he needed to fake it. But now his eyes had the look of a man who was tasting the bitterness of defeat for the first time in a long time. Any lingering doubts Odpor had harbored about his enforcer truly grasping the seriousness of this situation faded from his mind. Krillzoc understood his fate would be determined by what he said next.

"Chieftain Odpor, I have served you faithfully for ten years. I understand my past success cannot excuse my current failures. If you decide to dismiss me from your service, that is your right. If you choose to execute me for my incompetence, so be it. But I urge you to ask yourself if there is another man under your command who you feel is better suited to hunting down these Imperials and crushing the Resistance. If so, I wish him nothing but the best, for this is a cause I believe in more than any other. I await your judgement. No matter your decision, I thank you for the opportunity to fight against our Imperial oppressors for as long as I have."

He is not wrong. Who do you trust well enough to take his place? If Krillzoc is not up to this, is anyone else? Odpor could not remember being in the position of making such a difficult decision. Even making the ultimate decision to declare Qwitzite's independence from the Empire had come easier. He had no desire to kill or imprison Krillzoc, but the thought of appearing weak to his people was unbearable. If he allowed Krillzoc to live, let alone keep his command, what would the commoners whisper? Would they begin to suspect that the Resistance was correct about his fitness to rule? Would it shake their faith that seceding from the Empire was the right move? Would more dwarves begin to challenge his rule?

"Krillzoc, you have been devoted to me for a decade. I do not punish loyalty. I am disappointed with your recent failures; I do not deny it. To be clear, these blunders warrant your dismissal from my service, if not worse. But you came here today and owned up to your mistakes like a true man of Qwitzite. Every parent in this city should aspire to raise their children to possess a shred of your integrity. But I must stress upon you that this is the final opportunity I can give you. Do you understand?"

"Yes, Chieftain Odpor. I understand, and I thank you for your graciousness and mercy. Since I was old enough to know anything, I knew you were the right dwarf to lead our people into a new age of prosperity. The whispers from the traitors and fools never swayed me, and they never will. Every day since you have taken that seat as our leader, you have proven me right time and time again."

Your groveling is appreciated, but it will only get you so far, my old friend, Odpor thought. When Krillzoc had first entered his chamber, Odpor had not been able to imagine any scenario in which he would live to see another day. His enforcer had always had a silver tongue, but all of his arguments had been sound. Odpor had nobody else he could depend on to do what needed to be done. He had a plethora of dwarves who possessed the necessary callousness to serve as his lead enforcer but had yet to meet one who also owned the endless loyalty and ruthless calculating mind of Krillzoc. He doubted such a dwarf existed.

"Very well, Commander Krillzoc. You will retain your command for the time being. I am placing my faith in you; please do not make me regret this decision. Now, I want you to tell me your plan going forward. Show me I have not made the wrong decision."

"Chieftain, we have long suspected that the Resistance has housed the bulk of their forces in the city of Jezero, with assistance from our old friend Iskra. However, we have been unable to prove it. None of the dwarves we have interrogated have broken sufficiently to verify this. I propose that we cut off any hope Radig has of reaching the Imperial encampment while at the same time leaving his passage to Jezero wide open. It will be too tempting of an opportunity for him to pass up."

"So, you mean to allow them to escape Muog intentionally? I admit I am already skeptical, Krillzoc."

"The Resistance forces remaining inside Muog are petrified after we were able to round up so many of them and locate their headquarters in this city. Do not forget, Radig acted today with only the help of an Imperial captain. No fellow Resistance dwarves fought at his side other than Kalayo;

I saw this with my own eyes. This tells me that he believes all their forces inside Muog could be compromised. He has only two places to turn for help: the Imperials and Resistance forces outside of Muog. Even with his act of freeing their men, I doubt the Imperials would trust him. They have always viewed us as lesser beings, and Radig, foolish though he may be, understands this. So, he will turn to his fellow Resistance members. In doing so, he will confirm our suspicions of their location, and we can wipe them out in one swoop."

It was a bold proposal, one only Krillzoc would have had the nerve to propose to him. It was the reason he had been such a valued servant for so many years. So many men were capable of following orders without questions, no matter how vile and unsavory. But it took a man with a certain degree of self-assuredness to make such a proposal to Odpor, knowing how he would view it. Little though he relished the idea of allowing the Imperials to leave Muog alive, he had to acknowledge it was as sound of a plan as he had available to him. Sometimes short-term sacrifices had to be made in the name of long-term success.

"Very well, Krillzoc. I am listening. Precisely how would you go about doing this?"

"We quadruple the guard on all tunnels that lead toward the Imperial camp. Radig would never attempt to fight his way through so many men, especially knowing the type of reception he can expect from the Imperials even if he were to succeed. Remember, Radig knows about our arrangement with General Sylvester. A dwarf showing up in their camp and making wild accusations against one of their generals? They would execute him within a day, assuming they do not just kill him on sight."

"You believe this will motivate him to flee to Jezero instead?"

"It will, especially if we leave the path open for him. We leave a token force guarding the tunnel leading north, and it will be too tempting for him to pass up. We have long suspected that Iskra is leading the Resistance from Jezero. I propose we allow Radig to confirm these beliefs. Then we kill them all in one fell swoop. Why only eliminate a few of our enemies when we can eliminate the entire Resistance?"

Iskra. The very mention of the ancient dwarf's name brought a scowl to Odpor's face. He had tasked Iskra, a former adviser to his father, with ruling the remote northern city of Jezero. It was a move that had removed the troublesome old fool from under his feet without killing him. It was a decision he regretted every day, no matter how terrible the optics of killing such a loyal old dwarf would have been. It was a lesson he had not forgotten in the years since. Iskra had not hesitated to question his decision to rebel against the Empire, often and publicly. Odpor had long suspected his father's old friend of forming the Resistance but had never been able to prove it. That opportunity might have finally fallen into his lap, assuming Krillzoc did not fail him again.

"I cannot deny the wisdom in your plan, Krillzoc. If we have this opportunity to expose Iskra and the Resistance, we should not set it aside. I want you to assemble an attack force. I want to be ready to move against Jezero in short order if our suspicions are confirmed, before they can slip through our grasp. I want you to handpick your best trackers to keep watch on this tunnel day and night. Once Radig and the Imperials appear, they are to track them but not engage without orders from one of us. Radig can be our rat; it is a role he has already served well for Iskra. Now we need him to lead us to the cheese. It is a good plan, Krillzoc, but it is all for nothing if not executed properly. Do not fail me."

"I will not, Chieftain Odpor. I will never fail you again," Krillzoc replied, the deathly glare in his eyes revealing he had no intention of breaking that promise.

Chapter Six

G eneral Alexander Sylvester watched the sun creeping out of sight behind the western horizon, his mood blackening faster than the sky. For the second consecutive day, there had been no word from the city of Muog. Once again, no Imperial soldier had been thrown from the walls, to the delight of the common soldiers. He had handed that oaf Odpor everything he could have asked for, yet somehow the dwarf chieftain had managed to botch what should have been a simple task. By now, the spirits in the Imperial encampment should have been at an all-time low. Instead, the men were positively beaming, convinced their captured brothers-in-arms would soon be coming home. It was enough to make him feel sick to his stomach.

The command meeting earlier that day had gone quite well, much to Sylvester's chagrin. Supreme General Cadmus Twilcox seemed convinced the dwarves were too frightened of Imperial retribution to continue executing their men. The amount of undeserved praise the other commanders had poured onto the incompetent old fool throughout the morning had been nothing short of appalling. Twilcox's unmistakable aura of self-satisfaction had made the display all the more unbearable. It would not matter in the end; they would all have no choice but to follow him soon enough. One way or another, Sylvester would make it happen. He had come too far to accept anything less.

"General Sylvester, would you like your supper set at the table tonight, sir?" Captain Terrence Garrison had arrived, right on time, as usual. *At least Garrison is as dependable as always. There is always one thing I can count on.*

"Yes, Captain Garrison, that will be fine," Sylvester replied, turning away from the horizon and walking back into his tent.

He felt a sudden rush of gratitude for Garrison as he saw the man set about meticulously setting his table, ensuring his cutlery was placed in the exact spot he liked and pouring a glass of his favorite wine. He was fortunate to have such a faithful, unquestioning servant. Recent days could not have been easy for a man like Terrence Garrison. Everything his general had asked him had gone against every one of the oaths he had sworn upon joining the Imperial Army. It must've been a daunting prospect for any man to face, much less one as simpleminded as his faithful captain. But Garrison had wisely placed his trust in Sylvester, just as he always had. Sylvester wondered if this was a result of blind loyalty or Garrison truly believing their actions were necessary in service of the greater good. In the end, Garrison's motivations didn't matter. All that mattered was that Garrison continued to remain loyal and silent.

"Please have a seat and join me tonight, Captain Garrison," Sylvester invited. "Pour yourself a glass of that fine wine as well. I daresay you will find it to be an excellent vintage. You deserve a nice meal after all the hard work you have put in for me lately. I must confess, I feel the need for some company tonight, if you are so inclined. Some nights a man does not want to have supper alone. Do you know the feeling?"

Garrison looked perplexed but followed the order without question, just as he always did. Sylvester took his seat across from his loyal servant, shooting him a reassuring smile. He needed Garrison to know he appreciated his hard work. If Odpor was going back on their arrangement, he might well need to perform more unsavory tasks for his general. He had never invited Garrison to dine with him before, feeling it was best to keep a clear set of boundaries between them. Sylvester had always believed there was little to be gained by fraternizing too closely with your subordinates. But these were strange times, and Sylvester needed to keep his only true servant in the fold. Such small kindnesses could help to reassure Garrison that he was still doing the right thing.

"Please help yourself to as much food as you like, Captain Garrison. You're skin and bones. Twilcox continuing to allow these portions for senior command while our men are starving is ludicrous if you ask me. I find myself lacking an appetite this evening anyway. I know rations keep getting cut, but I want you to know how much I appreciate your service. It is invaluable to me and to the Empire."

"Thank you, sir. It has always been my pleasure to serve you."

"Yes, but you did not join the Imperial Army seeking pleasure, did you? You enlisted out of a sense of duty, a desire to serve your people. It's always been obvious to me, watching the selflessness with which you approach your service. You are quite rare in that regard, Captain Garrison, though I'm sure you realize this. It was much the same for me."

"What was it that made you want to enlist, General?" Garrison asked, surprising Sylvester. The man had never dared ask him such a personal question in all his years of service.

This is what happens when you lower barriers. They begin to think they can speak as your equal. Keep it up and he will think you are friends. Still, Sylvester saw no harm in answering the question.

It seemed like a lifetime ago, and Sylvester had to remind himself that it was. He had served the Empire for over twenty years, climbing his way swiftly through the ranks. His father had been a soldier but had never risen beyond the level of private, a relatively simple and unambitious man. He had returned to his home in Salvamoan once his tour of duty was complete, content to resume a life of poverty as an onion farmer. Alexander

Sylvester had never been satisfied in that life. He despised every aspect of it, especially the constant struggle in the name of barely surviving. Why should he work his hands to the bone so that he could continue to barely manage to scrape together a living? He was meant for more extraordinary things, and the Imperial Army had given him a path to achieving them.

When he enlisted as a private at the age of eighteen, Sylvester immediately recognized that he had made the right choice. He had always been intelligent, a gift which had been wasted on an onion farm in northern Salvamoan. Here, he could use his talents to their full potential and ingratiate himself with the people who mattered. In less than a year, he had been promoted to sergeant, primarily due to his knack for subtly calling attention to his fellow privates' wrongdoings. They had despised him for it, but once he had been promoted, there was nothing they could do about it. He had not enlisted to gain the friendship of commoners and infantry grunts. Alexander Sylvester had been meant for greater things. They were nothing more than a stepping stone to his eventual goals.

He rose through the ranks quickly after that, admittedly more as a result of his silver tongue than of any natural military prowess. In truth, he had never been much of a fighter. Even now, at the rank of general, he doubted he could defeat most of the common privates in this encampment in a straight fight. But his ability to see there were often better options than a straight fight had gotten him where he was, while most of his fellow privates had ended up dead in various wars and battles as young men. *The mind is a sharper weapon than any sword could ever be, if one knows how to wield it properly*, he had told himself repeatedly over the past two decades.

"Well, Captain Garrison, I felt I had a duty to serve my people, to defend those who could not defend themselves," he replied. It was the answer Garrison would expect, the one he would give himself if asked. He could never tell a righteous man like Terrence Garrison the truth—not if he planned to hold on to the other man's loyalty. A simpleminded man like Garrison could never understand the motivations of a brilliant man.

He could only understand the world from his own limited point of view.

Sylvester had received word several years past that his family farm had been the victim of raiders. His parents and younger brother had all been killed, and the remnants of the property had passed to him. He had sold what remained of the farm without hesitation, practically giving it away at the first offer. It didn't matter to him. He had no interest in profiting off it, and he certainly had no desire ever to set foot there again. As far as he was concerned, his family had nobody to blame for their fate but themselves. Ignorant fools, if they had possessed an ounce of ambition, they could have found a better life for themselves years ago.

"I'm glad you did, sir. This war has shown the men the value you provide to the Imperial Army. Serving the Empire is a great sacrifice to make. And matters are challenging, but without men like you, I shudder to think the state we would be in."

"The same can be said of men such as yourself, Captain Garrison. You have been of great assistance to me these past few weeks. The Empire owes you a debt of gratitude that it will never be fully able to repay, though I promise you, I intend to try. The value of men like you has gone overlooked by those at the top of the Imperial Army for far too long. It's long past time we rectified that."

"Thank you, sir. I did not enlist for gratitude or reward, but I appreciate you and everything you have done for my career."

As well you should, Garrison. You would still be a lowly sergeant if it were not for me, Sylvester thought, smiling all the while. He had been so fortunate to find a servant like Terrence Garrison; his unquestioning loyalty had proven useful time and time again. But while he could appreciate Garrison's loyalty, he still harbored no admiration for the man. Garrison was content to blindly allow Sylvester to choose his path for him. This benefitted Sylvester, but he would never be able to feel true respect for such a man. How could anyone be satisfied living a life dictated by another?

"So, what do we do now, General Sylvester? It seems as though

Odpor is not going to honor the rest of our agreement," Garrison said, shaking Sylvester out of his thoughts.

You will do what I tell you to do and nothing else, he thought blackly, the kind smile never leaving his face. *You should know by now to leave the thinking to me.*

"I have been thinking about that very thing all day. We find ourselves in a precarious situation, do we not? If Odpor does not deliver what he promised, we are right back where we started. And if he is not going to be a dependable ally, we will need to find another way to achieve our goals. I have given thought to going back into Muog to find out what is going on. However, with each passing day, it seems less advisable. Do you concur?"

"Yes, sir. I would not recommend you go back to Muog while we are uncertain about Odpor's intentions. For all we know, this delay is a ruse to get you to come back so he can take you captive as well. You would be a far more valuable hostage than any of those men. We wouldn't stand a chance of winning this war if they were to capture you."

It was true, and it was something Sylvester had been thinking about all day. What if Odpor was trying to lure him back into Muog? Had the dwarven chieftain somehow deduced Sylvester's plans to double-cross the dwarves once he had what he wanted? He wouldn't think it possible, but he had no way to be sure. He could send Garrison in his stead, as he had before, but Odpor would be too cunning to tip his hand to a man as simple as Garrison if treachery was his intent. The dwarves were not known as brilliant strategists, but Sylvester hadn't gotten as far as he had by believing in secondhand information. He had to operate on the assumption that Odpor was double-crossing him and doing so intelligently.

"Yes, Captain Garrison, I smell treachery afoot. Perhaps it was unwise to trust the dwarves in the first place, but I saw no better alternative at the time. Now it seems we have no choice but to search for one. Matters cannot be allowed to continue as they are in this camp. I'm sure you see how low morale has fallen. I fear Supreme General Twilcox will soon lead us into ruin. It may not be long before we have a full-blown mutiny on our hands."

"Well, sir, if I may offer a suggestion?" Garrison asked, much to Sylvester's surprise.

Sylvester had to struggle to maintain his benign smile. "Yes, of course, Captain Garrison. What is your suggestion?"

"You are quite well loved in this camp right now. While I understand that the delay in the executions is bad for us, your negotiations are seen as a big reason for that among the foot soldiers. They, of course, love and adore you for it. Of course, you're not getting the full amount of credit you deserve, but it is a start. I believe that if some misfortune were to befall Supreme General Twilcox, many of the men would call for you to replace him. I daresay they would be quite passionate."

Captain Garrison, maybe you are more intelligent than I have been giving you credit for, Sylvester thought. He would never have expected such an idea from the man's mouth. Garrison was fiercely loyal to him, but he had never been a man to make such a suggestion. He had always contented himself with silently following orders and waiting to be told what to do next. While the idea of Garrison thinking for himself did not sit particularly well with Sylvester, he could not dismiss the validity of what he had said. *A good idea is a good idea, no matter the source,* he told himself.

"What you just said took courage, Captain Garrison. You would be dragged off and executed if that had been spoken in the wrong company. Fortunately, I feel our thoughts on this matter are one and the same, and you can rest assured it will never leave this tent. Unfortunately, General Twilcox merely having an unfortunate accident is a difficult thing to make happen. He is a very cautious man, and he is always surrounded by men who safeguard him day and night."

"I understand, sir. It was just something to think about. A simple fall from his horse could change so much."

"You are right, but making such a thing happen without drawing attention to ourselves is no easy task. If Twilcox were to have an accident and I were to rise to power, it could raise suspicions in certain corners. Still, you have given me a great deal to think about, Captain Garrison. Perhaps together you and I will find an answer to our little problem. Let's continue to think on this and see if we can find a solution."

Garrison nodded his agreement. Sylvester fell silent, his thoughts racing. Garrison may have been a dull-witted fool, but he was onto something. With his own popularity at an all-time high, it was an ideal time to strike. Still, how could they possibly kill Cadmus Twilcox in a way that appeared to be a legitimate accident? Suspicion would fall on him immediately. The ordinary foot soldiers may love him, but the commanders must know or at least suspect his career aspirations. While they might not think him ambitious enough to attempt such a maneuver, once it happened, they would wonder. There would be questions, maybe even a full inquiry. He wanted Twilcox dead, but not enough that he was willing to risk his own imprisonment or death to achieve it. But he had never been a man to shy away from a challenge.

Enjoy your time at the top, Cadmus. It won't last much longer.

Chapter Seven

When Darian Tor came awake, his first reaction was surprise at the fact that he had been able to fall asleep at all. The last thing he could remember was Radig applying a strange-smelling salve to his head wound. He wondered if perhaps the salve had contained an herb that had allowed him to rest. If he had dreamed, he couldn't remember it. He sat up slowly, noticing at once that the throbbing pain where Krillzoc had struck him in the head, while still present, had subsided significantly. Captain Dunstan was sitting nearby and noticed he was awake within seconds. He rose and moved quickly to Darian's side, placing a steadying hand on his shoulder.

"How long was I out?" Darian asked.

"Eight or nine hours, I think. It's hard to keep track of time in this windowless room. I don't know how the dwarves do it, but it doesn't seem to be an issue for Radig or Kalayo. How are you feeling? Any dizziness or nausea? Try not to move too quickly—I don't want you to throw up."

"No, not yet, at least. A little surprised to still be breathing, if I'm to be completely honest. Feeling a great deal of confusion about everything that's happened today, but physically, better than I've been in quite a while. My head wound is feeling better, along with most of the cuts I got in the last two fights. The salve Radig put on them seems to be working. Based on the fact that this conversation is happening, I'm assuming we haven't been found yet?"

"Radig assures me Odpor's men won't find us here, that he and Kalayo are the only two who know about this place. I suppose time will tell, but it's been quiet thus far. We can only hope it stays that way. I don't see any better option for us at the moment. We must place our faith in them."

"I recall similar promises last time we escaped, but I'll take what I can get for now. We're not swinging from ropes on the walls, so that's already better than I expected out of this day," Darian said, looking around at the rest of them.

The rest of the Imperial soldiers were awake, staring at him intently. Kalayo was there as well, but there was no sign of Radig. It was all coming back in a whirlwind of thoughts and emotions: their death march to the wall, the appearance of Radig and Captain Dunstan, the intense battle for their freedom, and their ultimate escape. They had been full of questions upon their arrival, but Captain Dunstan had insisted on getting their wounds treated and them all getting some sleep first. Now those questions were returning in a rush.

"Captain, how exactly did you end up here with us?" Darian asked.

"Well, that's a bit of an unusual story. I'm not going to lie; I was just sitting here wondering how this all happened. As you said, it's been an unusual day. I wouldn't believe any of it myself if I hadn't lived through it. Radig came to me at camp and asked for my help setting you all free. If you had told me a few days ago that I would trust a random dwarf appearing to me out of the black of night, I would have laughed in your face. In fact, I probably would've said you were insane and sent you to the healers for an evaluation of your mental aptitude."

"But how did he know to come to you in the first place? How did he find you in the camp?" Darnold Dans asked.

"Well, suffice it to say, I was not particularly pleased with the army's lack of interest in getting you all out of here. I assume you've figured this much out by now, but they were quite content to allow you to be executed one by one rather than make a single concession to the dwarves. The price of your lives was considered smaller than the price of showing weakness. I couldn't stand by and let that happen, so I decided to try to come after you on my own. So, I was out in the neutral territory, searching for hidden tunnels into Muog. I was having no luck, but Radig came out of thin air like a ghost. Somehow, he knew my name and said that he had overheard you talking about me and how you felt I could be trusted. I'm glad to hear that. He said he didn't know which of his Resistance dwarves he could still trust, so he came to me instead."

"Well, I'm not sure why you trusted him, but I'm glad you did. I doubt we would have gotten out of that mess without you. Thank you, Captain Dunstan, sir," Preston said.

"I'm still not sure I understand why I trusted him, but here we are. I'm just glad to find some of you still alive. I wish I could have come sooner. And we can dispense with the formalities until we get back to camp, gentlemen. How are you all feeling? I can't imagine everything you've been through."

"We're still alive, so none of what we've been through really matters. We're the lucky ones, and the men who aren't here with us deserve justice. Now that we're free from the dwarves, I'm just angry. I'm ready to get out of here and lop General Sylvester's head from his shoulders," Berj said.

"Sylvester? What do you mean? He's been negotiating for your release; why would you say that?" Dunstan was perplexed.

"I suppose Radig didn't have enough time to fill you in on that part. It was Sylvester who tipped Odpor off about our mission in the first place. He's the one who got us captured and everybody else killed," Berj replied, shaking with fury. "The dwarves had an ambush staged for us as soon as we entered Muog. It turns out he's also the reason there was a trap waiting for our supply caravan as soon as we arrived at the front. Anything that's gone wrong of late, he's probably to blame."

Dunstan was quiet for a moment, looking to each of them in turn, receiving a nod of confirmation from each. "But Sylvester has been an Imperial general for years. He has over twenty years of service to his name. Why would he do this? It doesn't make any sense. What could he possibly gain?"

"From what Radig told us, it's a matter of career ambition. He wants to make Supreme General Twilcox look incompetent while appearing to be doing everything he can to save us. He seems to think winning the love of the common men to be the key to his rise to power. He is hoping the Emperor will promote him to Supreme General," Darnold explained.

Whatever Dunstan had been expecting to hear, it wasn't that. He let out a deep breath, and his shoulders seemed to slump. He began to pace back and forth across their tiny living quarters, apparently lost in thought.

His reaction isn't all that different from ours, thought Darian. *None of us wanted to accept the truth either, and when we did, it felt like a kick in the gut.*

When Dunstan finally spoke, his words came slowly. "I don't want to believe this to be true, but looking back now, it makes more sense than I care to admit. Only the highest command levels were aware of your mission into Muog; it wasn't common knowledge. If I were not your commanding officer, even I would not have known. In fact, from what I heard, Sylvester was one of the stronger supporters of sending you in the first place. Twilcox wanted it to happen, and Sylvester was in his ear, assuring him it was a good idea. Most of the other commanding officers felt the potential reward was not worth the risk and advised against it."

"In hindsight, I would have to agree with them," Preston muttered.

"Screw hindsight; any idiot could have seen it was a boneheaded idea from the beginning," said Berj. If his lack of decorum troubled Dunstan, the captain didn't show it. "Remember that talk we all had after we were assigned? We felt like we were being sent on a suicide mission."

Once again, Axel's death passed through Darian's mind, and he felt a burning hatred for somebody besides Krillzoc. The cruel dwarf would still pay for taking his friend's life if he had anything to say about it, but now there was another man to hold responsible. If it was the last thing he did, he would see Alexander Sylvester pay for his treason. The idea that Axel and the other soldiers had all died for one man's overzealous career ambitions was too much to bear. It was Sylvester's duty to command them with integrity, not sell them like cattle in the name of advancing himself.

Axel, my old friend, I'm so sorry this happened to you. You deserved so much better. I promise I will make sure those responsible pay for it. But while thinking it helped Darian feel slightly better, he knew the simple act of wanting it would not make it happen. They needed to figure out what they were going to do next. Looking for answers, he turned to Captain Dunstan.

"What should we do now, Captain Dunstan? We have to get back and expose Sylvester as the traitor that he is. If we don't, it's only a matter of time until more soldiers end up in danger because of him. If his goal is to seize power, he won't give up just because his first plan failed. He's probably already working out a new way to sacrifice more soldiers to advance his career."

"Radig is searching for a way to get us out of Muog right now. That's our first step; we are no use to anybody hiding in this house. In the meantime, you all need to rest and recover from your captivity. Radig's salves have worked wonders, but your wounds are still severe. However, even once we return to camp, we have to be very careful about how we handle this. We can't just walk up and accuse a general of high treason and expect anyone to believe us. If only we had some sort of proof."

"Radig was there when Sylvester made his deal with Odpor; he could vouch for what we are saying," Darnold pointed out. Kalayo let out a low snort of laughter but did not speak.

"Unfortunately, I think Kalayo is right to laugh at that idea, Private Dans. Radig is a dwarf and will be viewed as an enemy combatant, not a reliable source of information. We can vouch for him until we are as blue in the face as an ogre; it will make no difference. There is no way Twilcox would believe the word of any dwarf over the word of a distinguished general like Alexander Sylvester. The word of four privates and a captain with a questionable service record won't make much difference."

It was unfair, but Darian knew he was right. He had only been a soldier in the Imperial Army for a few short months, but he could already see much of the corruption and bigotry that had infiltrated its ranks. Sylvester had found a way to twist it to his advantage, and there was nothing they could do about it—not by using established channels, at least. It didn't matter to Darian. He would see Sylvester pay for his crimes no matter the consequences.

"So, what do you think we should do?" Darnold asked.

"I think that if given enough time, Sylvester will expose himself for the traitor he is. But we need to be careful not to show our suspicions when we return. We will be facing enough questions as it is; best we act as though we are clueless to his plans. It's our best hope of staying alive until we see an opportunity to move against him. They will want to know how you all escaped, and they will have noticed my absence by now. I didn't exactly ask for permission to come here with Radig. I might well be arrested for desertion upon our return, so I want to know that all of you know to keep your heads straight."

"Surely they wouldn't arrest you if you come back with us?" Preston said, drawing a laugh from the grizzled captain. "How could they punish you for saving our lives?"

"Orders are orders, Private Preston. Twilcox told me to sit back like a good little boy and wait for orders. Let me explain something I have learned throughout a long military career, something you will see for yourselves if you serve long enough. You're all intelligent enough that I imagine you have begun to suspect this on your own. Matters of right and wrong are less relevant to those in charge than seeing their orders obeyed. I don't like it, and I won't pretend I do. It's disgusting and a poor way of serving the Empire. But it's the way of the world, and while they have the power, we must do our best to conform to their rules. This was just one occasion where I couldn't keep my head down and follow along."

"You came after us even knowing you would probably end up locked up for it?" Berj asked.

Dunstan didn't answer right away. He seemed lost in thought, as though he was looking back on old memories. Darian remembered the stories about Dunstan's time serving in Thornata. Was he regretting his decision to come after them?

"The truth is, I probably should have retired years ago. I could see what the Imperial Army was becoming, but I was comfortable in my life. After all, what the hell else was I going to do for a living? It's not like a man of my rank can expect a generous pension. This is all I've ever known. I have never been a man who could set aside doing what is right in the name of following orders. I paid for it five years ago. After what happened up in Thornata, they made me reenlist. It was that or spend a few decades in a stockade, maybe hope to see freedom again in the last few years of my life. I couldn't do that, so I took the reenlistment. They were desperate for commanders, and I thought I was smart enough to keep my nose clean. I was determined to keep my head down, finish my term, and get out. Look how well that turned out."

Before he could elaborate further, a grinding sound of shifting stone erupted from one of the walls. The soldiers scrambled to their feet, reaching for the weapons they had stolen from their captors. Kalayo hurried to the wall, her ear pressing against the stone. A second later, she turned back to them.

"No need for your weapons. It is just Radig returning."

"How can you be so sure?" Darian asked, astonished that she could know that from simply pressing her ear against the stone.

"Dwarves cannot only see better than you; we can hear better too. If Odpor's men had found us, there would be more than one person out there."

Sure enough, Radig appeared in the small gap a moment later, the stones shifting back into place behind him an instant later. Darian couldn't help but be amazed once more at the ingenuity of the architecture in this city. He had never seen anything like these wonders of masonry before in his life.

Radig embraced Kalayo briefly, then motioned for the rest of them to gather around him. Reaching into a small sack he carried at his side, he withdrew a few loaves of bread and pieces of fresh fruit. Darian's stomach growled, and he realized for the first time that he had not eaten in over a day. As the soldiers began to devour the food ravenously, Radig began to speak.

"I am afraid the news is not great. Odpor has increased the security on every tunnel that leads in the direction of your camp. I fear we do not have a path to get there that would not take us through too many guards or under the sight of the archers on the walls. Odpor knows we are trying to get you back to your camp. He wants to make sure you do not make it home at all costs."

"What can we do? We can't sit here forever," Darnold said.

"From what I have found, we have one realistic option to get out of this city. I do not like it, but we may not have any other choice. Nobody knows about this safe house, but they will sniff us out if we stay here long enough. We have a few days at most, no more. Krillzoc is hateful and cruel, but he is also quite skilled at what he does. I have to give him credit for that much."

"What option is that, Radig?" Dunstan asked.

"I only found one tunnel with security that I honestly believe we could fight our way through. It leads out of Muog to the northwest. Once we are free, we could make our way north to the city of Jezero."

Jezero? Darian remembered seeing the name of the city on maps of Qwitzite, but as far as he could remember, there was no Imperial force stationed there. What good would it do them to flee to yet another city under Odpor's rule? No sooner had he thought this question than Captain Dunstan was asking it.

"It is not ideal, but you are wrong on one count, Captain Dunstan. Jezero is under the rule of a dwarf named Iskra. He is the equivalent of a governor in one of your other provinces; he manages all aspects of life in the city. Iskra also happens to be the man who first formed the Resistance against Odpor. While Odpor has long suspected him, he has not had sufficient evidence to move against Iskra. Attacking a city of his own people based on a mere hunch would be quite a bad look, even for a man as ruthless as Odpor, you see? Iskra is an older man and is beloved across Qwitzite. Killing him would spark a severe backlash. Odpor's followers are loyal, but that would test their loyalty, apart from the true fanatics like Krillzoc. Iskra would grant you asylum until we can find a way to return you to your camp, I am sure of it."

"No offense, Radig, but you also assured us Odpor would never find the last safe house you took us to," Berj said. "You assured twelve of us of that fact, and only four of us are still breathing. I appreciate everything you have done, please know that I do, but assurances only get us so far. How can we be sure this Iskra won't see us and immediately think of us as invaders? You say Odpor is suspicious of him? He could hand us over to Odpor to deflect suspicion from himself."

"It is a fair question; I take no offense," Radig replied, though Darian thought he caught the hint of a scowl flash across the dwarf's face. "Iskra is not a supporter of Odpor's plan to secede from the Empire. He will not view you as enemies but rather as potential allies. He is also a man of integrity and honor, and he would never turn away those who need his help. Kalayo and I will vouch for you. Unlike Odpor, Iskra takes the words of his followers seriously."

It was far from a convincing argument from Darian's point of view, but he didn't see many other options. If they could flee to Jezero, and if this Iskra did take them in, they would buy themselves time. They desperately needed more time to figure out what to do about General Sylvester anyway. As Dunstan had pointed out, merely marching into camp and pointing their fingers at him would likely end up with all of them in a stockade or a noose.

"As little as I like the idea of running away, I like it more than the idea of sitting here and waiting for Odpor to find us," Berj acknowledged, turning to Captain Dunstan for guidance.

Dunstan took his time answering, his face expressionless. Darian wondered if the captain was thinking about his past in Thornata. He knew that past mistakes would hang over his head if he were in Dunstan's position. It must've been challenging for the captain to make critical decisions with such a cloud hanging over his head.

"Gentlemen, I think Radig has presented us with the best option we have available. If Jezero is safe, even for a short time, it will afford us an opportunity to recover from our injuries and decide our next move. Are there any objections?"

Once again, Darian felt a swell of respect for the leadership of Thad Dunstan. The captain understood the unprecedented situation they found themselves in and was not ordering any man to do anything he was not comfortable doing. The Imperial Army would benefit significantly from more men like him in positions of power.

When no objections came, Dunstan spoke up once more. "All right, Radig. If you say this is for the best, we'll place our trust in you. You've gotten us this far. Let's see if you can get us out of here."

Chapter Eight

I t was the darkest of nights, or so Radig assured them, for their safe house had no windows for the Imperials to confirm. In the end, it mattered little. It would make no difference if someone spotted them, for dwarves possessed vision that was nearly as clear at night as it was in the light of day. They were in the dwarves' world, and the dwarves would always hold the advantage, as they had learned time and time again. But this was when there would be the fewest people out in the streets of Muog, presenting their best opportunity of escaping. While Darian was none too eager to fumble around in the dark, he had to admit Radig's plan was the best they had.

They had waited for two days due to Captain Dunstan's insistence that his men have time to allow their wounds to heal. Eager as they were to be out of Muog, they had all relented and agreed with his assessment of their health. They needed to be able to move fast or fight at a moment's notice, and they hadn't been in the best of shape. They wouldn't have lasted long if forced to run or to stand and fight. Two days later, while none of them were fully healed, each man swore they were well enough to survive whatever this night held in store for them. *Or so we can hope,* thought Darian. Radig had eventually relented to the delayed departure despite his concern that the delay would lead to their discovery.

"How are you feeling, Private Tor?" Dunstan asked him. He had been making his way to each man in turn, ensuring they were ready to go.

"Sore, angry, and ready to get out of this city. I'll be just as happy if I never have to set foot here again. I'll be ready if we need to fight, Captain Dunstan; you don't need to worry about me."

"A captain always needs to worry about his men, Private Tor. It's part of the job. The day I stop worrying about you is the day I am no longer fit to command you. Never forget that," Dunstan replied before moving over to Darnold Dans.

Darian thought about what Dunstan had said. In many ways, Thaddeus Dunstan reminded him of the man Axel Stark would likely have grown into had he not been robbed of his life by Alexander Sylvester and Krillzoc. The mere thought of the two men sent rage coursing through his body, just as it did every time they floated into his stream of thought. It was as though nothing else in his life mattered anymore. He lived only to see the pair of them served the justice they deserved.

He looked around the room at each of his companions, trying to get a measure of the state of each. Were they all ready for whatever this night held in store for them? Captain Dunstan was clearly prepared to move; his chief concern was the well-being of his men. The longer they spent in Muog, the higher their chances of being discovered and killed. It was still astonishing to Darian that Dunstan had risked so much to save a few lowly foot soldiers. He was the only one of the Imperials to still wear his armor and carry his Imperial-issued sword; Krillzoc had confiscated theirs when he'd captured them. Even now, after having had so much time to adjust to his new reality, that night felt like a lifetime ago.

Berj Jenson was stalking back and forth like a predator eager to escape from a cage. There was still a shining bruise on the side of his face where Darian had struck him, though the swelling had mostly subsided. The two had not discussed their fight; in fact, they had hardly spoken to each other since their escape. Darian had not forgotten Berj's comments about Axel, but he had managed to set them aside. He hoped that, in time, their friendship would be able to heal fully. In the end, there were few people he would rather have by his side in a nasty situation than Berj Jenson. His mouth may work faster than his brain, but there were few better in a fight. When the time came to deal with Krillzoc and Sylvester, Berj would be an ally he would want by his side.

Darnold Dans stood silently in a corner, his eyes sweeping the room, much like Darian's. Darnold had always been a slow, deliberate thinker. He undoubtedly wanted to have a measure of every person in the room and to know he could count on them in the worst-possible situation. His defensive fighting style had spared him from receiving injuries as severe as his comrades. It was well-deserved good fortune, which Darian envied every time an ache or pain raced through his body. If it came to a fight, they would likely need him to play a critical role if they were to survive. From Darian's view, Darnold Dans looked like he was prepared for such a challenge.

Max Preston was sitting against a far wall, his eyes focused on his feet. Darian was amazed at how much the young man had grown since their days in basic training. Harter Arsch had often commented that Max Preston would be the first dead body when a real battle came along, but Preston had proven him wrong time and time again. He had survived this long when so many others had not, and it had not been through mere chance. He had mastered his prior reckless urges and become a capable soldier. Darian was glad to have Preston by his side.

Radig and Kalayo stood together in a corner, conversing in low murmurs. Darian could only assume they were discussing the route out of Muog. There was still so much they did not know about these two dwarves. Radig had saved them twice now, though admittedly, the second time had been more about saving his wife. Both dwarves carried heavy weapons, Radig a mace and Kalayo an axe, and both had outfitted themselves in steel chain mail Radig had retrieved from a nearby stash. Darian believed they could trust the pair and hoped he was right. Radig and Kalayo were their only hope of getting out of Muog alive.

"If everybody could gather around please, I want to go over the plan one last time," Radig said, motioning for them to join him in the center of the one-room house. "First, I want to stress that we are only likely to have one chance at getting this right. We can attempt to retreat back here if we fail, but I do not like our odds. Once we are seen, the alarm will go up, and the streets of this city will be swarming with Odpor's men within minutes. I doubt we could get back here undetected, no matter how crafty we may be."

"I'm assuming you think we can get to this tunnel unseen, though?" Preston asked.

"That is the plan. As we have discovered of late, our plans have a habit of going horribly awry. If that happens tonight, I am going to pick up the pace. We essentially have to make a break for it in that scenario. I understand you are all injured, a few of you quite severely, but you will have to push on through the pain. It is up to each of you to keep up. We will not willingly leave anyone behind, but we each have a responsibility not to be a burden to the others. Understood?"

They all nodded their consent, though Darian knew all four privates were in silent agreement: they would never leave one another behind. If one man fell behind, his brothers would defend him until their last breath, no matter the circumstances. They had been through too much together to do anything else. For better or worse, they had been bound together by their shared struggles.

"There will be resistance in the tunnel, but it is clearer than any other path I have checked. I would anticipate about four guards. Captain Dunstan and I are in the best physical shape and will take the lead position. We have to dispatch them as quickly and quietly as possible. We are timing our departure to arrive just after these guards go on duty. That should ensure a several-hour head start before Odpor's men discover their bodies."

"Is there any chance the sentries above will spot us once we leave the tunnel?" Dunstan asked. "The walls provide quite a vantage point."

"It is minimal at most. This particular tunnel comes out far from the walls, and at much lower elevation. The guards up top will not be able to spot us, and the watch is focused toward your camp anyway. Odpor has little reason to send men north at this time, so our path should be clear. Still, we are going to have to march until dusk tomorrow. Odpor will send out search parties as soon as they discover the dead guards, and we need to cover as much ground as possible before that happens. They will know where we are heading in short order. Our only chance is to outpace them. It is going to be a long few days, so I hope you all rested while you had the chance. I want to put as much distance between Muog and us as possible before we take a break. Once we leave this room, there is to be no speaking, understood?"

Radig paused for a moment, looking around to see if there were more questions. When none came, he motioned them all to form a line behind him as he made to open the door. Radig and Captain Dunstan took the lead, while Kalayo brought up the rear. The Imperials had to duck into a bowlegged crouch to squeeze their way through the dwarf-sized door. Kalayo closed it behind them with a quick movement of her hand, leaving no trace of the concealed chamber.

Hopefully we don't have to try to flee back here, thought Darian. *If Radig and Kalayo don't make it, we won't be able to get inside, even if we can find it.*

They emerged into a narrow alley, which was fortunately utterly devoid of any sign of life. Radig turned to the right, not waiting to see if they would follow. They had no choice now; their escape from this cursed city depended solely on the two dwarves. They shuffled along quickly, knowing a guard could turn into the alley and spot them at any moment. One cry of alarm would be the end of them. Darian was right in the middle of the group, with Max Preston in front of him and Darnold Dans behind. *We've survived so much together, and we will survive this too,* he told himself. *Whatever this blasted city has to throw at us this one last time, we'll get through it.*

Every time they came to an intersection, the Imperials held their breath as they darted across, their hands never straying far from their weapons. Occasionally, Darian would steal a glance back, reassuring himself that Darnold, Berj, and Kalayo were still there. He soon lost track of time and all sense of direction. Radig was taking them along a complex and winding path, one he had assured them was the least likely to be occupied. Still, it only took one dwarf stepping out of their well-concealed doorway at the wrong moment to spell disaster.

The darkness only complicated matters further. Radig and Kalayo may have seen as clearly in darkness as in broad daylight, but their Imperial companions were not so fortunate. On several occasions, Darian feared he had lost sight of Radig up ahead, but each time, their guide slowed his pace to allow his charges time to catch up. He wondered for a brief moment if Radig was regretting his decision to free them from that prison. It had undoubtedly proven to be more trouble than he had anticipated. Radig and Kalayo could have fled the city days earlier without so much trouble had they been on their own. Or he might still be comfortably embedded under cover among Odpor's guards. Had Radig's plan at least had the desired effect of sowing discord among the dwarves loyal to Odpor? Darian did not know and knew he was unlikely to find out.

After what felt like an eternity of twists and turns through the stone streets of Muog, Radig brought them to a halt in front of an un-adorned wall. There was nothing to indicate to Darian that this wall was different than any other they had passed, though he had learned by now that few things were as they seemed in Muog. Radig immediately went to work, his hands moving in intricate motions across the stone's surface. Within seconds, a doorway had begun to appear. Like every other door they had encountered in Muog, the Imperials had to stoop low to make their way through. Once again, Kalayo closed the entrance behind them, leaving them in near-total darkness. There was a long pause until Max Preston drew Darian in close and whispered into his ear, his voice barely audible.

"Radig says there is a long staircase leading downward, right in front of us. He cannot risk any light yet, so we must move slowly. There's a steep drop on each side. There is no handhold, because of course there isn't. Why should anything ever be easy for us? Pass it on to the others."

Darian whispered the same message to Darnold, who, in turn, passed it on to Berj. Radig could apparently hear the message being passed along and began to advance immediately once it had been delivered, not waiting for an acknowledgment. Darian probed cautiously with his right leg in the darkness, searching for the drop. He found it at last and cautiously took one slow step down. Then he took another, and then another, each time holding his breath, hoping he would not plummet forward into the void.

If their trek through Muog had felt protracted, the journey down this long stone staircase felt never-ending. To their credit, the dwarves had built the steps symmetrically, each the exact same width and height as the one before, though this did little to ease the nerves of descending them in the darkness. With each step, Darian expected one of his comrades behind him to tumble forward, sending them all plummeting into the darkness. To his relief, it did not happen, and finally, he reached out cautiously for the next step and found it was not there. Taking a deep breath, he inched forward carefully, fearing the step may just be wider than the others, but was thankful to find he was on even footing once more.

"Cover your eyes; Radig is going to give us some light," Preston whispered, a message Darian passed on to Darnold Dans before clenching his eyes shut tight.

He opened them slowly, finding what appeared to be a dimly

glowing pebble resting in Radig's hand. The light it gave off was a faint but welcome sight for the Imperials. Darian turned to look back at the stairs and was amazed. They stretched so far that he could not see the top. The trek might not have lasted as long as it had seemed, but it had indeed brought them deep underground. Radig beckoned for them all to lean in close, his voice little more than a murmur.

"We are almost out of here. There are four guards stationed up ahead. A few hundred more feet, around a corner, and we will be right on top of them. I wanted your eyes to have a chance to adjust to the light before we reach them. When we close in on them, I am going to make it much brighter. This should catch them off guard and give us the advantage. Dwarf eyes are sensitive to sudden changes in light. Let Captain Dunstan and I do the fighting unless it appears we are in grave danger or we call for your help. Understood?"

They nodded as one, and Radig began to lead them forward once more. In the dim light, Darian could see they were approaching a bend in the tunnel and tensed, half expecting the guards to come walking around the corner at any moment. Captain Dunstan silently drew his sword, and Radig already had his heavy mace gripped tightly in his hand.

This is it; we are finally getting out of Muog, Darian dared tell himself. After so many days spent feeling assured of his inevitable death within the city's walls, it already felt as though a heavy weight was lifting from his shoulders.

As soon as Radig turned around the corner, the light emanating from the pebble in his hand intensified. Even Darian, whose eyes had already adjusted to the dimmer light, had to briefly squint against the brilliance of its glow. Radig charged forward with the light held high above his head, Captain Dunstan on his heels. As he rounded the corner, Darian could see four dwarven guards in the distance, their heads turning involuntarily away from the light in Radig's hand. *Not a bad trick to have up your sleeve, Radig.* It had helped them escape the battle under the walls of Muog, and now it was going to free them from this cursed city once and for all.

Radig crashed into the first guard, his mace coming down in a ferocious strike. His victim never had a chance, the blow shattering his skull in an explosion of blood and bone before he could think to bring his shield up to defend himself. Radig never hesitated, turning to his next opponent, the mace lashing out again. This foe was more prepared, his shield in place, and Radig's attack glanced away harmlessly. The guard thrust his shield forward, and now it was Radig who was in danger, backpedaling and trying to avoid the axe swing coming for him.

Captain Dunstan was there in an instant, his sword coming down on the dwarf's arm as he swung at Radig, the axe clattering to the ground with a cry of pain. Radig sprung forward to finish him as Dunstan turned to engage the remaining two guards. He deflected one sword strike and slipped away from another before his own sword found its mark, catching one of the guards clean through the chest, punching through his hard leather armor with a powerful thrust. The second guard swung at Dunstan with an axe, but the captain was too quick. Stepping inside the dwarf's reach, he drew a dagger from his belt, thrusting it cleanly into his opponent's throat before the attack could find its mark.

Darian was reminded of their battle on the way to Muog, when the dwarves had attacked their supply caravan. He had been left in awe of Dunstan's combat prowess and felt similar amazement now. The guards had outnumbered him and Radig four to two, but Dunstan had quickly dispatched two of them and allowed Radig to defeat a third.

Don't be too awestruck. He earned those skills the hard way. You better hope you never see as many fights as he has in his life, he reminded himself. There was a time in the not-so-distant past when he would have longed to have Dunstan's skill with a blade. Now he understood better the cost of acquiring such talent and was perfectly content never to see another fight once Sylvester and Krillzoc were dealt with.

The fight had lasted only seconds, but Radig was still anxiously watching the tunnel behind them, searching for any sign that anyone had heard them. Apparently satisfied they had not, he motioned for them to follow again, this time holding up the pebble and flooding the tunnel with light. They hurried along, stepping over the bodies of the four fallen guards. Radig made no effort to conceal the bodies; to do so would've been a waste of time. Their absence would tell the story of what had happened just as well as their corpses. Their time was better invested in covering as much ground as possible. They soon came to another downward staircase, though this was a much shorter and less nerve-racking journey thanks to the light now shimmering brightly in Radig's hand.

After another long walk of several hundred yards, they arrived at one last staircase leading upward. With Radig still leading the way, the party hurried up, eager to be back in the fresh air again.

The dwarves are incredible to be able to build these tunnels, but I don't know how they stand spending so much time underground. Not having the sun overhead feels so unnatural. When they reached the top, Darian squinted to see what Radig was doing with his hands. Yet again, the dwarf's movements were so fast and intricate that he could not follow them. How did he remember the exact actions for each doorway? Were there markings that told him what to do? A moment later, an opening appeared in the earth above them, and at last, they were free of Muog.

Darian took a deep breath of fresh air for what felt like the first time in a lifetime. Since entering Muog on their ill-fated mission, every time they had been outdoors, he had felt little appreciation for something as simple as fresh air. They had been in a perilous situation each time. They still were, he reminded himself, but this time felt different, just by virtue of being outside the city walls. This was the type of victory that had once seemed impossible. His thoughts turned to Axel, dead in that city, dead so the rest of them could have a chance at life. It was a sobering moment, thinking back to the night they had entered Muog thirteen strong. A bad ending had always been a strong possibility, and they had all known it. But in his wildest imaginations, Darian could never have concocted a tale of despair like the one they had just lived through.

"I can't believe it. I thought we would all die in that blasted city. No offense, Radig and Kalayo, but I would be just as happy never going back!" Max Preston declared, putting words to Darian's thoughts.

"None taken, but I would keep my voice down if I were you, Private Preston," Radig warned. "Patrols do not usually come through this area, but we cannot be too cautious."

"Fair enough," Preston replied, dropping his voice to a whisper.

"We need to get moving. The farther we are from Muog, the safer we will be. We will be heading northwest toward Jezero. If we make good time, we can be there in four days. Any questions before we get underway?"

Radig waited for a moment, but no questions were forthcoming, everyone apparently eager to be on their way. With Radig in the lead, they set off for the northwest. They knew their ordeal was far from over, but they felt more reason for optimism than they had since before their capture.

It's time to turn the tables on these bastards, thought Darian, eager as ever to serve justice to those who deserved it.

Chapter Nine

T he sun had not yet fully risen when Krillzoc stepped into the home of Odpor. Unlike his last visit, he was not fearful of how the dwarven chieftain would respond to the news he bore. A less cunning and charming man than Krillzoc would never have been able to talk Odpor out of his plan of removing him from power. Any other dwarf would never have left their last meeting alive; Krillzoc was certain of it. But Krillzoc had served Odpor longer than any other dwarf, and he knew precisely how to appeal to his sensibilities. The shame he had felt at his failures was insignificant compared to the rage and hatred he held for those who had caused them. Now he found himself delighted to have the opportunity to inflict his revenge upon those unfortunate souls. They would pay the price for his humiliation, and if he had his way, they would beg him to end their suffering long before they were done paying that price.

Odpor was already waiting for him in his throne room. He must have woken early to receive the news, good or bad. His face was an unreadable mask as Krillzoc strode around the reflection pool to approach his chair, sinking into an informal bow. Krillzoc caught the hint of a grin on Odpor's face; he must already suspect what Krillzoc had come to tell him.

"Chieftain Odpor, I come bearing news of the Resistance and the escaped Imperials."

"Indeed? Then tarry not, Krillzoc. Tell me, what news do you bring?"

"Our suspicions have proven to be correct. Late last night, Radig and Kalayo led the Imperials through the northern tunnel and out of Muog. The scouts I placed on the exit spotted them during the early-morning hours and confirmed that they have set out toward the northwest, toward Jezero. The scouts are following them and will continue to bring us updates as necessary. I have made it clear that they are not to attack or interfere without authorization."

"Excellent work, Krillzoc. How many casualties did we suffer in the tunnel?"

"Only four; I lessened the security to the point that Radig would not be able to resist." Krillzoc could hardly contain his delight. "I had asked our commanders specifically to station men who would be no great loss to our cause in this tunnel."

"A necessary sacrifice. Their deaths will be the beginning of the end for the Resistance. All four are to receive a hero's burial, understood? They may have been incompetent buffoons in life, but we must show our appreciation for their service publicly. Make sure it is known all throughout the city who was responsible for their deaths. Any opportunity to turn public opinion further against the Resistance should not be squandered. See to it that their families receive double the standard payout."

"Yes, Chieftain Odpor. Do I have your leave to begin mustering an attack force to move against Jezero?"

Odpor did not answer immediately, and to Krillzoc, it seemed the chieftain was considering his options. Surely Odpor had no plans of allowing the Imperials to escape? They had finally received an opportunity to prove Iskra's treachery, and they could not pass it up.

"Not yet, Krillzoc. Let us wait until we have confirmation that they have reached Jezero. They will be on edge upon their arrival, as will Iskra, searching for any hint of a threat. Best if we lull them into a false sense of security. I would not want them to flee Jezero prematurely. That being said, I do want you to begin exploring options for moving a sizeable force out of Muog discreetly. It would not do for the rest of the Imperial Army to spot our actions and attack when they believe us to be vulnerable. Soon enough, my friend, we will crush Jezero and the Resistance, and then we will return and put an end to the Imperial Army as well."

They were on the verge of the open war Krillzoc had always craved. To this point, the war with the Imperials had consisted of small guerilla attacks against their forces. While he reveled in every opportunity to draw Imperial blood, he had long been losing his patience. He despised sitting back inside the walls of Muog, waiting to see the Imperials' next move. From the beginning, he had urged Odpor to muster an army and meet them head-on, though the chieftain had preferred a cautious, more strategic approach. Odpor's reasoning was that since the Imperials could never hope to breach the walls of Muog, the dwarves should sit back and allow their adversaries to make the first mistake. It was an intelligent strategy, but Krillzoc had never considered himself a scholar.

"I have another job for you in the meantime, Krillzoc."

"Your wish is my command, Chieftain Odpor. What do you require of me?"

"I believe an alliance with General Sylvester still makes sense for us. Or rather, the appearance of an alliance with General Sylvester still makes sense for us. However, he has not returned to negotiate with me again. I can only assume the lack of executions has led him to believe that we are going back on our end of the deal."

"He would be a fool to believe such a thing. A dwarf always lives by his word, especially one of your noble stature."

"True, though I have never suspected the man of being anything other than a fool, Krillzoc. But you should never underestimate the value the right fool can provide when properly utilized. I want you to enter the Imperial camp tonight and speak with him on my behalf. I hope you understand this for the honor it is. I would entrust such a task to no other dwarf."

Krillzoc was indeed honored beyond words by the trust Odpor was placing in him, only days after threatening him with imprisonment or execution. Odpor was often a difficult man to serve, and he expected nothing short of perfection from those who served him. But he could also show himself to be just and merciful, as he was now. Krillzoc had infiltrated the Imperial encampment countless times before; to do so again would not be so difficult. Still, he could not risk failure, not with the amount of faith Odpor was placing in him. Executing a small-scale assault was one thing; negotiating with a high-ranking general was another. He would need assistance to ensure success, as unpalatable as the thought was.

"Your trust in me is an honor beyond measure, and I give you my word as a dwarf that I will not fail you. What message do you wish for me to deliver to Sylvester?"

"Be truthful with him; explain what has happened with his captive soldiers and the Resistance. Hopefully this honesty will assist with building his trust. Tell him I still believe we have the potential for a fruitful partnership. If he wishes to take the place of Cadmus Twilcox at the top of the Imperial Army, there are other means of doing so. Some of those means are far more direct than the clever games he has tried to play thus far. I am sure you take my meaning, Krillzoc."

"Yes, of course I do, Chieftain Odpor. I will not fail you."

"I know you will not. I leave the specifics of the following operation to you. Such a task falls under your purview, after all."

With a second bow, Krillzoc turned and left the room to set about his work. There was much he needed to accomplish before leaving for the Imperial camp later that night.

His first stop was a nondescript building not far from Odpor's home, one that would seem unremarkable to any who did not know what it possessed. This was where the dwarves had stored their official records for centuries. Krillzoc was not the type of man to lay out intricate plans, but the success of this attack was crucial. If they were going to assault Jezero, he needed to find out everything he could in advance. He had visited the city only once, years before, and had been far from impressed. Unlike Muog, its physical defenses were sorely lacking, but he still needed to be aware of any traps that may be lying in wait.

After two hours of poring over various scrolls and schematics, Krillzoc left the records office. He was confident he knew the tactics Iskra would employ to try to defend Jezero from an assault. Even better, he was confident in his ability to counter those defenses. Now he needed to assemble the force that would overwhelm those defenses. He would have to choose carefully, for they needed to leave Muog adequately defended in the event that the Imperials finally decided to attack. He was not sure of exactly how many fighters Iskra had under his command, which further complicated matters.

He arrived at the barracks before noon, calling out to several commanders to join him in his office. He stepped into the small room, taking a seat behind the desk he seldom used. Krillzoc had never been a dwarf to lead from behind a desk; he preferred to be either on the front lines or in an interrogation chamber. His natural talents were in the arts of ending lives and inflicting pain. But there were a lot of moving pieces, and he could not be everywhere at once. He had no choice but to delegate some responsibility, something he despised doing. He had always felt that if he wanted something done correctly, the only way to be assured of it was to do it himself. That was not an option here, so he would have to delegate and be sure those assigned to these tasks understood the consequences of failure.

The three dwarves he had called arrived within minutes. Every dwarf in these barracks knew better than to keep Krillzoc waiting for long.

Once they were gathered in the cramped office, he began to lay out his plans.

"My friends, Chieftain Odpor has entrusted me with a task of great importance. I shall require all of your assistance to complete this. Understand that failing me means you are failing Chieftain Odpor himself. I trust you all understand the consequences of such a failure?"

"Yes, sir," all three replied in unison, exchanging nervous glances. Krillzoc smirked in satisfaction. He did love to see his men squirm under pressure. He had always believed that men who understood the repercussions of failure would perform better in the name of avoiding it.

"I need one of you to oversee the construction of siege equipment. This is not any normal siege equipment. In fact, it is quite unlike anything you have ever seen before. I have plans for you; I brought them from the records office. This will need to take place outside of the city walls, far beyond the range the Imperials normally patrol. You are to use only dwarves whose loyalty is beyond question, and they are not to utter a word of this to another soul. Word of this getting to the Imperials or the Resistance would be disastrous for us. Do I have a volunteer for this task?"

After a brief pause, the dwarf on the far left stepped forward. Krillzoc handed him the plans, smirking at the astonished look on the man's face as he examined them.

If you think you are surprised, wait until you see the faces of those filthy Resistance traitors when they see this in action.

Iskra was a filthy traitor, but even Krillzoc had to acknowledge he was no fool. He would prepare Jezero for any foreseeable assault. But he would never see this coming.

"I need another one of you to begin preparing the assault force that will be using this equipment. We are moving against the Resistance in force. Again, the loyalty of the dwarves involved cannot be in question in any way, and they need to be ready to deploy at a moment's notice. We need the most vicious dwarves in the army because this force will need to be smaller than I would like. The bulk of our forces need to be here to defend Muog against the Imperials."

Another dwarf stepped forward to volunteer his services, and Krillzoc sent him on his way. This left only one, a grizzled veteran named Gornash. Krillzoc was delighted with how things had unfolded. Gornash was the exact man he wanted for this particular assignment.

"Gornash, I will be leading the assault on the Resistance myself. While I am gone, Chieftain Odpor will need someone to stand in my place and lead the defense of Muog if necessary. This will be your duty. You will be responsible for the security of the chieftain himself as well. Do you feel you are up to the task?"

"Yes, sir," Gornash replied, his face expressionless.

Of course you are; I would not have selected you otherwise. Krillzoc could not have been more pleased with Gornash to serve as his proxy while he was away. The dwarf possessed the necessary mercilessness to do the job effectively and none of the ambition to seize it for himself permanently. He would not seek to supplant Krillzoc while he was away. Krillzoc would not need to worry about a struggle for his position once he returned. Gornash would serve Odpor well enough that Krillzoc would not incur the chieftain's wrath for the choice but not well enough for Odpor to consider a changing of the guard. The fact that Odpor had been so close to replacing him was still fresh in Krillzoc's mind.

With the necessary tasks delegated, it was time for Krillzoc to plan his trip into the Imperial encampment that night. It had been quite some time since he had entered the camp himself, and he would need guidance, especially to reach a high-ranking general's tent undetected. The dwarf he needed would not be found in the barracks but likely at one of the taverns nearby. This was not a man he savored the thought of doing business with, but he was the best at what he did.

To Krillzoc's relief, he found the man he sought at the first tavern he checked. The room went silent as he entered, as such places usually did.

Krillzoc's reputation preceded him everywhere he went in Muog, and he was perfectly fine with that. His contact was sitting alone at a table in a corner, sipping an ice-blue drink so pungent that the mere smell of it nearly brought tears to Krillzoc's eyes as he took a seat opposite the man.

"What do you want, Krillzoc? I am a bit preoccupied at the moment, if you have not noticed," the dwarf said in a tone Krillzoc would have accepted from almost nobody else.

You are fortunate that I need you, you rat-faced bastard. One day I will finally be able to cut your throat and be done with it.

"Good afternoon, Haggart. I require your services tonight."

"Why should I care about what you require, Krillzoc? What have you ever brought me? Nothing but misery and scorn. Go begging elsewhere and leave me in peace," Haggart said, making no effort to conceal his disdain.

"I could have your tongue torn out for speaking to me this way. Do you understand that, you drunken fool?"

"How about you get up and do it, then?" Haggart said, his voice rising with each word. "Go on, Krillzoc. Show me what a big, strong, important man you have become. Hell, come take a swing at me. If you hit me hard enough, it might even sober my sorry ass up. That is what you always say you ought to do, right? I am right here. Give it your best shot!"

Heads were starting to turn in their direction, and Krillzoc felt his face go red. He would never have swallowed such insults under normal circumstances, but these circumstances were far from ordinary. Beyond that, as skilled of a fighter as he was, Krillzoc understood that he was talking to one of the few dwarves in Muog who might actually be able to best him in single combat. Haggart appeared to be unarmed to the blind eye, but Krillzoc was no fool. He would wager his life there were at least a dozen razor-sharp blades hidden somewhere on the drunkard's person. It seemed Haggart had consumed enough alcohol to make the rash decision to use one of them if pushed too far.

"Haggart, I did not come here to fight with you," Krillzoc began, trying to soothe the drunken fool. Haggart was having none of it.

"No, you came here to use me and throw me away, just like you always do. Why would I expect anything else from you by now? It has always been that way, has it not, Krillzoc? You have had no qualms about using us where convenient to further your career ambitions. And once you have gotten what you want, you vanish again, off to bigger and better things. My curse is being the last one left for you to torment with this nonsense. I ought to pluck one of your eyes from your skull for having the nerve to show me your face, you blood traitor. But Mother always said that family was the most important thing in the world. So, turn tail and run back to Odpor before I drink enough for my hatred of you to outweigh my love for her."

"What happened to her was not my fault, brother. Blame me all you wish, but you know it to be true. I sent her gold every month," Krillzoc tried to reason, but now Haggart was on his feet, remarkably well-balanced for a man so deep into his drinks.

"Oh, yes. You thought the little trinkets you sent could make everything better. Ever bother to show your ugly face? No, but I suppose it was buried too far up Odpor's rear, was it not? You should know something, *brother.* Even in those last days, while she was wasting away, she never lost hope for you. 'Oh, he will come,' she kept telling me. 'He would never let his mother go to her ancestors without seeing the face of her youngest son one last time.' But you never did, did you, Krillzoc? I should have killed you back then. It would have been an insult to her memory, but it would have made the world a better place. Get it over with already. What did you come here to ask me?"

"I need you to guide me into the Imperial encampment tonight," Krillzoc said, deciding it best not to further pursue the argument. "There is a general named Alexander Sylvester. I need you to show me to his tent and stand guard while I am inside."

Haggart stumbled back into his chair, laughing. He was red-faced from the liquor, and Krillzoc wondered briefly if his brother would even be able to maintain his consciousness. Haggart had always been simpleminded, but since their mother's death, he had found a mean streak as well. Still, Krillzoc had little choice. If he wanted to get close to Alexander Sylvester, his brother was his best hope of doing so.

"Why do you think I would do that for you, Krillzoc?"

"I will pay you more for one night of work than you make in a year."

"There it is again. Always thinking you can buy your way out of any problem. How did we end up so different, Krillzoc? We had the same upbringing, the same blood. I will be honest with you: I am tempted to accept your offer. If they catch us, at least I can die smiling, knowing that you will go with me. Family should die together; Mother would approve, would she not?"

"Then do it, Haggart. Help me. If you are lucky, you will finally see me get the justice you feel I so rightly deserve. If you are not so fortunate, you will still be paid handsomely for your efforts. You have nothing to lose."

"Meet me here at dusk. I will do as you ask. Hell, I might even bring you back in one piece, against my better judgment. Once again, you will have Mother's talk of family and loyalty to thank for it if so. You had better have my money in your hand, or I walk."

Haggart did not wait for a reply, downing the remainder of his drink in a single swig and rising from the table. He was out of the tavern a few seconds later, leaving Krillzoc alone. Countless eyes continued to dart cautiously toward him, averting the second he turned in their direction. Everyone in the tavern had just watched Haggart make a fool out of him.

Cursing his hated brother, Krillzoc stormed from the tavern, hoping all the while for one of these fools to give him an excuse to make an unpleasant example of them. None of them did, his reputation intimidating enough that none dared to level a taunt at him despite Haggart's public insolence. The jokes would no doubt begin as soon as he was out of earshot.

He and Haggart had been close once, though it felt like he had lived several lifetimes since then. His elder by four years, Haggart had taught him everything, including how to fight. As a young dwarf, it had seemed there was nothing Haggart didn't excel at. But as he matured, Krillzoc realized that despite all his ability, his older brother possessed not an ounce of ambition, no desire to further his station in life. Haggart had joined the dwarven army the moment he turned of age and quickly found renown as the best tracker the force had ever seen. A man of his skills should have risen through the ranks in a matter of years, but Haggart had no interest in promoting or in bettering himself.

Krillzoc had always been a polar opposite in that regard. For as long as he could remember, he had dreamed of clawing his way out of the poverty and squalor of his youth. Haggart might've been content with living a simple life among the commoners, but Krillzoc had always been destined for better things. Yet, to his frustration, his own military career had been rather ordinary—at least until Odpor came to power. By ingratiating himself with the new chieftain, he had assured his meteoric rise to power. In doing so, he had left what remained of his old life behind.

Their mother had been a simple woman, content in her mundane life, much like Haggart. Krillzoc had sent her gold monthly, bearing love for the pitiful woman despite her countless flaws. But that was not enough for Haggart, who felt Krillzoc had betrayed his family by leaving them behind to serve Odpor.

Was I so wrong to bring a shred of honor and dignity to our family, you ignorant oaf? Krillzoc had long ago shed any desire to reconcile with his stubborn brother, but if he was going to succeed tonight, he needed Haggart's help. Despite his many shortcomings, his brother was the one man who could assure him safe passage in and out of the Imperial camp.

Forcing Haggart from his mind, Krillzoc set out to prepare himself for the night ahead. He could not allow his brother to distract him from what was truly important. The future of the dwarven people could depend on this meeting. Odpor had placed a great deal of trust in him after multiple failures. Krillzoc understood all too well what one more failure would mean for him.

Chapter Ten

With each passing hour, General Alexander Sylvester found himself sinking deeper into the pits of despair. He had been sitting with Captain Terrence Garrison for hours, brainstorming ideas to achieve the ends they desired. Hours later, they were still no closer to a solution than when they had started. As long as Cadmus Twilcox continued to draw breath, Sylvester would have no choice but to live in his shadow, kept from reaching his full potential. It was a fate he refused to be relegated to, no matter the price. Furthermore, the Imperial Army would not survive another year under Twilcox's sheer incompetence; he was certain of that much.

"Twilcox could come down with a severe illness from something in his food," Garrison suggested.

It had gone this way for most of the night, Garrison throwing out pitiful suggestions and Sylvester poking holes in them. Garrison had suggested everything from an unfortunate fall from a horse to a hired assassin from the Brothers of the Night. None of them had been able to pass Sylvester's intense scrutiny, and neither would this one.

"The top-ranking general of the Imperial Army suddenly becoming ill from food poisoning would draw far too many questions. There would be immediate inquiries, and all of the food in the camp would be inspected within hours. Besides, getting access to his food would be much more difficult than it sounds. Twilcox doesn't eat the same mush as the men under his command, the filthy hypocrite. He has a private chef, a man who has served him for close to fifteen years. Drawing suspicion onto such a man and away from ourselves would be a tall order. What would the chef stand to gain by murdering his source of income? I also don't think we will be able to bring the chef over to our cause. By all accounts, Twilcox treats him like a son. It can't be done."

For the first time since you entered my service, I wish you were sharper of mind, dear Terrence, Sylvester thought. It was not fair to Garrison; Sylvester had never asked him to be a man of strategy before. But he still could not help but feel frustrated with his longtime servant. His job was to do whatever the general required of him. Now his general needed him to devise a way to kill a man, and thus far, he had proven himself less than useless. Were he reporting to any other commander, Garrison would be scrubbing latrines or serving slop in the chow hall. Instead, he sat in counsel with the most brilliant military mind of their era and was squandering the opportunity.

"Rations are at an all-time low. Morale is low among the men, and tensions are running high in every corner. What about a brawl breaking out that Twilcox just happens to be near, and he tragically dies in the scuffle? Such fights are quickly becoming a common occurrence."

"We would be forced to place our trust in the type of soldiers who tend to have loose tongues. The type of man who would accept payment for this type of a job would never be trustworthy. The Imperial Army would be none too kind to men who instigated a fight that caused the death of their Supreme General. It would only be a matter of time before one of them spilled the truth in the hope of leniency. It's likely they would all talk, and their similar stories would be enough to raise suspicions. Maybe nobody would take their statements seriously, but that's a chance we can't afford to take."

"Perhaps I could provide a solution to your problem," a voice said from the tent's entrance.

Sylvester and Garrison spun, shocked to find not an Imperial soldier but a dwarf standing just inside the entryway to the tent. Garrison sprung to his feet, placing himself between the dwarf and Sylvester, his sword clearing its scabbard. Sylvester could not help but feel touched as he rose to his feet; Garrison had never hesitated to rise to his defense. The captain had hurried to place his own body between the attacker and his general. The dwarf was not holding a weapon, though he did have a sword strapped to his waist in plain sight. He raised his hands disarmingly, flashing them a smile that didn't seem to reach his eyes.

"Relax, Captain Garrison, I mean you no harm. If I had come here looking for a fight, I would not have declared my arrival, would I? I would have cut you both down before you were aware of my presence. Come now, you are both smart enough to understand this."

The dwarf was familiar. Sylvester could vaguely remember him as being present for his meetings with Odpor. Why would Odpor risk sending one of his top commanders into the heart of the Imperial encampment? He had all but given up hope of the partnership with the dwarves ever bearing him any fruit. He didn't know why Odpor had halted the executions of the captured soldiers, but he had little use for allies who couldn't keep their word.

"Remove the sword from your belt and lay it on the ground, dwarf," Garrison commanded, clearly not the least bit assuaged by the dwarf's reassurances.

"My apologies, Captain Garrison, but that is not going to happen. I have come here to speak with your general in good faith. That said, I have no intention of leaving myself defenseless in a camp full of men who would love nothing more than to kill me. There are two of you and I am alone; that is all of the assurance I can offer you."

"You will drop the weapon now, or you will not live long enough for me to tell you again!" Garrison took two steps toward the dwarf, his sword held defensively in front of him.

"General Sylvester, my name is Krillzoc, and I am here to speak with you on behalf of Chieftain Odpor. I assure you that I mean you no harm, but if Captain Garrison takes two more steps in this direction, you will need to find yourself a new servant," the dwarf warned, his steely eyes never leaving Garrison.

Sylvester hesitated for a moment, trying to get a measure of Krillzoc. To come alone into his tent was a bold move, one Sylvester did not doubt Odpor had authorized himself. But was Krillzoc being truthful about the reasons for his visit? Or was this an elaborate assassination attempt, a way of Odpor terminating their partnership permanently? The only way to be sure was to hear what Krillzoc had to say. Alexander Sylvester had never been a man to take unnecessary risks, especially where his own safety was concerned. Every move he had made in his career had been one of deliberate calculation, down to the last minutia. He despised making crucial decisions without time to think through all possible ramifications.

Still, would Odpor send one of his top commanders for what would likely end as a suicide mission? The dwarves were resourceful, and Krillzoc was likely no exception. But killing an Imperial general in his own tent? Nobody could escape the manhunt that would ensue, no matter how clever. Furthermore, taking a long, hard look at Krillzoc, Sylvester doubted Garrison would be his equal in a fight. If he allowed Garrison to attack, it would only assure his demise. The smartest move was to hear what Krillzoc had to say.

"Stand down, Captain Garrison; let's hear Krillzoc out. You are welcome to keep your weapons, Krillzoc. I ask only that you remain standing where you are until we are sure of each other's intentions. And I'm sure I don't need to remind you that one shout is all we need to bring this entire camp down upon you," Sylvester said, his mind made up.

It was apparent that Terrence Garrison was none too fond of the order, but he would never disobey a direct command. Stepping slowly backward away from Krillzoc, he sheathed his sword, still leaving himself planted firmly between the dwarf and his general, Krillzoc smirking all the while. Sylvester felt another swell of gratitude for the eternal loyalty of his most faithful servant.

"Thank you for receiving me, General Sylvester. As I said, Chieftain Odpor has sent me here this evening to negotiate a new partnership," Krillzoc said.

"It's funny you mention that, Krillzoc. I could have sworn I had already struck a bargain with Odpor. I was under the impression we had already formed a partnership. Yet, for days now, he has failed to live up to his end of that bargain. Would you care to explain why that is?"

"Your men escaped from the prison complex we held them in with the help of a member of the Resistance. This is a group of radicals who are determined to disrupt Odpor's rule by any means necessary. They do not share his vision of an independent Qwitzite. We found and killed most of them in a battle but were also able to recapture several. However, they escaped again, once again with help from the Resistance and a man appearing to be an Imperial captain."

An Imperial captain inside Muog? Sylvester's mind immediately shot to Thaddeus Dunstan, the outspoken fool who had advocated so passionately on behalf of those captured soldiers. The man had a history of going against orders; was it possible he had done so again? You could never be sure what type of drastic action a principled fool might take. Still, throwing away a decades-long career over the lives of a few ordinary foot soldiers? It was so outrageous to Sylvester that it bordered on unbelievable. *Nevertheless, I better have Garrison look into this. We need to be sure of Captain Dunstan's movements.*

"Perhaps Odpor should not have made an agreement with me if he was unable to honor his end of the bargain. This is the first I am hearing of this Resistance," Sylvester said. If he was going to be convinced to partner with the dwarves again, he would need certain assurances that they could deliver on what they promised.

"With all due respect, General Sylvester, I would remind you that it was you who first proposed such a partnership, not Odpor. If you did not equip yourself with the necessary information beforehand, who is truly to blame? Any ignorance on your part of what is going on inside Muog is not our fault, nor is it our concern."

"Mind your tongue, dwarf, or maybe I'll remove it for you! You are speaking to an Imperial general!" Garrison snapped, taking a menacing step forward. If Krillzoc found the threat or the gesture the least bit intimidating, he did not show it. Sylvester placed a restraining hand on Garrison's shoulder, again thinking that his captain would not stand a chance against this dwarf in a fight.

"As you say, Krillzoc, I did extend the offer to Odpor. However, he was under no obligation to accept it. If he felt he was perfectly capable of winning Qwitzite's independence without my help, he should have done so. To accept an agreement when you cannot hold up your end of the bargain is shameful."

"The remaining soldiers were on their way to their executions when your captain interfered with our operations. Perhaps you should keep your men in line, General Sylvester," Krillzoc retorted.

This one is good, Sylvester thought. Odpor had indeed chosen his representative well. Few men would have the nerve to speak to a general, even of the opposing force, in such a manner. He could shout for assistance at any moment, and Krillzoc would die. Yet Krillzoc showed no fear. Sylvester had to respect it, albeit begrudgingly.

"Very well, Krillzoc. You say some of my men escaped with help from this Resistance and a mysterious Imperial captain. How many? Where are they now? What is Odpor doing to recapture them?"

"Four of them escaped, along with the captain. We believe they have hunkered down in a safe house inside Muog. They cannot hide forever. Sooner or later, they will have to show themselves, and when they do, we will put an end to them."

Krillzoc was a talented liar—Sylvester could see that much—but not good enough to fool him. There was something the dwarf was hiding from him. Whatever had happened to those men, they were not merely cowering in a hole in Muog, and Krillzoc knew it just as well as he did. But it didn't matter much at this point; four foot soldiers were the least of his worries. Unless they returned to the camp, they posed little threat to him. He needed a way to dispose of Cadmus Twilcox, and Krillzoc had suggested he had a way to do it. It was time to cut to the chase.

"You said you had a proposal for me, Krillzoc. Let's hear it."

"Chieftain Odpor still feels it would be best for all parties if you were in command of all Imperial forces. The pair of you agreed to as much in your previous discussions, did you not? I could not help but overhear your difficulties finding a way to rid yourselves of Cadmus Twilcox. You cannot do it yourselves; you must realize this by now. There is no way for you to kill him without drawing intense scrutiny upon yourself. There is another way, however. What if we did it for you?"

"How do you plan to do that?" Sylvester was skeptical. If the dwarves were able to launch an attack that would kill the Imperial Army's top commander, why had they not done it long ago? "It seems as though you would have done this already if you were truly capable of doing it."

"Because we need your help, General Sylvester. Twilcox does not move about your camp often; he prefers the security of his tent, where he is surrounded by guards at all hours. We need you to tell us where he will be and when he will be there. We need you to give us a time and place where he will be as lightly guarded as possible. If you can do this, we can eliminate him for you. Nobody would question his death at the hands of dwarves other than how we got into the camp, but we have been able to do that for months without issue. There would be no reason for additional scrutiny in your direction as you work to succeed him."

It was almost too good to be true, and Sylvester quickly reminded himself of how well the last bargain he had made with Odpor had played out. While it was tempting to jump on this offer and never look back, he knew he had to take a more levelheaded approach. It was a pretty promise, but could the dwarves actually keep it?

"Why should I believe this will end any differently than when I trusted you last time?" he asked.

"To be blunt, General Sylvester, your request last time was ludicrously overcomplicated. This is a much simpler affair. Give us a time and a place, and this man will die. That is all there is to it. No lengthy captivities or theatrics to worry about this time around. Forgive me for saying so, but I found the whole scheme to be ill-advised. I have always found simpler plans to be far more effective."

Sylvester was still skeptical, but the allure of finally seeing Cadmus Twilcox dead and gone was proving to be too much for him to resist. With Twilcox removed from the picture and Sylvester's popularity among the men skyrocketing, his ascension to the rank of Supreme General would be assured. Odpor must've been convinced he would keep his word of putting an end to the fight against the independence of Qwitzite.

"Am I to assume that Odpor is content with my end of our previous deal? You will kill Cadmus Twilcox for me, and I will convince the Emperor to end this war against you?"

"That is all we request of you, General Sylvester. From my point of view, this is a no-lose deal for you. Until we have held up our end of the deal, you have to do nothing. All of the risk is in our hands."

Oh, you simpleminded fool, I will not be holding up my end of the deal regardless. I look forward to wiping your cursed city and all of you growth-stunted abominations off the face of this earth. Sylvester could scarcely believe such an opportunity had fallen into his lap. He could have everything he wanted while risking nothing to get it. He had always believed such an opportunity would arise, but he had begun to lose faith after so many repeated setbacks.

"Very well, Krillzoc. You may report to Chieftain Odpor that we have an agreement. Slay Supreme General Twilcox, and I will convince the Emperor that this war is a lost cause," Sylvester said, nodding in agreement. "I will have command of the Imperial Army, and Qwitzite will have its independence within weeks."

"He will be delighted to hear it, General Sylvester. This leaves only the matter of Supreme General Twilcox's whereabouts."

"Twilcox inspects this encampment once every week, though he changes the day to prevent attempts such as this. His next inspection will take place in five days, more than enough time for you to plan your assault. He will be at his most vulnerable when passing along the northwestern boundary of the camp. I assume you have a place you can lie in wait? You can expect his arrival shortly after midday."

"Excellent. I will begin putting our plans into motion. As I have promised, Cadmus Twilcox will die, assuming your information is accurate. May I make one last suggestion to further ensure your ascension, General Sylvester?"

Who does this dwarf think he is to advise me of anything? Sylvester had rarely heard such a ridiculous statement but decided to handle the matter diplomatically rather than admonishing the fool. It would not do to jeopardize the newly rebuilt relationship now.

"I would be delighted to hear your suggestion, Krillzoc," he said, hoping his tone was convincing.

"Intervening yourself in a valiant attempt to save Twilcox's life would ingratiate you even further in the eyes of the Emperor and soldiers. It would also help to deflect any lingering suspicion of guilt. If you would like, I will select two dwarves for this mission whom you should be able to defeat easily. They will be told you are the target, and all others will be ordered not to touch you. Killing these two dwarves should do a great deal to help your cause."

"You would send two of your men for the sole purpose of me killing them?" Sylvester was skeptical. Was this some clumsy attempt at a double cross?

"Is this so different from our partnership thus far, General Sylvester? You sacrificed the soldiers who came into Muog and those guarding your supply caravan. You did this in the name of the greater good. Are two lives such an unbearable sacrifice? I think not, though you are under no obligation to accept my suggestion."

Alexander Sylvester had rarely been so elated. Everything he had ever wanted had just fallen into his lap. He did not bother to look to Captain Garrison; the other man's opinion was irrelevant. He could hazard a guess at what Garrison thought; he would urge caution in making another deal with the dwarves. It was why he would only go as far as Sylvester allowed him to go in the Imperial Army. Victory required bold decision-making, and greatness required the will to take action. Few men were undaunted in the face of such risks.

"Krillzoc, I do believe we have a deal."

Chapter Eleven

F or five days following their late-night escape from the dwarven capital city of Muog, the party of Imperial soldiers and Resistance dwarves marched toward the city of Jezero. They slogged on each day, rarely stopping for even the briefest of rests. To the surprise of the Imperial soldiers, they had quickly left the barren plains and bare hills of southern Qwitzite behind. For the past two days, they had traversed through rolling green hills and dense pine forests. More than one of them had commented on the shocking change of scenery only for Radig to shake his head in exasperation.

"What, did you think all of the people of Qwitzite lived in a barren wasteland devoid of all life?" he asked. "Our ancestors arranged Muog in its location due to the fantastic natural defenses it provided, which I am sure the commanders of your army would have to admit was a good strategy. A capital city should always be easy to defend, especially for people like the dwarves, who are bound to be the target of attacks. Dwarves, despite the many misconceptions about us, actually love more natural surroundings. This is why you saw so many flowers and gardens inside Muog. Many of the dwarves who live there leave Muog once they reach old age, preferring to live out their final days surrounded by living things."

It was indeed a surprise to Darian Tor, though he did his best not to show it. All he had ever known about the dwarves involved their skills as warriors or stonemasons. To be told they would find a major dwarven city amid this lush forestland was the last thing he had expected to hear. He recalled their first journey to Muog after they had completed their training. Captain Dunstan had made him realize how little he knew about the people they were coming to conquer during that journey. The longer he spent with Radig and Kalayo, the more he realized they were still an enigma.

He remembered how he had told himself he would make an effort to learn more about the dwarves during his time in Qwitzite. He realized he had still learned very little other than that they allowed their women to fight beside them in battle. But now, only a few short weeks later, Darian found he didn't much care to learn any more. The dwarves had surprised him in many ways, but his thoughts were elsewhere. While he bore no animosity toward most of the dwarves, his mind had room for only one thing: vengeance for the death of Axel Stark.

The passage of time had done nothing to ease his rage over the murder of his oldest friend. On the contrary, his anger had only burned more intensely with each passing day. His need to take revenge upon Krillzoc and Alexander Sylvester was all that was keeping him on his feet after the ordeal he had been through in Muog. He considered every day they were allowed to continue breathing to be an insult to his dear friend's memory. One way or another, he was determined to kill both of them, even if he did not live to tell the tale. If he could die knowing justice had been served, he could die content.

They made camp shortly before nightfall, just as they had every other night. Captain Dunstan assigned them each to a watch, allowing each man to get enough sleep while also ensuring they were well protect-ed. Despite their arduous march, this strategy had allowed most of their injuries to continue healing, albeit slowly. Not willing to risk a fire, Radig withdrew some cold rations from his pouch. He passed some around to each man—bread that was growing staler by the day, as well as a few strips of strange dried meat that none of them had ever had before. None of it was particularly appetizing, but Darian reminded himself the underwhelming rations were preferable to swinging from the walls of Muog in a noose.

"We will arrive in Jezero by midday tomorrow," Radig commented, breaking the silence as they ate.

"Are you still confident we haven't been followed?" Dunstan asked.

"As confident as I can be. I am no tracker. Odpor is arrogant, but he is no fool, and he has some of the best trackers and spies in Qwitzite at his service. He knows we would not sit and hide in Muog forever. There are only so many places for us to go, and he has long suspected Iskra of leading the Resistance. But once we reach Jezero, we will be secure. He will deduce where we have gone sooner or later, make no mistake, but we will be safe enough. Odpor cannot muster enough of a force to attack Jezero without leaving himself vulnerable to an assault by your Imperial friends."

"That's reassuring," Berj Jenson muttered.

"I never claimed to have a perfect plan. But this is the best option we have available to us. If anyone feels they have better, feel free to speak up, though I have heard no input thus far among the numerous questions and complaints," Radig shot back, his eyes meeting each of them in turn.

Radig was clearly growing frustrated with the constant questioning of his plans, but Darian felt such frustrations were unwarranted. After all, the last time they had just followed along with Radig, they had ended up recaptured, with Axel and the rest of their fellow soldiers dead in a supposed safe house. He knew Radig was doing his best, but the dwarf needed to understand the reasons behind their lack of confidence.

"What kind of welcome can we expect once we reach Jezero?" Darnold Dans asked.

"It is hard to be certain. Iskra will welcome you with open arms; I am sure of that much. He has never been one to turn away any potential ally, even Imperials. Some of our fellow Resistance dwarves and the civilians may be less welcoming, as you caught a glimpse of on the night I freed you from the first prison. But Iskra commands enough respect that they will accept his decision, even if they do not agree with it."

"Why? We all have the same enemy, don't we?" Preston chimed in.

"Having a common enemy does not automatically form a friendship," Kalayo cut in. "Being opposed to secession does not mean these dwarves bear any love for the Empire. For decades, the Empire has been content to collect excessive taxes from the dwarves, yet what do we receive in return? They send us no crops if we are in a drought. They provide us with no military support if bandits are raiding our villages. Even those who oppose Odpor grow tired of being overlooked by those in power. What has the Empire ever done for us?"

"Why do you oppose Odpor if you despise the Empire so much?" Darian asked.

"Odpor is an unstable madman; you have seen it with your own eyes. What good would it be for us to trade a far-off tyrant who disregards us for one closer to home?" Kalayo asked.

"I hope you can all understand. We do not want to secede from the Empire. We feel we are stronger and safer as part of the Empire. But the dwarves will only tolerate the mistreatment from Valdovas for so long," Radig added. "How would you feel if you were in our position?"

Darian could understand their frustrations, even if he had difficulty finding much room for sympathy when he was so consumed by anger. The dwarves experienced hardships he could relate to, but they were not his concern. All that mattered was taking his vengeance on Krillzoc and Sylvester for Axel's death. Anything else was a distraction he could not afford to carry in his mind.

***

They woke shortly before dawn, eager to see this journey to Jezero reach its end at last. With Radig leading the way, they set off to the northwest. They made their way through dense pine forests and wide-open meadows with gently rolling hills on both sides. They reached Jezero before midday, just as Radig had promised they would. After the last few weeks, Darian Tor did not think anything could surprise him anymore, but the sight of Jezero proved to be yet another shock.

They came out of the forest and onto the edge of a rise overlooking the city. There were none of the high stone walls he had expected after Muog. In fact, Jezero did not look all that different from the small village where Darian had grown up in Verizia, though on a much larger scale. The most shocking sight was the vast lake on the city's western edge. The houses and buildings ran right up to the edge of the crystal clear water. Looking down from above, Darian could even see the reflections of the buildings and tree-lined hills in the water below.

I would never have imagined such a place when I thought of Qwitzite.

Unlike Muog, which they had mostly only seen under the guise of night, Jezero was bustling with life. Darian could see dwarven men, women, and children moving to and fro in the streets, going about their everyday lives. It was a stark contrast to Muog, a city living under the threat of siege. There were even a few fishing boats out on the lake. The Imperials had never imagined they would find an entire city of dwarves living quaint, ordinary lives amid the chaos of this war.

Radig led them down from the rise and toward the main gates of the city. As they drew close, it became apparent that Jezero did have a wall, though not nearly as formidable as Muog's. It rose just barely above the heads of the approaching Imperial soldiers. As they approached the gates, several dwarven soldiers moved to block their path.

"We have not seen you in quite some time, Radig, Kalayo. We did not think to see you return with such company," one of the guards greeted, his suspicious eyes never leaving the Imperials. His fellow guards had moved into a line alongside him. They had placed their hands on their weapons, but as of yet, none of them had drawn.

"I did not have a chance to send word ahead. We need to see Iskra right away. Things have not been going well in Muog. These soldiers were captured by Odpor's men in a raid orchestrated by one of their generals. I could not allow such an alliance to form without resistance. Please admit us; we have no time for delays," Radig said.

"You think we are going to allow a bunch of Imperial soldiers to meet with Iskra? You have gone mad, Radig." The dwarves made no move to admit them into the city, all of them staring at Radig with bewilderment in their eyes.

"That is not your decision to make, and I would urge you to mind your place. Iskra leads this city, and you know damn well that he will want to see us immediately. If Iskra finds out that you have delayed us by denying these men entry, I would hate to see his wrath," Kalayo shot back, speaking up for the first time.

The guards were exchanging nervous glances, and it was apparent they had no idea how to handle this situation. They weren't eager to allow Imperial soldiers into their city, but they also seemed uncomfortable challenging Radig and Kalayo. At last, the lead guard spoke once more.

"If they surrender their weapons, we will admit them."

"That's not going to happen," Captain Dunstan said, interjecting before Radig or Kalayo could respond.

This statement did nothing to improve the demeanor of the guards blocking their path. Several of them moved in closer, as though Dunstan had just confirmed the Imperials' ill intentions for their city. Dunstan didn't back down, meeting their gaze with a fierce glare of his own.

"Do not be ridiculous, my friends. There are five of them, and how many hundreds of our men are inside Jezero? Stripping my companions of their weapons does nothing to protect the people of this city. It is merely a symbolic gesture meant to make yourselves feel more comfortable. We are wasting valuable time. May we please enter? We have matters of great importance to discuss with Iskra. Delay us further and I will be sure to name each and every one of you as a cause of our tardiness," Radig said.

After several more uncertain glances among themselves, the guards stepped aside to allow them into the city. Radig led them forward once more, never looking back, though Darian could feel the guards' eyes on his back as they stepped forward.

These dwarves sure have a lot of love for the Empire, he thought sarcastically.

Matters did not improve as they made their way deeper into the city; it seemed as though they drew a glare from every dwarf they passed. There was even an occasional insult hurled their way, but Radig pressed on, paying them no mind.

At least they aren't throwing things at us like the dwarves in Muog.

The streets of Jezero bore some similarities to those in Muog. Finely crafted stone buildings lined cobblestone streets, along with carts and stands selling wares of every sort imaginable. Gardens and flowers seemed to be even more common here, and the difference that struck Darian Tor the most was the demeanor of the people. Unlike the dwarves of Muog, these people had not lived with the shadow of war hanging over their heads, and it was apparent in the way they carried themselves.

Iskra's home was not what any of them expected to find. From their experience, important people tended to have large, elaborate homes, usually with extensive security. That was not the case with Iskra, whose simple stone house blended in perfectly with those surrounding it. Apart from a few climbing plants making their way up its plain white walls, there was nothing to set it apart from any other building on the street. Radig motioned them to follow him up to the door, which he tapped four times.

The door swung open almost immediately, revealing an ancient dwarf with a kind face. His snow-white beard nearly reached his knees, and he wore only a simple brown robe. He smiled at Radig before his eyes turned to the rest of them. To Darian's surprise, the dwarf did not meet them with a scowl but rather a curious grin. Stepping aside, the old man motioned wordlessly for them to enter, then closed and latched the door behind them. While larger than the safe houses they had squeezed their way into in Muog, the Imperials still needed to crouch to make their way inside.

Radig led the way into a simple sitting room, not all that dissimilar from the one in the house Darian had grown up in. The Imperials each took an awkward seat in the dwarf-sized chairs, their eyes trying to glance discreetly around the room to take it all in. Iskra was a man of simple taste, judging by his home. There was no expensive artwork or decorations. There was only a stone table, a few simple cloth rugs to adorn the floors, and a few potted plants sitting upon shelves on the walls.

"Welcome to my home, my new friends. I apologize if the welcome you received out in the city was not warm, which I must imagine it was not. We do not see many Imperial visitors here in Jezero. I am Iskra, and I am responsible for the people of this city. I do not yet know your story, but I know Radig and Kalayo would not have brought you here without a good reason. Tell me, Radig. What brings you here?" Iskra's voice sounded surprisingly young and spry for a man of his advanced age.

"I am sorry to arrive here unannounced, Iskra. We would have sent word, but things have not been going well in Muog. We could not risk a message being intercepted. We cannot even be sure which of our dwarves in Muog we can trust anymore," said Radig.

"I assumed as much. No apology is needed, my friend. Our communication from Muog grows less frequent by the week. What has Odpor done now?"

"He made a pact with an Imperial general," Radig began, causing one of Iskra's eyebrows to climb nearly into his hairline. "The general betrayed these men sitting here, along with their comrades. He revealed their mission to Odpor, allowing Krillzoc to capture them. He wanted Odpor to execute them one by one as a way of destabilizing the control of Cadmus Twilcox. He would then seize power for himself and supposedly persuade the Emperor to grant Qwitzite its independence.

"I set them free from their prison, hoping to sow some discontent with Odpor's rule in the ranks of the common people. But they found us before I could get the Imperials out of Muog. You know how effective Krillzoc is at extracting information from people. I suspect some of our own people may have met unfortunate fates in his questioning. These are the men lucky enough to survive the second capture. It was too dangerous to try to get them back into their encampment, so we brought them here."

Iskra did not reply immediately, instead turning his gaze on each Imperial soldier in turn. Darian felt uncomfortable as the old man's piercing gaze met his, but he refused to look away. Taking a deep breath, Iskra began to speak once more.

"It sounds as though you made the best decision available to you from a wide array of undesirable choices, Radig. I am sorry you men have found yourselves caught up in this mess. The betrayal of a man ranked above you must wound you all quite deeply. It is a pain I can sympathize with all too well, unfortunately. You are all welcome to stay here in my home as long as you wish. I promise that no harm shall come to you here. We will make every effort to ensure you can return to your camp safely when it is possible."

"Thank you for your hospitality, Iskra, though we hope not to intrude upon it for too long," Captain Dunstan said. "We need to get back to our camp and figure out what we are going to do about this treasonous general."

"Yes, that will be complicated for you, I am sure. Still, the hospitality of Jezero is yours for as long as required. As I am sure you saw on your way in, most of the people of this city bear no love in their hearts for the Imperial Army. You are welcome to move about the city as you please, but I would stress caution and advise that none of you venture out alone. I will make it known that you are welcome guests, but I cannot guarantee that all of my people will see eye to eye with me on this."

"We are free to roam the city? Doesn't that risk Odpor finding out where we have come?" Berj Jenson asked.

"I can understand your trepidation, my good man. However, I fear Odpor already knows where you have come. Concealing your presence will do us little good. He has long suspected me of being the head of the Resistance. At this point, nothing will dissuade him from that belief. Even had you fled elsewhere, he would still believe me to be harboring you."

Good, maybe he will send Krillzoc after us again. I would love nothing more than one last chance to kill that sneering bastard, Darian Tor thought. This was a foolish line of thinking, and he knew it, but he did not much care at the moment. Every night when he went to sleep, the images of Axel Stark's death were there to greet him. He would never be able to rest in peace until those responsible had paid the price.

"You must all be hungry. I cannot imagine you had many feasts on the march from Muog or during your captivity, for that matter. Please join me for lunch in the kitchen," Iskra said, shaking Darian out of his dark thoughts.

The Imperials followed Iskra into his kitchen, finding it every bit as plain and unassuming as every other part of the house they had seen. Taking seats around a wooden table, they watched in amazement as Iskra set about the kitchen preparing the meal himself. No Imperial dignitary would ever be caught dead preparing his own food, much less for guests. Darian begrudgingly had to admit that he found himself rather liking Iskra already.

Before long, the aged dwarf had served them a lunch of fresh vegetables, fruits, and fish. The soldiers devoured it all ravenously. For the four younger men, it was the first full meal they had enjoyed since before their capture. Even in the Imperial encampment, their meals had been far from a satisfying affair.

"I do hope you enjoyed everything," Iskra commented as he cleared the table. "The fish come from Lake Isabella; I am sure you saw it on your way into the city. It was named after the first woman to rule Qwitzite. It was said her eyes shone like sparkling sapphires, much like the lake."

"The dwarves had a female ruler?" Max Preston asked. The rest of them were equally surprised. It had been shocking enough to find women fighting alongside the men, but in positions of power as well? Thinking back to what he knew of his home province's history, Darian couldn't recall any female ruler of Verizia.

"Yes, close to four hundred years ago," Iskra replied with a knowing smile. "We have actually had several chieftainesses since, though none quite as famous as Isabella. I understand in the bulk of the Empire, men and women traditionally fill separate roles. Here in Qwitzite, we did away with such traditions centuries ago and found we have become stronger for it overall."

Having seen Kalayo in battle, Darian had a hard time finding room to disagree.

Rising from the table, Iskra led them to the second level of his home, showing each man a small bedroom he could use for the duration of their stay. The furnishings appeared comfortable, if slightly undersized, for the five guests.

"Do watch your heads; I know our ceilings can be quite low for men such as yourselves. My apologies in advance for the numerous times I am sure you are doomed to bump your heads. Do not hesitate to come to me with anything you need. I will send for a healer to come and check on your wounds. It appears Radig has done a good job tending to them as best he could, but one can never be too cautious. We will leave you to rest for a while. I am sure your ordeal has been exhausting." With that, he headed back down to his sitting room to meet with Radig and Kalayo.

Darian lay awake in the bed Iskra had provided him, staring at the ceiling a few feet above his head. He was so far away from the destiny he had been foolish enough to believe was awaiting him in the ranks of the Imperial Army. He had imagined himself returning home to Verizia in a few years, his family and friends hailing him as a hero coming home. Instead, all he would have to return to were questions about Axel and why his oldest and closest friend was not coming home with him. For the first time, he thought about Axel's family. They would not know about his death yet; how could they? Even the Imperial Army did not know his fate outside of the men in this house.

He rose in the bed, looking about for what he needed. He found a small sheet of parchment quickly enough. After a few more minutes, he found a quill and a small bottle of ink in a cabinet near his bed. Sitting down awkwardly at the dwarf-sized table and chair, he began to write.

To Parnax and Kelissa Stark,

I am writing with the news I hoped I would never have to deliver. Your dear son, Axel Stark, was killed in battle in the dwarven city of Muog. He died fighting bravely, protecting the men under his command from harm. He was my dearest friend, and my most profound regret is that I was unable to save him. Every man, woman, and child in the Empire owes him a debt of gratitude for his courageous sacrifice.

With deepest sympathies,

Darian Tor

Finished with the brief note, Darian reread it to himself several times. It felt woefully inadequate, but what else could he say? One sentence bothered him in particular, the last one. The Empire owed Axel a debt of gratitude for his sacrifice? What had he sacrificed himself for exactly? To save his men, of course, but why had they even been there in the first place? How were their actions making the Empire a better place? Ultimately, they were there to serve the sinister plans of a treasonous Imperial general and nothing else. Why was the Imperial Army in Qwitzite to begin with? So they could continue to collect taxes from people they had neglected and oppressed for decades? It made Axel's death feel meaningless, which Darian could not bear.

He stepped out of the bedroom, finding Iskra walking down the hallway. The elderly dwarf greeted him with a smile.

"Having trouble sleeping?"

"I was wondering if you have a way to send a letter to Verizia. Krillzoc murdered a friend of mine in Muog, and I wanted to let his family know," Darian explained, trying his best to keep his voice neutral, not wanting to show any sign of weakness.

"Of course, my young man. I am sorry for your loss. We have a line of communication that runs north into the province of Floresta. I can have them take your letter and see that it finds its way safely to Verizia."

Darian scribbled down the location of Axel's family and handed over the note. Iskra folded it gently into his robe, not looking at it. Thanking the dwarf, Darian stepped back into his room and closed the door. He collapsed onto the small bed, and realizing he was entirely alone for the first time since he had arrived in Salvamoan for his Imperial Army training, he began to cry.

Chapter Twelve

Two days after their arrival in Jezero, the Imperial soldiers decided to venture out into the city for the first time. Heeding Iskra's advice that they would be better off not traveling alone, all five Imperials agreed to go together. The days of rest in Iskra's home had done wonders for their injuries, as had the full meals the Resistance leader prepared himself three times a day. So, after lunch, they decided to set out to explore their temporary home and get a breath of fresh air in the process. Shortly after leaving the house, they encountered Kalayo, who agreed to show them around the city. As she took the lead, Darian couldn't help but wonder if she was coming along at Iskra's request to ensure they were not accosted by dwarves who may not be overly fond of Imperials.

Darian had not spoken to the others about the letter he had sent to Axel's family. In fact, he had not spoken much to any of them about anything. While the time at Iskra's had been restful for him, and he understood the time to heal was necessary, he had never been more eager to get back into the fight. Krillzoc and General Sylvester were not going to kill themselves, and his mind could not be at peace until they were both dead.

Kalayo led them through numerous cobblestone streets, pointing out various landmarks as they passed. They passed through streets full of markets, dwarves moving about their daily lives as though there were no war at all. The glares of the dwarves followed them everywhere they went, but this time they hurled no insults. Darian could only assume this was due to Iskra making it known that they were welcome guests in the city. From what he could tell, the old dwarf commanded a great deal of respect among his people, even if his subjects did not agree with this particular decision. After spending two days in his home, it was clear to Darian why Iskra's people adored him so much. His kindness and hospitality toward them had been more than they would have expected to find in the home of any Imperial, let alone a dwarf.

As the afternoon wore on, they found themselves walking along the shores of Lake Isabella, discovering the waters to be even more beautiful up close. They were so crystal clear that while standing on the docks, the Imperials could even make out the fish swimming near the lake's bottom far below. Kalayo was able to identify each type of fish through the water, leaving the Imperials amazed.

"It's remarkable to me that this place seems so untouched by the war," Darnold Dans commented as they continued along the water.

"Well, it has not been wholly untouched. Many of the warriors who live here were called to defend Muog when the siege began, and they are still there. The longer the war wages, the fewer of them will return. It has made life more difficult for those who remain. Still, Iskra does what he can to keep this city insulated from the troubles of the outside world. For the most part, he succeeds. He is the ruler Qwitzite should have had. We have left behind many of your more asinine Imperial traditions, but somehow, we still abide by a line of succession for our rulers. I think of the prosperity and peace we could have if circumstances were different, and it pains me. Many dwarves feel the same way."

"Many provinces hold elections to select their leaders now," Darian said. "Of course, the Emperor is still a position passed down within the same family. But in Verizia, we have elected our rulers for close to a century now. It is the same in the neighboring province of Thornata, though their rulers have not always ruled uncontested, have they, Captain Dunstan?"

"I don't think there will ever be any such thing as an uncontested ruler," Dunstan replied. "Unfortunately, in Thornata, power was seized by a power-hungry madman. His name was Idanox. I never had the pleasure of meeting him personally, though I heard civilians cheering in the streets as his headless body was carted past them. Tells you everything you need to know about the man, doesn't it? But from what I understand, he felt his vast wealth gave him a right to rule to fellow Thornatans, though he proved to be ill-suited to the task. Still, he managed to rally a rather sizeable number of his countrymen to overthrow and murder their elected duke."

"It sounds like he and Odpor would have gotten along well," Berj Jenson quipped. "Wealth, blood—what's the difference? Neither of them produces suitable rulers. All they give us are fools with an overinflated sense of self-importance. How many failed regimes will it take for people to realize it? How many common people have to suffer and die first?"

They continued along the waterfront, which seemed to stretch on forever. Darian found himself lost in thought. The lake brought back memories of the rivers and canals of Verizia, waters he had explored with Axel in their youth. On numerous occasions, one of them had nearly ended up drowning, usually through acts of their own recklessness. On one misadventure, Axel had turned up with a dilapidated boat he had found abandoned on a riverbank. From the appearances of it, its previous owner had deserted it for good reason. The pair had done their best to fix it up and then had taken it for a ride down a canal. They had ended up walking several miles home after the boat had fallen apart completely.

For the first time, Darian found memories of Axel bringing him happiness rather than anger or grief. He wished his friend were here and could see the beauty of Jezero for himself. So many things had been stolen over the past weeks, but simple moments like these pained him the most. He paused for a moment, feigning interest in a nearby building while truly working furiously to fight back the tears threatening to well up in his eyes. Darian knew his world could never return to the way it had been, but he was grateful to at least possess memories of better days. If he survived what was still ahead of him, maybe they would one day provide some comfort for him.

"Does anybody else hear screaming?" Max Preston asked.

The group came to a halt, all listening intently. Sure enough, within seconds, Darian thought he could make out the sounds of far-off screams. They were distant, but to him, they sounded like the cries of children.

"Something is wrong. This way!" Kalayo cried, speeding off in the direction of the cries. All five Imperials followed without question. Immediately, Darian wondered if Odpor had decided to strike out at them already.

How could he have mustered a force so quickly?

They sped through the twisting cobblestone streets, and the farther they ran, the more traffic they found surging in the opposite direction. Something terrible was happening to make all of these dwarves flee; that much was clear. The six picked up their pace, the increasing volume of the cries telling them they were drawing close. They turned a corner to find the commotion source, a stone courtyard in front of a small building that appeared to be a school.

Close to a dozen dwarven children were standing in the street outside the school. Darian was no expert on dwarves but estimated them to be roughly ten years of age, judging by their size compared to the adult dwarves he had met. Ten rough-looking dwarven warriors stood behind them, shouting out to a crowd of terrified onlookers.

"These are the children of Resistance traitors, and if they are not stamped out now, they will grow into traitors as well," shouted a young dwarf who appeared to be the leader. "Odpor is the one true ruler of Qwitzite, and it is time we do our part to enforce his rule. If Iskra and his band of treasonous cowards are unwilling to learn for themselves, we will teach them a hard lesson here today! Ah, look here! What perfect timing! Here are the Imperial invaders that Iskra has so willingly welcomed into our fine city." He pointed toward the Imperial soldiers with his sword, and they felt every eye turn toward them.

"Release these children at once, you sniveling cowards!" Kalayo cried, stepping forward and drawing her axe. The Imperials moved to support her, drawing their swords. "Is the murder of children what your precious Odpor stands for? Is this the way of life you want for our people?"

"You should be ashamed to find yourself in such company, you stupid woman. Step away, or we will be happy to put an end to you and your Imperial friends once we have finished cleansing this school of the blood of traitors. This is your only warning. Run off and hide behind Iskra's legs."

Kalayo never hesitated, nor did she run off and hide. She did not bother to reply, at least not with words. Instead, she sprung forward so fast her Imperial friends could barely keep up. She shoved two of the children aside, driving her axe forcefully into the head of the leader of the dwarves, splitting his skull before he could raise his sword to defend himself. Darian was not far behind, charging recklessly into the line of dwarves. These men supported Odpor, one of the men responsible for Axel's death. They were willing to murder innocent children to send a message to their enemies. He knew all he needed to know about them.

I've watched enough innocent people die for Odpor's pride. Not today.

He rushed headfirst into the first dwarf he saw, completely ignoring the attack the man was launching at him. It likely would have been fatal if it had landed, but Darian's strike found the mark first, and he drove his sword deep into the dwarf's gut. Wrenching his weapon free, he was already looking for his next opponent and found one quickly. Once again, he charged forward, disregarding the sword coming his way. The blade struck a glancing blow on his wrist, opening a shallow cut. Darian's sword delivered a far more grievous wound, catching the dwarf clean through the neck.

A third dwarf was coming forward to meet him, a challenge Darian welcomed with open arms as he ignored the throbbing pain emanating from the wound in his wrist. Two vicious swings of his sword, and the dwarf was dying on the street in a rapidly expanding puddle of blood. A fourth dwarf met the same fate a few seconds later, Darian paying no mind to the minor wound he'd received on his right leg in return.

He spun on the spot, searching for another foe, but there were none in sight. They had defeated all ten of the Odpor loyalists, four of them dead at his hands. The battle had only lasted a matter of seconds. As his breathing slowly returned to normal and the pounding in his head began to subside, Darian noticed Darnold Dans watching him closely, his face an unreadable mask. Looking past Darnold, he began to count the children, relieved to find ten terrified but unharmed faces gawking back at him.

Darian sheathed his sword, his head throbbing. A rush of anger had struck him unlike any he had felt since the night he had watched Krillzoc murder Axel Stark. Onlookers were beginning to pour out into the street, several of them rushing forward to shower him with thanks for saving their children. One older woman actually hugged him, pulling away with tears in her eyes. Kalayo walked up, wiping blood from her axe as she did.

"You fought well, Private Tor. These children would probably all be dead if it were not for you Imperials. You stepped forward to defend the children of those who have done nothing but treat you with scorn and hatred since you arrived in this city. You have my thanks. Dwarves can be stubborn, but they recognize courage, and they respect and honor those who show it. I have a feeling you will have the thanks of everyone in Jezero before too long."

"They are only children. It wouldn't be right to hold their parents' actions and words against them," Darian said. His voice seemed to tremble as the words left his lips, but he could feel his rage finally beginning to subside, the throbbing in his head fading away altogether.

"This is the first time the Odpor loyalists have been this brazen here in Jezero—that I have heard of, at least. Hopefully it will be the last," Kalayo said, grasping his shoulder for a moment before moving away to thank Captain Dunstan.

"That's a nasty cut," a voice said from behind him. Darian turned to find Darnold Dans standing there, pointing toward the wound on his leg. He was still staring at Darian inquisitively. Darian looked down at the injury for the first time, realizing it was bleeding much more profusely than he would have suspected.

"Stings a little bit, but it's not too bad. Can you help me wrap it? I'm sure Iskra has a poultice or something that will help it heal faster, but it's probably best if I don't drip blood all over the streets on our way back. Some of them have finally just stopped hating us. Let's not ruin the goodwill so soon by making a mess."

Darnold nodded and used a strip of cloth to bind Darian's wound as best he could. Darian winced a few times, trying not to show how badly the wound was hurting. Once Darnold was finished, he placed a reassuring hand on Darian's shoulder, his voice lowering.

"Are you doing all right, Darian? I've never seen you fight like that before. You ran into that line of dwarves recklessly; I would expect that from Berj, but not you."

"Yes, Darnold, I'm fine. I suppose it was just the urgency of the situation. The lives of these children were at stake, weren't they? If a few cuts are the price I have to pay to save them and rob Odpor of a few of his loyalists in the process, I would say it's worth it. Wouldn't you?"

Darnold examined him a moment longer, and Darian hoped he would buy the lie. Darnold merely nodded, then moved off to see if he could help elsewhere. He knew Darnold meant well but couldn't help but be annoyed by his friend's questions. What business was it of Darnold's anyway? Who was he to judge the way Darian had fought? How many of those children might have ended up dead if he hadn't fought so recklessly? What did it matter what his motivations were?

***

Iskra prepared a particularly spectacular feast in their honor that night. When they had told him what had transpired, he had been furious at the nerve of the Odpor loyalists but immeasurably grateful for their intervention. Radig returned to the house late in the day, heaping praise upon them and reporting that public perception of the Imperial soldiers was already beginning to shift in the city. Most of the people of Jezero now regarded them as nothing short of heroes.

"It seems the secessionist fools not only failed to deliver their message but managed to make the five of you hundreds of new friends in the process!"

Darian took his leave from supper early, insisting he was fine and just wanted rest after the trying day. He retreated to his room, closing the door firmly behind him. He could not stop thinking about what Darnold Dans had said after the battle. Had he truly been acting recklessly? That was not like him; he had always been levelheaded, even in the most intense situations. His early defensiveness had evaporated, replaced by a nagging fear. If he could not keep control of his emotions, was he a danger to his friends? He had already lost Axel, and he could not bear the thought of losing another friend, much less if he ended up being at fault. They were counting on him to be there to fight beside them, to protect them at all costs. He couldn't do that if he couldn't control his emotions.

He was still wrapped up in these thoughts when there came a knock on the door. He opened it, surprised to find Captain Dunstan waiting in the hallway.

"May I come in for a few minutes? I was hoping to have a word with you," Dunstan said.

Darian stepped aside to allow the captain into the small room. He took a seat at the dwarf-sized table, and Darian joined him a moment later, wondering how ludicrous the pair of them would look to an outside observer, grown men sitting in these chairs that appeared to be meant for large children. Darian did not speak, assuming Dunstan would give the reason for this visit when he was ready. He suspected he already knew the reason anyway. After a long moment, the captain began to speak.

"Private Dans came to see me a few hours ago," Dunstan began, confirming Darian's suspicions. "He was concerned by what he saw out of you in the fight on the street earlier. He said you were fighting recklessly, with no regard for your own safety. He feels your injuries were avoidable. That doesn't sound like you. Do you feel this is true?"

"I was worried about the children, that's all," Darian said, his eyes not meeting Dunstan's.

"As were we all, but you would've been no help to them if you'd gotten yourself killed in your charge, Private Tor. You have been quite reserved since we left Muog. What's on your mind?"

What was on his mind? Was Dunstan an Imperial captain or a counselor? They had saved the children; his feelings were of no concern to anybody but himself. Darian had no interest in discussing what was on his mind with Thaddeus Dunstan—or anyone else for that matter. How could he possibly begin to understand what Darian was going through? Apparently realizing Darian was in no hurry to answer, Dunstan started talking again.

"You and Sergeant Stark were close, were you not? You grew up in Verizia together, correct?"

"How did you know that?" Darian asked, surprised.

"A good captain takes the time to learn things about the men under his command. I have always attempted to be a good captain, though I would certainly never claim that I have never fallen short. I actually addressed this with Sergeant Stark before your departure on that ill-fated mission. When he requested you and I found out you were old friends, I had concerns. I wanted to be sure he could make impartial tactical decisions where you were concerned. He assured me he could, and I believed him."

This was all news to Darian. Axel had never mentioned having any such conversation with Captain Dunstan. Still, it wasn't all that surprising when he thought about it. Dunstan had shown more of a capacity to care for his men than any other Imperial commander Darian had encountered during his short time in the army. The fact Dunstan was sitting next to him in this remote dwarven city having this conversation at all was a testament to it. Darian could not imagine another commander taking the risks Captain Dunstan had by going after them. Not a single other officer in the Imperial encampment had possessed the courage to advocate for them.

"I keep replaying his death in my head, over and over, every moment leading up to it, everything that happened. Maybe if I had done things differently, he would still be alive. Maybe if I had fought better, I could have saved him. I wonder all day, every day what I could have done to save him. But I couldn't. He's gone, and now all I can think about is making those who are responsible pay for it. It's all that matters to me now. It's consuming me; it's all I can think about. When we fought those dwarves today, their support for Odpor sent me into a rage. I want Odpor dead. I want Sylvester dead. I want anyone who supports either of them dead."

"Sergeant Stark deserves justice, and I will do everything in my power to ensure he gets it. You have my word, not as an Imperial captain, but as a man. My word is one of the few things of value I have left at this point, and understand it's not something I give cheaply. But you need to understand that vengeance and justice are two different things, Private Tor. You are being driven by a need for the former, not a desire for the latter. I have seen it many times before throughout my career."

Darian would never have expected to hear this. How could Dunstan possibly think he wanted revenge more than justice? It was nothing short of outrageous to suggest such a thing. *Who does he think he is? And to think I respected him as a commander. He is nothing but a doddering old fool. He has no idea what is going on inside my head.*

"No doubt you think I am wrong. You are probably thinking all sorts of horrible things about me right this moment for even suggesting it," Dunstan said with a knowing smile. "I understand. Look at me, Darian. Do you think I have gotten to my age without walking in similar shoes? We always look back, wondering what we could have done differently. I'm not immune from such doubts—far from it. But the past is gone, Darian, and what's done will always be done. Killing Odpor and Krillzoc will not make you feel better about it, nor will killing Sylvester. I'm not saying they don't need to die for their crimes. Obviously, they do. Just don't lose sight of the true reason why. For justice, of course, but also to protect the men, women, and children who would become their victims in the future. We cannot bring Sergeant Stark back, but maybe we can spare more families the grief his will face when they learn his fate."

Darian was still uncertain of what Dunstan meant. If revenge and justice produced the same results, what did the technicalities matter? What was important was Odpor, Krillzoc, and Sylvester dying. Everything else was irrelevant; how could a man as experienced as Dunstan not understand this?

"You know, I've spent a lot of the past five years wondering if I should have handled matters differently up in Thornata," Dunstan said, catching Darian by surprise.

"I don't know much about what happened up there—only that there was a civil war and you led Imperial troops into battle without authorization from Imperial High Command. We heard a few rumors in Verizia but never many details. The Thornatans keep to themselves,"

Darian said.

"That's the gist of it. Imperial High Command certainly didn't care much for any details beyond those. A nasty group of bandits took over the province—called themselves the Hoyt. They launched attacks against Imperial border fortresses, including the one I commanded. Imperial soldiers were killed. Was I supposed to sit back and allow other fortresses to be attacked, more men to die? I thought not. But I went even further than that, leading the surviving men into battle, seeking justice for those the Hoyt had already killed. In the end, most of the Imperial soldiers stationed in the province ended up dead, either in their fortresses or in the Battle of Oreanna, under my command. I was the one who made those decisions, and it was my responsibility to own them. And here I am, the disgraced captain, sent into another war to teach me a lesson."

Upon hearing more of Dunstan's story from the man himself, Darian did not feel like the captain had made the wrong decision. The more he learned about how Imperial High Command handled such matters, the more he questioned whether joining the Imperial Army had been a mistake. It had seemed so simple a decision when he had made it. He could follow in his father's footsteps and Axel's as well. What better path for a young man to take to find himself? At that moment, just about any other path felt preferable.

"When I wasn't much older than you, I was serving as part of an advance force in a border skirmish. The Obalans had dispatched a group of mercenaries to seize several farming villages that were rightfully a part of Kardia. Understandably, the Kardians were outraged and appealed to the Empire to intervene on their behalf. When we arrived, our mission was to drive the mercenaries from the villages. A larger force would be following us and stationing there to keep the peace.

"It was a rather simple operation, right? But when we arrived, we saw with our own eyes the types of things the mercenaries had done to those innocent villagers. To this day, I don't know if those who survived the brutality were the fortunate ones or not. Killing a person is far from the worst thing you can do to them, and I will leave it at that. But when I saw those broken people, those who survived and those who didn't, it enraged me."

Darian couldn't help but lean inward, entranced by the captain's story. "What happened next?"

"The mercenaries came out to negotiate a surrender with us, smirking with pride all the while. I'll never forget the leader's face. I never learned his name, but that face will be in my mind until the day I leave this world. The joy he extracted from the suffering he had caused was sickening."

"He sounds like Krillzoc."

"I haven't had the pleasure, but all your descriptions of this sadistic dwarf remind me of this man. I wanted him dead the second I laid eyes on him. When the fighting broke out, I rushed for him. I broke his defenses easily, and I cut him down with that smirk still plastered across his face. I've never taken such pleasure from watching the life leave another man's eyes. We overwhelmed the mercenaries with only two casualties on our side. One of those was a young man named Garreth. He was a friend of mine. He was from Floresta, the son of a fruit merchant. We had been friends all through training; he was always quick with a joke. From what I heard, he died shortly after the fighting started, right after I rushed in to kill the mercenary leader."

"But you don't know if you could have saved him by staying back and being more patient," Darian pointed out.

"You're right, I don't. And I never will. Could I have saved Garreth? Maybe, maybe not. But I do know I will spend the rest of my days asking myself that very question. All because I allowed my anger to take control."

"From what you've told me, the mercenary leader deserved his fate."

"Be careful trying to determine what another person deserves. People rarely get what they deserve in this world, for better or for worse. But does it make a difference that he died by my hand? He was doomed from the moment the battle began, but Garreth might not have been.

"Remember one thing, Darian. From what you and the others have told me, Axel Stark gave his life so the rest of you would have a chance to survive. Here you are today, still breathing. From everything I know of him, his life was no small gift. Are you willing to throw away his sacrifice to give yourself the pleasure of revenge? Or are you going to honor it by fighting for something greater than yourself?"

With that, Dunstan rose and left the room, leaving Darian Tor with more questions swirling through his head than ever before.

Chapter Thirteen

Darian Tor woke the following day feeling better than he had in a long time. His talk with Captain Dunstan had not solved any of his problems, but it had given him a new outlook on them. In Dunstan's words, what was done was done, and there was no changing it now. All he could do was try to live each day as Axel would have wanted. And bring those responsible for his friend's death to justice, of course. He could continue to live his life full of hatred and rage, or he could turn that energy toward achieving something positive. He understood this renewed sense of purpose would change nothing of what had happened over the past few weeks. Still, perhaps it could serve as motivation to change what would happen next.

He descended the stairs into the kitchen to find his three fellow privates already seated around the table. There was no sign of Iskra, Captain Dunstan, Radig, or Kalayo. But there was food waiting, so Darian took a seat and began to dig in. He had not eaten as much as he should have since their arrival, his appetite sparse, but this morning he found himself downright ravenous. His friends watched him with a hint of amusement on their faces as he ate enough for two men. When he finally pushed his chair away from the table, he found he was feeling even better.

"Now that Darian's all done stuffing his face," Berj Jenson said, "I was hoping we could have a little chat, just the four of us."

"About what?" asked Max Preston.

"Well, we've been here for three days now, and we've done nothing other than save some schoolchildren. While I'm happy we could be of assistance, I can't help but wonder what we should do next. Odpor almost certainly knows where we are by now, and he could come after us at any time. Iskra has even told us as much," Berj said. "It doesn't seem like sitting around and waiting for that to happen is our wisest option."

It was true, especially after encountering the Odpor loyalists the day prior. If they had somehow managed to elude his detection here prior to yesterday's confrontation, word was no doubt on its way to him now. Their days of being able to hide peacefully in Jezero were numbered; there was no way they weren't. The last thing any of them wanted was for the innocent people of this beautiful city to pay the price for harboring them. They needed to decide on their next steps soon.

"We still need to figure out what to do about Sylvester," Darnold Dans pointed out. "If we just march into camp with some story of our escape, it's only a matter of time before he tries to come after us. He doesn't know how much we know or don't know, but he can't take any chances; he's in this too far. Anyone who might pose a threat to him will have to go, and we would certainly fall into that category."

"Darnold is right," Darian said. "Sylvester would much rather see us all dead than take the slightest risk on us knowing about his plans. He will make a move on us shortly after our return—I'm sure of it. Either we will be attacked and killed or thrown into the stockade on imaginary charges. But I don't think we've been looking at this deeply enough."

"What do you mean? How could we be looking at this any deeper?" Berj asked, one eyebrow arched.

"He means that simply knowing Sylvester's immediate plans is not enough," a voice said from the doorway. The four turned to find Captain

Dunstan entering the room, followed closely by Radig and Kalayo. "We need to know what his endgame is if we are to figure out a way to stop him. What is his ultimate goal?"

"We know his endgame. He wants Supreme General Twilcox's job," said Preston.

"Yes, but for what purpose? Is it solely to stroke his own ego? That's possible, but not likely in my view," said Dunstan. "Sylvester is without doubt an ambitious man, but he is also a cunning one. No matter how strong his lust for power may be, he would not risk his life to come into it unless he had larger ambitions, ambitions he could only accomplish with that kind of power at his disposal. I fear his rise to the rank of Supreme General is only the beginning of his plans."

It was a question that had plagued Darian the night before, ever since his talk with Dunstan. Sylvester was power hungry—that much was clear—but was he simply seeking power for power's sake? Would he be content to seize it and hold it? It didn't feel right. A man as ambitious as Sylvester would have additional plans, things he wanted to do with his power once he came into it. But what would those ambitions be? They had only known the man for the span of a brief conversation in Muog; there was no way for them to be sure.

"Whatever it is, I doubt it is good for the dwarves," Radig said. "Sylvester told Odpor he wanted to see an end to the war. He said he would try to convince the Emperor to allow the secession of Qwitzite. From the beginning, this has never felt right to me. Why would he do this? To save the lives of Imperial soldiers? All of you are evidence of how much those lives truly mean to him. No, there is something else up his sleeve, something that will benefit Sylvester immensely—I am sure of it."

"It seems more likely he means to betray Odpor," said Kalayo. "What better way to gain the Emperor's favor than by winning this war shortly after being appointed as Supreme General?"

She's right. Sylvester must be planning to double-cross Odpor, Darian thought. No other possibility made sense. Sylvester challenging the Emperor's decisions immediately upon coming into power was nonsensical. It would do nothing but ensure his reign over the Imperial Army would be short-lived. The man had not risked everything to gain power only to see it ripped away in the name of advocating for the dwarves. If Odpor believed otherwise, he was a fool.

"Is there a way to expose Sylvester to Supreme General Twilcox and Odpor? Reveal his intentions to both of the men he is trying to betray?" Darian asked.

"Odpor would not listen to a word anyone here has to say," Radig said. "Honestly, I doubt he believes Sylvester fully anyway. It would not shock me if he was planning a betrayal of his own against Sylvester. From what I heard while I was still in his employ, he views the man as nothing more than a smooth-talking buffoon. He accepted Sylvester's help because he had little to lose by doing so, with plenty of potential gain. But Odpor is cunning; he knows better than to trust Sylvester. In my opinion, he likely wants Sylvester to replace Twilcox because he thinks an Imperial Army under Sylvester would be easier to defeat. Still, any partnership beyond that is far from Odpor's mind."

"He would be a fool to believe this," said Dunstan. "Twilcox is a more traditional soldier, no doubt about it. He has a better head for standard military strategy. But Sylvester is ten times as cunning as Twilcox could ever be, and he's shown he will not let trivial things such as honor or morals stand in the way of his goals. I believe Sylvester will be a far more dangerous adversary than Odpor is giving him credit for."

"This may be true, but an army undergoing a leadership change will still lack the stability of one under a steady commander," Kalayo said, a point that was hard to refute. "It will take time for Sylvester to consolidate his power."

They were still debating the various players' motives in this intricate game an hour later when Iskra walked in to join them. The ancient dwarf's face was troubled, filling Darian with immediate concern. The kindhearted dwarf had never shown any such emotion to them before. Something serious must've been weighing on his mind.

"My friends, I have some rather sobering news. Or a sobering lack of news, I should say. I have not received a single word out of Muog since your arrival. I can only assume Odpor and Krillzoc have managed to suffocate our few remaining lines of communication."

"Were you expecting to hear anything in particular?" Max Preston asked.

"No, but I typically receive a report on their various doings from our spies in the city every week. This week's report is three days late, and I have begun to suspect it will not arrive at all. I do not like not knowing what Odpor is doing."

"You think Odpor is planning something." Radig made it a statement rather than a question.

"His war with the Imperials has been at a standstill for months. There will be whispers among the commoners in Muog. Even those who feel secession is the right decision will begin to doubt him after such a long period of inaction. Any faith he will have drummed up by capturing you will evaporate quickly after word of your escape spreads. So, what will he do? He does not have the numbers to assault the Imperial encampment directly. He could hurt them, maybe he could even defeat them, but not without suffering horrific casualties. His advantage in that battle lies solely with the power of Muog's formidable defenses. So, I believe he will choose a different target, one that will instill faith in those who are beginning to question his abilities and fear in those who oppose him."

"You think he will attack Jezero? Could he get away with such a move? Attacking a city of his own people?" Dunstan asked.

Darian was skeptical as well. He didn't doubt Odpor's willingness to slaughter his own people but rather his confidence in facing the potential ramifications of such a move.

"I feel we should not discount the possibility. If he feels it is the only way to cling to power, he will not hesitate. Furthermore, he knows I am leading the Resistance, or at least he suspects it strongly enough to believe he knows it. If he feels killing me would end the Resistance, that would be all the motivation he needs. Odpor has never lacked a willingness to make bold moves. He often fails to think them through completely, this is true. Perhaps attacking Jezero would have ramifications he cannot foresee. Though I suspect that is a fact that will be of little comfort to our corpses."

The thought of Odpor sending a force against one of his own cities was still hard to imagine for Darian. But then he realized the Emperor had done essentially the same thing to Muog in response to a challenge of his power. Was it so outlandish to believe Odpor would do the same? He had sacrificed smaller numbers of his soldiers in the guerilla-style attacks he had already mounted against the Imperials' encampment. Remembering Odpor's smile after mercilessly sending a defenseless soldier to his death off the walls of Muog, Darian realized it was not such a stretch.

"How vulnerable is Jezero to an assault?" Berj Jenson asked.

"You have seen for yourselves in that attack on the schoolchildren. His loyalists are already here, though we cannot possibly say how many of them. You passed through our walls on your way here, and they are far from formidable. This city was built as a home for the common people, not a fortress to defend from military assaults. That said, we do have a few tricks up our sleeves. But we have nothing that can surprise them if they take the time to do their research. A sufficiently large force would overwhelm us with little difficulty."

"What type of tricks do you have up your sleeve exactly?" Darnold Dans asked.

Iskra did not answer, not right away. He exchanged a long glance with Radig as though they were trying to determine if the Imperials could be trusted with this information. Darian did his best not to take offense at the hesitation. *I suppose even saving the lives of all those schoolchildren only buys us so much trust.*

"There is a wide trench surrounding the city. You would not have seen it; it is perfectly concealed, and you walked right over it without issue. We dwarves are quite industrious, in case you have not noticed. I could have this trench opened with a simple command, forcing any attackers to climb down and back out. This would be a delaying action and little else. However, there is a gate connecting this trench to Lake Isabella. We open the gate and flood the trench, drowning anybody unfortunate enough to be inside."

It was something, but it was not enough to inspire a great deal of confidence in the Imperials. Surely Odpor and Krillzoc could find a way to circumvent the trench. And even if many warriors would drown in the flood, weighed down by their armor, it would be nigh impossible to time the attack to kill all of them at once. Some would survive, and they would not give up so easily. They would find a way to cross the flooded trench and proceed with their attack.

"But surely Odpor knows about this trench?" Dunstan asked.

"I cannot say for sure. The trench was dug well over a century ago, and Odpor has never been one to study history. But there are records of this city's defenses in the archives in Muog. If they bother to look, they will find it. I think it would be unwise to assume they will not."

As arrogant as Odpor and Krillzoc were, Darian also did not think it wise to wager on such an oversight. Odpor understood he needed a victory, and he would leave nothing to chance. He would study his records and find everything he needed—Darian was certain of it. No matter what the defenders of Jezero tried, it would not be enough to hold back Odpor's wrath.

"Could they attack from the water?" Captain Dunstan asked. "There are no walls along the shores of Lake Isabella."

"They would have to either haul boats all the way here or build them close to Jezero. If they were to camp in the nearby forests to build watercraft, they would be vulnerable to guerilla assaults, much like they have done to your encampment," Radig said. "I do not see Odpor doing that, though we cannot rule it out altogether. I think he would prefer to come straight at us and raze this city to the ground in a single swoop. Do not forget his display with you on the walls of Muog. Optics are important to Odpor. He wants to win decisively, and he wants everyone to see him doing it. He believes such displays are a good way to show off his power and reinforce that nobody can stand against him."

The more Iskra and Radig had to say, the deeper Darian's spirits sunk. He had finally begun to find himself again here in Jezero, and he had no desire to see the beautiful city destroyed or its people killed. It was so bitterly unfair. Most of these people wanted to live their lives in peace, and Odpor refused to let them do so. Iskra wasn't much better in his eyes. Who was he to lead the Resistance from this sanctuary while using these innocent people as a shield? Unable to contain himself any longer, he decided to give voice to these thoughts.

"So, what are you going to do, Iskra? You can't just sit here and wait for Odpor to come to you. The people in this city would pay the price. If you want to protect the people of Jezero, maybe it's time for you to stop hiding here and take the fight to Odpor."

His fellow Imperials were all staring at him, their mouths agape. Iskra had been kind to them, and Darian's brash statement was one seemingly more likely to come from Berj Jenson. Darian had never been one to challenge an authority figure openly. Radig and Kalayo looked downright furious at his nerve, but Iskra was smiling at him.

"You are not wrong, Darian Tor. In fact, you are wise beyond your years. That is why I feel we need to put a plan into place and start carrying it out at once. The time for sitting and waiting is coming to an end. If we do not remove Odpor from power soon, we may never have the opportunity to do so again. I was actually hoping you and your friends would agree to help us."

It was not the response Darian had expected. He had suspected the elderly dwarf would be furious with him for having the nerve to say such a thing. Most of the authority figures he had ever dealt with did not care for being told what to do or being called out on their failings. Apparently, Iskra and Captain Dunstan were cut from a similar cloth.

"As Darian has said, we cannot simply sit here, waiting for the hammer to fall on top of us. First and foremost, we need to begin working on a plan to evacuate the city as efficiently as possible. There are too many dwarves here who want no part of this war, and we should not force it upon them. If we were to do so, how would we be any better than Odpor? If the attack comes sooner than expected, we need to be ready to get them to safety."

"Evacuating Jezero would be no easy feat," Radig said. "Close to forty thousand dwarves live here. Even with those who have been forced to leave to defend Muog, there have to be close to twenty thousand at present, if not more."

"Would it be easier to bury twenty thousand corpses?" Iskra asked, and Radig had no reply. "Very well. Then we will begin planning to evacuate. Radig, Kalayo, I need suggestions on where to take these people. I would prefer a longer, more staggered evacuation. Moving them all at once would provide Odpor and Krillzoc with a soft target to attack. Please report back here with your suggestions at dusk."

Radig and Kalayo did not look overly thrilled with their assignment, but both left without another word. Iskra had enough of their respect that they would not challenge him on this. Darian understood they were more interested in winning the war against Odpor than they were in helping people flee the coming battle. But the last few weeks had taught him that wars were not always worth the cost paid. If they could save thousands of lives, they would thank him one day, assuming they all lived long enough to see that day arrive.

"Thank you for speaking up, Darian Tor. It takes courage to do so in these situations, and I appreciate your willingness to step forward," Iskra said, smiling warmly at him. "There is more work to be done. I will begin rallying those who are willing to stay and fight. The time is fast approaching when we will have to make our move against Odpor in Muog."

"You are going to bring the fight to him?" Preston asked.

"We are not going to have many other options, Private Preston. With the resources of Muog available to him, Odpor could allow this war to drag on for decades if he is willing to do so. I am not willing to see my people live like that, all in the name of his pride. This war will not end until Odpor is dead, and he is unlikely to come here himself and let us kill him. We could wait for him to die of old age, but I, for one, am not willing to see the people of Qwitzite suffer for that long."

"Do you have any ideas for how you are going to pull this off?" Berj asked.

"One matter at a time, Private Jenson. Private Tor was right when he pointed out that this city's innocent civilians need to be our top priority. This is what separates us from Odpor. He cares not for the blood of the innocent. He is willing to see as much of it spilled as necessary to fulfill his own ambition. We are not so callous. We have a cause worth fighting for, and this is exactly why we will defeat Odpor."

Darian felt his cheeks go slightly red at Iskra's praise, but he still could not help but feel proud. He felt like Axel Stark would have spoken out if he were in the same position, and that thought made him happy. His friend's future had been stolen, but if Darian lived his own life in Axel's way, his friend's memory would live on for a long time.

Chapter Fourteen

One section at a time, the attitude and general demeanor of the Imperial encampment shifted. As it did with every inspection, the whispers began to spread rapidly as soon as it started. Supreme General Cadmus Twilcox had begun his weekly assessment of the camp, and nobody wanted to draw his attention in their direction. The camp's mood had been dark for weeks, but every last man knew better than to show the slightest hint of this to their commanding officer. Twilcox was a career soldier, having served for close to forty years, but he bore little in the way of love for the men under his command. They were nothing more than tools he could use to complete a job. In the eyes of Cadmus Twilcox, every man was an expendable asset, and they all knew it.

Every last man dreaded these full-camp inspections. Each time, it seemed Twilcox searched for any excuse he could find to have a man flogged or thrown into the stocks for a few days. During his last examination, he had rebuked a young private for close to an hour over the unacceptable state of his uniform. The poor soldier had not noticed the smallest of dirt stains on his shoulder and had paid the price for it. The hatred and scorn of his men meant nothing to Twilcox. If anything, he carried it with him like a badge of honor. He had never believed a beloved commander could be an effective commander. It was common knowledge that he saw love as something you should receive from your mother, not your fellow military men. Would you follow your mother into a war? He did not need or want love; he required obedience. These inspections were an opportunity to reinforce to each and every man the power he held over them.

General Alexander Sylvester rode at the right hand of Cadmus Twilcox, hardly able to believe the day was upon him at last. The moment he had spent his entire adult life working toward had arrived. In a matter of hours, Twilcox would be dead, and his ascension to the top of the Imperial Army would be assured. Decades of hard work and sacrifice were finally about to pay off. He stole the occasional glance at his superior, taking great satisfaction from the fact that the fool had no idea he was living his last few hours.

In typical fashion, Twilcox was taking his sweet time with the inspection. At his current rate, it would be close to two more hours before they reached the northwestern edge of the encampment. Sylvester hoped Krillzoc's assassins would not grow impatient and leave, or worse yet, suspect him of treachery. Would the carefully laid plot be thwarted due to Twilcox's stubborn desire to inflict his insufferable presence upon his men for as long as possible? It was an unbearable thought to Sylvester. If he hadn't known any better, he would've suspected Twilcox was wise to his plan. He tried to move the procession along at every turn, and at every turn, Twilcox resisted him.

So, the hours stretched on, hours spent under the burning-hot midday sun. Sylvester surmised that Twilcox must be in an especially foul mood today, even by his standards. Every company they inspected, he found some minute detail to criticize, drawing the men's scorn. Sylvester bore no more love for these simple men than his superior, but he had long understood the value of their love and loyalty. If you could convince them that you cared about them, they would do anything for you, and they would do it with a smile on their face and love in their heart. What did it matter if it was all a charade? Perception was far more important than reality when it came to dealing with simpleminded men such as these. Treat them as Twilcox was, and they would be all too happy to see you bleeding out, face down in the dirt. Treat them well, and they wouldn't hesitate to fall down and die to defend you.

"I'm surprised you haven't found an excuse to run off yet, Alex," Twilcox commented as they rode between companies. "It has always been quite apparent how little patience you have for these inspections. Isn't there some other urgent business for you to attend to?"

"I don't see anything more urgent than making sure the camp is at the ready, Supreme General," Sylvester forced himself to say professionally. Nobody dared call him Alex other than Twilcox. *Laugh it up while you still can, you senile old fool. We'll see who is laughing while you are dying in the dirt. Enjoy every minute you have left; I'm afraid they are running out.*

"No? It seems like every other inspection, your friend Captain Garrison comes running up with some terribly urgent matter requiring your immediate attention within an hour of getting underway. You know, I've always meant to ask you about that man. A rather simple fellow, isn't he, Alex? I've always wondered why you never found a brighter man to work under you."

"Captain Garrison has always served me well, Supreme General. I've never seen any reason to replace him," Sylvester said. It was somewhat surprising to him that a man like Twilcox could not see the value of a more simpleminded servant. Twilcox had made the worst mistake a man could make. He had placed his trust in someone more intelligent than himself. Today it would cost him his life.

"No? Well, suit yourself, Alex. I would be happy to find you a more suitable officer to attend to your needs. You work hard; why make yourself work harder by accepting incompetent service?"

"Thank you, Supreme General. That will not be necessary. As I have said, Captain Garrison performs his duties admirably and has always been a faithful servant."

"See, that's where you are going wrong, Alex. You treat his loyalty like it's some great attribute on his part. In case you haven't noticed, they are all loyal. They have no other choice; it was in the oath they swore. Look around you. Take a long, hard look at some of these men. When the alternative is swinging from a noose or rotting in a cage, any one of these men will follow any command you give them. They won't question you. They won't talk back to you. It's a beautiful thing, is it not?"

Sylvester did not reply, too confounded by the other man's blatant ignorance to find a suitable answer. He wondered if Twilcox would realize the truth of what was happening in his last moments. Would he suspect that Sylvester was behind his demise? In a way, Sylvester hoped he would. He wanted Twilcox to realize as he took his last breath that it was Alexander Sylvester who had finally put an end to his miserable existence. *Maybe you will even recognize in those moments that your own arrogance allowed me to do it, you blithering old fool.*

The sun was already dropping when they finally reached the northwestern edge of the encampment, over an hour later than usual. Twilcox immediately went to work, ridiculing several sergeants for their unshaven faces. Meanwhile, Sylvester's eyes were continually sweeping their surroundings, searching for any hint of Krillzoc's men. He spotted no signs, but he knew the dwarves were exceptionally skilled at remaining undetected. If they were indeed going to hold up their end of the deal, Sylvester would not see them until they did it.

He felt around for his sword on his belt, reassuring himself that it was there. Krillzoc had assured him that only two incompetent warriors would attack him. While fighting had never been his greatest strength, he should be able to dispatch them. In doing so, he would win the love of the lowly foot soldiers, a general willing to fight beside them for a change, to put his own life at risk to defend their own.

Captain Garrison had not been pleased when Sylvester had commanded him to stay clear of the proceedings. He would have felt better having the loyal captain by his side, but it could not be so, not this time. He needed the men to see him fighting beside them, not standing by as Garrison protected him from harm. Garrison would also be at risk in the struggle, and he could take no chances with the life of his most faithful servant. Now, more than ever, he would need a man like Garrison. Once his ascension was official, there would be a fresh promotion awaiting the man with endless devotion. Major Terrence Garrison would have a critical role to play in the future of the Imperial Army.

He was so lost in his thoughts that it caught even Sylvester by surprise when the attack came.

I should have been watching more closely. Well, at least my reaction will appear genuine.

Twilcox's bodyguards were the first to go down, dragged from their horses and hacked to bits before they knew what was happening. The dwarves had appeared as if from nowhere. Twilcox spun away from the unfortunate soldier he had been criticizing for the state of his uniform, his mouth agape. The young man died first, a tragic but necessary sacrifice, an axe splitting his skull before he could even register what was happening. Twilcox met the same fate a few seconds later, a spear driven straight through his chest before he could reach for a weapon to defend himself. Sylvester felt a rush of joy unlike anything he had ever felt before wash through him as Twilcox collapsed, a pool of blood forming around his slumped figure. It was time to finish this charade.

"The Supreme General is down! On me, lads! We have to get him to a healer!" he cried, ripping his sword from its sheath and leaping from his horse.

One by one, every Imperial soldier in the vicinity rushed to join him, inspired by his courage in the face of danger. One dwarf lunged for Sylvester, his axe swinging sloppily for the general's legs. Sylvester sidestepped the clumsy attack with ease, his sword coming down on the dwarf's head before the fool could recover. A second dwarf was now lumbering toward him, this one brandishing a mace as though he had never held a weapon before in his life. Krillzoc had chosen his would-be assassins well.

Once again, Sylvester avoided the incoming attack without difficulty, his counter leaving the unfortunate dwarf bleeding out on the ground. The Imperial soldiers surged forward, inspired by their general's exceptional bravery and skill. They had overwhelmed the dwarven assassins within seconds, with no need for Sylvester to put on any more of an act.

"Send for a healer at once! Supreme General Twilcox is gravely wounded," he ordered a nearby soldier as he rushed to kneel by the fallen general's side. Pulling his dagger, he hastily cut a strip from his own tunic, using the cloth to apply pressure to Twilcox's wound. It was all for naught, of course. Twilcox was as good as dead already—it was apparent to see—but he needed to complete the farce. *Farewell, old friend. You will do far more for the Imperial Army in death than you ever could have done in life.*

***

Sylvester stepped out of Cadmus Twilcox's tent hours later, straining to maintain the somber expression on his face. Inside, he had never felt so gleeful in his entire life. He had just finished meeting with the other three generals stationed in the Imperial encampment. Stories of his bravery during the attack had spread through the camp like wildfire. The other generals had voted unanimously to name him as the interim commander of the invasion force until the Emperor could name an official replacement for Twilcox.

The message to the Emperor in Valdovas had been sent earlier that day. It had included the written recommendation of over two dozen of the camp's senior officers that Alexander Sylvester be elevated to the rank of

Supreme General. It was only a matter of time until the promotion was official.

As he made his way through the encampment toward his tent, every man he passed stopped what he was doing to snap a salute in his direction. A few even broke decorum to shout words of encouragement or thanks. Each time, he nodded solemnly in response, doing his best to maintain his mourning demeanor in the wake of the tragic death of his predecessor. Though he doubted anything could stop his promotion now, it was still best if he gave off the outward appearance of grief in the midst of this horrific tragedy.

Krillzoc had held up his end of their bargain to perfection. Not that it would do anything to save the dwarves, of course. They had proven themselves too troublesome for Sylvester to reconsider his prior determination. They would need to be dealt with swiftly and decisively. It would not be too difficult to persuade the Emperor that their extermination was necessary. The resources of Qwitzite were far too valuable to yield, and the dwarves would never be willing subjects of the Empire. Nasty business, but it would show the Emperor that he had selected the right man for the job.

In a matter of weeks, he would accomplish what Twilcox hadn't been able to do in months. Not only would the war be over, but Alexander Sylvester would immediately find himself as one of the Emperor's most trusted and valued servants. His rise to the rank of Supreme General and victory in Qwitzite would only be the beginning.

As he approached his tent, he found Terrence Garrison waiting, his face quizzical. Sylvester motioned for the man to join him in the tent.

"It is done, Captain Garrison," Sylvester said as they took their seats at the table. "The recommendation has been sent to Valdovas. In the meantime, I have been named the interim commander of this army. I have said this before, but it needs to be said once more. I appreciate your loyalty during these trying times. I could not have achieved any of this without your hard work. It is a relief to finally see that our struggle has not all been for naught."

"It has been my honor, Supreme General Sylvester," Garrison said, and it sounded even better than Sylvester had anticipated. "I hope to continue serving you for many years to come."

"And you shall, Captain Garrison. I do believe I mentioned seeing a promotion in your future. I will be submitting that form tomorrow morning. Now, please fetch me a glass of wine and one for yourself. I do believe a toast is in order. We have much to celebrate this evening, you and I."

Chapter Fifteen

D arian Tor looked down across the city of Jezero, feeling for the first time in a long time that he was genuinely making a positive difference in the world. One by one, the members of the large party of dwarven citizens stepped forward to thank him, many of them embracing him in the process. Once they had done so, each moved on to do the same to Berj Jenson, who looked decidedly uncomfortable with the added attention and praise. Darian smiled at each and every person who thanked him, wishing them well on their journey north.

The Imperial soldiers had been assisting the Resistance for the better part of the last week with the evacuation of Jezero. With such a sizeable portion of the Resistance's forces tied up in other essential tasks, Iskra had asked if the Imperials would be willing to provide extra security for the fleeing civilians. They had been quick to agree, quite eager to do something besides sitting around and waiting for something terrible to happen. So, they had taken turns coming out in pairs to help escort those unable or unwilling to fight safely out of the city.

Iskra had gone to work quickly after their meeting, arranging asylum for the people of Jezero in the distant city of Dranath. Dranath sat on the far northwestern border of Qwitzite, bordered by the province of

Floresta on the north and the immense Thrawll Desert on the west. Odpor was unlikely to send forces so far from his safe haven in Muog, and if he did, the people would be able to flee into Floresta. Odpor may have been bold, but sending forces into a neighboring province was a prospect even he would balk at. Within another week, Jezero would be nearly deserted. Only Resistance members who were willing to stand and fight would remain. They could only hope it was soon enough. Thus far, the scouts had seen no signs of an imminent attack, though there were whispers of a force massing in the forests north of Muog.

"It's quite a change from when we first arrived here. Remember when they wanted nothing more than for us to die a most unpleasant death? I never thought I would see so many of them smiling at me," Berj said, walking up to Darian as the dwarves moved off to the north.

"Well, to be fair, they have little reason to have any love for Imperials. Who knows? Maybe our presence here will help bridge the divide in the future. Maybe we're changing the world, Berj."

"We can hope so, but I'm not so optimistic. Whenever commoners like you and I make a positive difference, those bastards in power always find a way to muck it up, don't they? Such is the way of the world, and that won't be so easy to change."

"Well, if we have anything to say about it, there will at least be different bastards in power by the time we're done. They may end up being no better than our current group, but at least there will be some measure of justice for those who deserve it," said Darian.

Looking down at Jezero from the top of the hill north of the city, Darian hoped Berj was wrong. If his time in this beautiful city had taught him nothing else, it had shown him that these people deserved better. He realized that all across the Empire were people not so different from these dwarves, who wanted nothing more than to live a peaceful, prosperous life. As long as tyrants like Odpor and Sylvester were allowed to remain in positions of power, there would be no positive change for anyone. As long as there were evil men vying for power, innocents would suffer in their struggles for power. He was more determined than ever. If the world would not change for the better on its own, he would do everything in his power to make it happen.

Darian and Berj turned to make their way back into the city. Four Resistance fighters would escort the civilians the rest of the way to Dranath, hopefully returning in time to help defend Jezero. Captain Dunstan and Max Preston would leave upon their return to accompany the next group, then Darian would head out one last time for the day along with Darnold Dans. By rotating the trips, they had managed to keep themselves well rested. Radig felt it was only a matter of time before Odpor moved against Jezero, and they all needed to be prepared in case it happened at an unexpected moment. Little though he wanted to see it happen, Darian was inclined to agree. It wouldn't be much longer before they would be forced to fight or flee.

"You and I haven't talked much since leaving Muog. I suppose that's my fault, isn't it?" Berj said, breaking the silence. "I was a real ass back in that cell."

"It's all in the past, Berj," Darian replied. He had not forgotten Berj's comments about Axel but had managed to forgive them. They hadn't been in their right minds in that cell, and he could not hold anything Berj had said against him. A year prior, every one of them would have still been considered a child by law. How could he condemn such a person for their words in the midst of such a wretched situation? They'd all thought they were mere hours away from death.

"It is, but that doesn't mean I don't need to apologize for it. Axel died for us, and I disrespected his sacrifice. I deserved everything I got and then some more. I've never regretted saying anything so much in my life."

Darian shot Berj a reassuring smile and clapped him on the back. It was strange; just over a week ago, he had felt a wave of burning anger he had thought would never subside toward virtually the entire world. Now he felt no need to hold grudges, least of all against a good friend like Berj. He had not forgotten their time together in Krillzoc's torture chamber on the night of their capture. They each bore a brand in the same spot, a macabre mark that would bind them for life. Life was too short to be angry with friends, especially when your life was as dangerous as theirs.

"Axel was a good man. He didn't deserve to die the way he did," Darian said. "But it wasn't your fault. It wasn't mine either, even though I've had a hell of a time convincing myself of that. In the end, there are only three people responsible for his death: Odpor, Krillzoc, and Sylvester. Before I take my last breath, I intend to make sure they answer for it, all of them."

"I would love nothing more than to help you do that." Berj returned his smile. Darian thought for a moment that there was no man he would rather have by his side for the battles ahead.

"Dunstan was right about the dwarves, though, wasn't he? For the most part, at least. I made plenty of smart comments about how naive he was for believing that nonsense, but now I have to admit it. For every sick, twisted lunatic like Krillzoc, we've met countless others who seem to be normal, good-hearted people," Berj said. "I look at Jezero and think I would be happy to live out the rest of my life here with these people."

"There is so much we don't know about them, but it's been good to learn what we have. They aren't so different from the people who live in my village in Verizia. Iskra is a good man, maybe the best man I've ever met. Kalayo is brave, selfless, and friendlier than she likes to let on. Radig is a bit of a puzzle, isn't he? But he's saved our necks enough times that I think he is trustworthy. I imagine living through everything he has would give anyone a gruff exterior."

They walked on in silence for several minutes, each man lost in his own thoughts. They had escorted the dwarven civilians nearly two miles outside of the city, so there was plenty of time to gather their thoughts on the trek back. Darian thought mainly of the task ahead, the continuing evacuation of Jezero. Investing himself in the mission of saving these people had given him a renewed sense of purpose. He could not go back in time and save Axel, but he could help ensure that none of these people suffered an equally meaningless death. If Axel was his inspiration for it, what better legacy for his friend to leave behind?

"Do you smell smoke?" Berj asked, interrupting his train of thought.

Darian came to a halt, sniffing the air. Berj was right: there was a scent on the air. It was faint, and still a long way off, but it did smell like smoke. He scanned the horizon, searching for the source. When he did, his heart sunk like a stone. A black plume of smoke was rising into the bright afternoon sky, emanating from the eastern edge of Jezero. An accidental fire? Perhaps, but Darian's instincts told him something more sinister was at play.

"Let's get down there and see what's going on," he said to Berj, taking off at a run without waiting for a reply.

"Darian, slow down!" Berj cried, scrambling to keep up. "You don't know what you're running into."

It was a rare occasion that Berj Jenson was the voice of reason. Darian knew he was right, but still, he did not slow his pace. He had promised himself and Axel's memory that he would do everything in his power to keep as many of the people of Jezero safe as he could. If he did not hurry to the spot of the potential danger, he was breaking that promise. He desperately willed his feet to move faster.

They entered the northern gate of Jezero, noting as they did so that the guards who were normally posted there were absent. Whatever was happening was dire enough to draw them away from their post. *Unless they didn't leave willingly.* Darian turned down a main thoroughfare, leading the way east through Jezero. He didn't know exactly where he was going, but he allowed his nose to lead the way through the streets. The more pungent the stench of smoke became, the closer he knew they were to their objective. The nearer they drew, the more dwarves they encountered fleeing in the opposite direction, their eyes wide with terror. Before long, the sound of clashing weapons rose into the air, ringing out above the mayhem of the fleeing crowds.

Tearing out into a major intersection, they suddenly came upon their destination, a scene of utter chaos unfolding before their eyes. A large building was engulfed in flames, the smoke billowing from its rooftop growing darker by the second. To make matters worse, the buildings on either side also appeared to be in imminent danger of going up in flames. Darian followed the sounds of the clashing weapons, finding Captain Dunstan, Darnold Dans, and Max Preston in the midst of a desperate struggle.

It was impossible to determine who was fighting on which side. The scene was utter pandemonium. The street was flooded with dwarves fighting one another. Some belonged to the Resistance and others to Odpor—that much was clear—but for Darian, there was no way to discern which was which. It did not take long for one of the Odpor loyalists to reveal himself, racing toward Darian and Berj, brandishing a heavy mace.

Berj stepped forward to meet the assailant, his sword clearing its sheath as he did. He met the dwarf a few feet in front of Darian, his sword deflecting the mace's swing and countering in what seemed to be a single fluid motion. The dwarf never stood a chance; Berj's sword slipped under his guard and punched through his ribs. He collapsed at their feet, blood staining the cobblestones beneath him.

More dwarves had taken notice of them and were moving to attack. *At least we know which side they're on*, Darian thought, bringing his sword up into a defensive position. Two assailants were on top of him in seconds, both lashing out at him with razor-sharp swords. He deflected one attack and managed to sidestep another, but the dwarves pressed forward, sending him reeling backward before he could conceive a counterattack. He was forced to give ground steadily, barely managing to keep himself alive but never able to launch an attack. He was being forced to give up more ground by the second, steadily being backed toward the wall of a nearby building where they could finish him off easily.

It was Berj Jenson who saved him, charging into the midst of his battle like a wild bull. His sword hacked the life out of one of Darian's attackers before the dwarf could register what was happening. Berj was gone a split second later, pulled into combat with another foe, but he had given Darian the opening he needed to rid himself of his second attacker. Countering one last strike, he was finally able to step into an attack of his own. The dwarf barely parried his first attack, but the second broke past his defenses, Darian's sword finding a home in his shoulder. The dwarf continued to lash out at him despite the grievous wound, forcing Darian to draw his dagger and shove it into the side of the dwarf's neck to finally put an end to him.

Darian spun in every direction, trying to assess the current state of the battle. He saw the axe out of the corner of his eye just in time to slip underneath it, an act of pure instinct. The swing had been a wild one, leaving his attacker exposed. Darian cut the life from him without hesitation, his counter an act of reflex, then stepped away as the dwarf fell to the street. Assuring himself there was no imminent attack coming toward him, he paused for the briefest of moments to take in the scene around him.

The fire had only intensified, spreading to several buildings now. Captain Dunstan was leading a counterassault against the Odpor loyalists, though how he could tell who they were was a mystery to Darian. He started forward to join the battle, but something caught his eye in the chaos. In a window of one of the burning buildings was a dwarven child, her face taut with horror as she screamed for help. The fire would reach her within minutes, and she was too small to hope to escape on her own. The window was two levels above the ground with only the stone street beneath her; she could not survive a jump from the window.

Darian didn't hesitate. He bolted through the midst of the battle, ducking under and around countless attacks, never sure if the man he was passing was friend or foe. He tore out of the struggle, racing for the open doorway to the building as fast as his legs could carry him. He lowered his shoulder and blasted through a pile of stone debris in the entryway, breaking through on his first try. He stumbled into the building, winded from the force of the impact. He tried to take a deep breath to recover and immediately regretted it, thick smoke flooding his lungs and sending him into a coughing fit.

The heat was unimaginable, and Darian was forced to squint against it as tears flooded his eyes. There were flames everywhere he looked, creeping closer to him with each passing second. His gaze cast about, desperately searching for stairs leading upward. It did not take him long to find them, though his vision was growing more obstructed. The combination of the smoke and the tears it was bringing to his eyes was nigh impossible to see through. Blinking furiously, trying to maintain what little vision he still possessed, he staggered up the stairs more by feeling his way rather than seeing it. Twice he was forced to place a steadying hand on the wall, and twice his skin screamed in protest as it made contact with the scorching-hot surface. Each time he pulled his hand away, it required a great effort, and he knew without looking to confirm that he had left bits of his flesh behind.

By the time Darian made it to the top of the second flight of stairs, the heat and smoke were so oppressive that he could hardly breathe. How many windows to the left of the entrance had the child been? Darian racked his brain, trying to remember, but the fire was stealing his ability to think clearly. With no other options, he started to shout.

"Where are you? Where are you? Where are you?" he shouted, his voice growing hoarser with each repetition.

Somehow, the child made her cries heard over the roaring flames and collapsing walls. The voice seemed to be coming from the second wooden door. Darian stumbled forward, crashing into the door. He realized his body must be beginning to fail him when he could not break through on the first attempt. *Is this how I'm going to die? Burning to death in this hallway?* Refusing to accept defeat, he charged forward one more time. This time he was successful, and he smashed his way through the door, feeling several splinters embedding deep in his flesh as he forced his way through and paying them no mind.

He could barely keep his eyes open through the heat, smoke, and tears, but he seemed to have smashed his way into a small living area. Each breath was becoming more painful to draw, but he staggered forward, desperate to find the trapped child. It did not take him long to find her, curled into a fetal position underneath the window, crying in terror. The flames were advancing into the room now, and they were already within feet of the girl. Darian threw himself on top of the child, hoping he could protect her from the burning inferno.

"Put your arms around me and hold on tight," he gasped, his voice so raspy he could hardly understand himself. Each word was agony to produce. To his relief, he felt the girl's arms tighten around his neck.

It was clear to Darian that returning the way he had entered was no longer an option. Even if they could get out of this room, the fire had almost certainly already enveloped the stairs down to the street. There was only one way out now, and though he dreaded it, Darian didn't hesitate. He lifted the dwarven girl in his arms, finding it took every last ounce of strength he could muster. He turned to put his back to the window, holding her firmly to his chest. Sliding onto the windowsill, he found himself wishing he could take one last deep breath. Knowing there was no time to waste, he pushed off the windowsill as hard as possible, tumbling out into the void.

The fall lasted longer than he expected, the girl screaming in terror the entire way. He held her as firmly as he could as she thrashed in sheer panic, determined to keep her on top of him, hoping his body would dull the force of her impact enough that she would survive the fall. The ground arrived abruptly, driving every last ounce of air from his lungs as he struck. It didn't hurt, at least not in the way he had expected. There was no sharp explosion of pain but rather a startling numbness followed by a dull throb that intensified slowly. The girl clung to him, still crying, which gave Darian comfort. At least she was still alive, though he found he couldn't move to make an assessment of any injuries she might have suffered from the fall.

Captain Dunstan's face appeared through the smoke over his head, his eyes grave with concern. Max Preston appeared a second later, reaching down and prying the crying dwarven girl from his arms. His vision was blurring into a singular hazy image, and Darian was hardly aware of what was happening. After a few moments, it felt like he had been lifted and carried away from the fire. As soon as they set him down, a hazy face of a frantic dwarven woman appeared above, tearfully thanking him for what he had done. He couldn't reply, couldn't speak at all. Each time he tried, his throat screamed in horrible agony.

The Imperials carried Darian back to Iskra's home, the battle over. The journey was a blur to Darian, and he faded in and out of consciousness multiple times. They laid him down in the bed he had slept in since their arrival, all of them sitting at his side. A dwarf healer arrived several minutes later, scrutinizing him. Darian could hear his comrades frantically asking if he would recover, but the healer paid them no mind, merely examining Darian silently, his bearded face swimming in and out of sight. After a few minutes, he produced several balms and began applying them to burns Darian hadn't even been aware he had suffered.

"He is quite fortunate to still be alive at this point," the healer said, speaking for the first time.

"He will survive, though?" asked Captain Dunstan.

"I am a healer, not a fortune teller. But he has a chance. You will have to keep him in bed as much as possible for the next few days. These balms will heal his burns, but he needs rest. The inside of his throat is also burned, which is why he cannot speak. It happens when you breathe in the smoke and air from such an intense blaze, and these burns are quite severe. I have something for that, but he will have to drink it, and it will not be a pleasant experience for him, though it will help. Could two of you assist?"

Darian didn't understand the request until Berj Jenson and Max Preston stepped forward and restrained him as gently as they could manage. The balms had done a great deal to numb his burns, but the pressure of his friends holding him against the bed caused them to flare in pain again.

The healer raised a small vial to his lips, urging him to drink. Darian managed to open his mouth wide enough for the healer to pour the liquid down his throat, then immediately regretted it. The pain intensified; it was unbearable. The taste was beyond vile.

This is too much; please just let me die, he thought, unable to put it into words. He thrashed out, but Berj and Preston managed to hold him in place. *Let go of me, you bastards! Just let me die!* But the pain began to subside within a minute, and slowly but steadily, his throat began to numb.

"I know, lad, it is unpleasant, but you should start feeling better soon. Starting in the morning, he can have water, but only water tomorrow. I will return to check on him, and he will likely need another dose of that medicine, though it will not be so unpleasant the second time. But I am hopeful he will be able to bear soft food again in two or three days. For the time being, he is out of immediate danger. He has several broken ribs and possibly an injury to his back as well. I do not want to risk sitting him up yet, so I will bind them tomorrow and assess any other bone injuries he may have. Just keep him as still as possible. The medicine I just gave him will make him fall asleep soon, and he should be out for a good long while. Thank you for what you did, young man. It is a miracle the girl survived. I daresay you will be viewed as quite the hero by the people of Jezero for many years to come."

With that, the healer was gone, leaving Darian alone with his fellow soldiers. They had each dragged a chair into the tiny room to keep him company, and none showed any sign of leaving now. Captain Dunstan sat near his head and placed a reassuring hand on his shoulder.

"You are quite the hero, Private Tor. Iskra is extremely grateful for what you did back there. I'm sure he will be in to see you himself once you have had the chance to rest. We managed to clear out the Odpor loyalists, but we were alarmed when none of us saw you. We were worried you had fallen in the battle and were checking the bodies. Imagine our surprise when you came plummeting from the sky. The child will be fine; thanks to you, it seemed as though her injuries were minor."

The girl had survived; that was all Darian had needed to hear. He was in agony, but it was worth it. He realized, lying there in pain, that this might be the best thing he had ever done. Just as the healer had said, he began to feel the medicine taking effect, his eyelids growing heavy. Within minutes, he had drifted off into a painful yet relieving sleep.

Chapter Sixteen

O dpor could not recall the last time he had felt so ecstatic. The Imperial siege of Muog had not been easy on him. Being forced to sit behind his walls with invaders on his doorstep had been unbearable, but he could see the future becoming clearer with each passing day. His faithful servants in Jezero had been sowing chaos in his name. Their actions in the streets of the Resistance-led city were laying the foundation for his attack force, which would soon be ready to march. Already, that traitor Iskra had begun the evacuation of those too cowardly to stand and fight. To top it all, he had finally received word that Imperial Supreme General Cadmus Twilcox was dead.

Krillzoc was standing to his right, fully back in his good graces. Odpor was delighted to have had his trust in his most valued servant validated. Any who might have questioned his decision not to have Krillzoc killed would have no choice but to acknowledge their error in thinking now. After all this time, how could anyone question the wisdom of his decisions? Before long, Jezero would fall, and the remainder of the Resistance along with it. With Twilcox dead, the Imperial Army was no longer a significant threat. Alexander Sylvester was not nearly as brilliant as he believed himself to be, and he would prove to be the downfall of the

Imperials. Everything was unfolding in the best possible way.

"Chieftain Odpor, General Alexander Sylvester of the Imperial Army is at the main gates, requesting an audience," one of his stewards announced.

This caught Odpor by surprise. He had not expected a visit from Sylvester, and certainly not so soon after the death of Twilcox. The overeager fool would draw suspicions from his own forces, coming to parlay with the enemy so soon after they had killed his former superior. Still, Odpor supposed Sylvester's standing among the Imperials was not his concern and ordered the steward to admit the fool to the city. If Sylvester wanted to alienate himself in the eyes of his men, who was Odpor to deny him? Perhaps they would hang him as a traitor and plunge their forces into further disarray.

"He made no mention to me of coming for a parlay after Twilcox was dead," said Krillzoc, who appeared just as surprised as Odpor. "It does not seem like a well-calculated move on his part."

"I am not shocked. Men like Sylvester get clever ideas in their heads and decide to act on them impulsively. It happens all the time. In his eyes, he can do no wrong. The death of Twilcox has likely only intensified his arrogance. He no doubt dreamed of this moment for years. I suspect he means to walk in here and gloat about this glowing victory he has won. Say nothing, my friend. The less we give away to him, the better. He will understand who has truly been pulling the strings soon enough."

Krillzoc nodded his agreement, and they waited silently for Sylvester's arrival. It came roughly fifteen minutes later. He strode into the room like a conquering hero, his face portraying a smugness that bordered on criminal.

Live it up while you still can, you arrogant fool. Enjoy this prize we have won for you; the days you have to do so are numbered, thought Odpor. Once again, Captain Garrison accompanied Sylvester, though his expression bore none of his general's pride. Garrison had struck Odpor as a simple man from their limited interactions. Such a man was undoubtedly a good servant for Sylvester, whose overblown ego would never allow him to have an intelligent servant.

"Greetings and salutations, Chieftain Odpor. I must admit, when Krillzoc came to offer me this new bargain, I was skeptical. But your men performed their jobs to perfection. In fact, it was a privilege to see them in action. I believe this is the beginning of a beautiful new partnership," Sylvester said, beaming all the while.

"Welcome, General Sylvester. We had not expected to receive you again so soon. I wonder if your men might view this visit with skepticism, considering the recent demise of Supreme General Twilcox?" Odpor asked. "I have to assume most of your army is quite displeased with the dwarves at this moment."

"Were they more intelligent, I would share your concerns, Chieftain Odpor. Fortunately, not many men have been blessed with our mental aptitude. My fellow generals begged me to come here and request a temporary halt to hostilities between our forces. They view my negotiating prowess as the only hope of a peace being brokered between our two sides."

And I am sure you never hesitated to jump at the opportunity to inflate your undeserved reputation. It took every ounce of self-control Odpor possessed to refrain from scowling. What kind of fool did Sylvester take him for? Odpor was tempted to order Krillzoc to put a painful end to the insufferable man right then and there. But an Imperial Army under Alexander Sylvester's command was an army they could more easily defeat in battle. Better to let Sylvester believe the dwarves were falling for his little charade hook, line, and sinker.

"Is that a fact? I assume you want me to honor their request. I imagine us launching more attacks after this meeting would do your standing in the encampment no favors."

"I cannot imagine it would. The officers have already sent their recommendation to the Emperor that I should succeed Twilcox. It should only be a matter of days now. Once it is official, you have my word. I will immediately get to work on persuading him to end this senseless war once and for all. It's long past time for the Imperial Army to go home and leave the dwarves to live their lives in peace. My men are weary of this senseless conflict, as am I."

Oh, yes, I am sure you will. Odpor had seen through Sylvester's deceit from the start but had been all too happy to allow him to hang himself slowly. Sylvester was the type of man who always believed he was the most intelligent man in any room. Such men were rarely correct in their assumptions, and this was one such case. By the time he realized the error of his ways, it would be too late for him to save himself.

"Very well, General Sylvester. If you are giving your word, that is enough for me. You have mine that there will be no attacks against your forces for the time being. You have given me no reason not to trust you to this point. I am assuming you will resolve this matter within a fortnight?"

"I would assume so. The Emperor will be decisive in naming me as Twilcox's successor; I'm sure of it. Once he does, it will not take me long to persuade him of the error of this war. I can be quite convincing when I need to be."

"I do not doubt it, General Sylvester. If you are agreeable, there is one more matter I would like to discuss with you before you take your leave. We continue to hunt for the Imperial soldiers who managed to escape Muog. What course of action would you like us to take once we find them?"

"Kill them at once, but please keep it quiet this time. There will be no need for further public executions. Better if their fate remains a mystery in the encampment. I would ask for their return, but with this treasonous Captain Dunstan involved now, it is hard to be sure how much they do or don't know or suspect. I no longer need them to earn additional favor among the ranks. They are a variable that is too unpredictable to bring into the Imperial camp at this point. Better to put an end to them and remove any doubt."

"As you wish, General Sylvester. I think you are right; I believe this is the beginning of a partnership that will ensure both of us get what we have always wanted."

"When two brilliant minds such as ours come together, is there any other possibility?" Sylvester asked. "Thank you for your time, Chieftain Odpor. When next we speak, it will be to bring an end to this ill-advised war once and for all."

The two Imperials departed without further comments, leaving Odpor feeling more gleeful than ever. He had suspected Sylvester to be a fool from the beginning, but this meeting had confirmed those suspicions beyond any doubt. The death of Cadmus Twilcox had been the death of the Imperial Army, and they just didn't realize it yet.

"What are your thoughts, Krillzoc?" he asked.

"May I speak bluntly, Chieftain Odpor?"

"I demand nothing less."

"I think General Sylvester has managed to get his head so far up his own backside that he would not see the truth of things if we held a massive sign up to explain it for him."

Odpor burst into a fit of gleeful laughter. He had expected to leave the meeting with Sylvester feeling irritated with the man's bravado but found he was feeling quite the opposite. Sylvester's smugness was so absurd that it was downright comical. When the time came, he hoped his men would be able to capture Sylvester alive. If there was ever a man who deserved a few days in Krillzoc's interrogation chamber prior to his demise, it was Alexander Sylvester. But more pressing matters required his attention; there would be time to daydream later.

"Now that the Imperials are gone, how go your preparations for moving against Jezero?"

"The force can be ready to march as soon as tomorrow. Our men have been working day and night to get everything prepared. Iskra will have no answers for our offensive."

Finally, we will put an end to the Resistance. Poor Iskra has no idea of the horrors we are about to unleash on him and his merry band of traitors. The agreement to abide by Sylvester's temporary peace agreement had been an easy decision to make. With Krillzoc and a large portion of his forces away dealing with the Resistance, it was better not to draw the wrath of the Imperial Army. The halt of assaults against the Imperials had already been decided prior to Sylvester's arrival, but what harm in giving the conceited fool another false sense of achievement? It was still improbable the Imperials would ever be able to breach Muog's defenses, but why take the risk?

"Excellent work, Krillzoc. I want you to leave tomorrow and see this matter finished as quickly as possible. The sooner our forces are consolidated back here, the sooner we can give the Imperials the surprise we are preparing for them."

***

Alexander Sylvester waited until they were well into the neutral territory before turning to Terrence Garrison with a broad smile. The meeting with Odpor had gone far more smoothly than he could have hoped. He had feared convincing Odpor to cease hostilities would be like pulling teeth, but the simpleminded dwarf had given in without much in the way of resistance. The man was even more dimwitted than Sylvester had initially suspected.

"Captain Garrison, I believe that went as well as anyone could have hoped," he declared.

"Yes, sir. I was surprised Odpor agreed to your request for peace so easily. Do you think he was being genuine?" Garrison asked.

"Oh, I think he was being quite genuine. Odpor is a fool, but he still has eyes. Even the densest man to ever live could see the dwarves have no hope of winning this war. At best, they can continue to force this senseless stalemate for another year or two, which benefits nobody. I don't think we will see any of their surprise assaults for a while. I am his only plausible path to victory, even if he would never admit it."

To his surprise, Garrison did not appear to be reassured. Was his most faithful servant beginning to doubt him at the moment of his greatest triumph? No, that could not be the case. Garrison was likely just feeling the strain of the past few weeks. It was nothing that his upcoming promotion could not solve. He had already sent the initial paperwork. Garrison's promotion would come soon.

"What will be our first move after your promotion is official, sir?" Garrison asked, catching Sylvester off guard. Garrison was the type of man who was usually content to sit back and await his next orders.

"I plan on drafting a letter to the Emperor recommending the extermination of the dwarves. This war has gone on for too long as it is. We cannot allow it to take any more Imperial lives or waste any more Imperial resources. The Empire needs Qwitzite's resources to begin to recover from the cost of this madness. Millions of crowns have been squandered in this struggle. Twilcox was too weak to see it, but I'm not. We need to bring this province under control, and the dwarves have proven they will never be willing to accept Imperial rule. They have to go."

"You think the Emperor would agree to such a move? While the dwarves have been rebellious, they are still an invaluable workforce. Where will the workforce come from to take advantage of Qwitzite's resources? The Empire depends on them, in the gold and gem mines in particular." Garrison said.

"Where there is a will, there is a way, Captain Garrison. Perhaps we will be able to bring in ogres to work the mines. I assume it's not so much different from the rock scratching they do in Gryttar, and they would even be paid a little for it. If we manage them well, we can assure they never get the same grandiose ideas of independence as the dwarves. One would assume any life outside of a fighting pit would be a desirable-enough existence for an ogre."

"And how will we go about exterminating the dwarves? To date, we have been unable to find a way to breach the walls of Muog."

"I am still working on that plan. I will be requesting additional forces from the Emperor, obviously, but even more men may not be enough. Odpor may open his gates to us in the name of signing a treaty, but I don't think we should count on it. We may need to capture a few of their scouts and torture them into giving up the locations of their tunnels. Such practices are illegal, of course. But what the Emperor doesn't know won't hurt him. Twilcox may have been too weak to do what is necessary, but I assure you I am not."

***

Garrison did not comment further on their walk back to camp, but he was uneasy with the plan. Odpor may not have been a good man, and he may well deserve what was coming to him, but was that true of all the dwarves in Qwitzite? Did every last man, woman, and child deserve to be slaughtered so the Empire could get back to mining and logging in the province? Garrison had not met many dwarves, but he could not imagine that to be the case. As with any other group of people, there would be both good and bad among them. They would all die for Odpor's crimes, and he, Terrence Garrison, would be complicit in their deaths.

They were drawing near to the Imperial encampment when General Sylvester made a comment about being hungry. Ever the servant, Garrison assured the general he would have his supper delivered without delay. He had tethered himself to General Sylvester so many years ago because he believed in the man and the good he could do for the Empire. Was Alexander Sylvester still the same man he had been back then? And if he was, how blind had Garrison been not to see what lay hidden beneath his surface?

Chapter Seventeen

D arian Tor did his best to walk without a limp as he strode into the building where Iskra had summoned them to gather with Resistance leadership. His body still ached with every step, but he was determined to project an image of strength in these trying times. Nearly every dwarf he had passed in the streets of Jezero had beamed at him, some of them approaching to shake his hand and thank him for saving the small girl from the burning building. Each time, his companions shook their heads with exasperation, but in truth, they were all just relieved to see him back on his feet again.

It had been ten days since he had plummeted from that window with the dwarven girl, and each day he had made remarkable strides in his recovery. His body was still in near-constant pain, but the healers who visited daily assured him that he was out of immediate danger. He would likely bear aches and pains from the ordeal for the rest of his life, but he would recover for the most part, thanks to the efforts of the dwarven healers. Captain Dunstan had told him such pains were part of a soldier's life and that he still limped when it rained from a twenty-year-old wound. If you lived long enough as an Imperial soldier, it was inevitable. Such scars were the price you paid for holding on to your life.

Three days earlier, his throat had finally felt well enough to swallow solid food, and he had hardly stopped eating since. His friends had watched in amusement as he had shoveled down helping after helping of everything he could get his hands on. He paid them no mind; if they had eaten nothing but cold mashed-up potatoes and peas for a week, they would be doing the same. He was surprised at how quickly his body had lost its strength, and he was eager to build himself back up as soon as possible.

The evacuation of Jezero had continued, forcing his friends to work extra shifts with him out of commission. He had insisted for the last week that he was well enough to help, but Captain Dunstan had ordered him to stay in bed. Thus far they had spirited over half of the city's population to safety. Darian only hoped there was enough time to save the rest before the inevitable attack came. When Radig had told them of Iskra calling this council, he had not appeared to be in a happy mood but had refused to provide any insight as to the purpose. Was Odpor finally making his move against them? Darian was surprised it had taken so long. What could Odpor have up his sleeve that could take so long to prepare?

They stepped into a large round chamber, finding a massive table at its center with close to a dozen dwarves already seated, including Radig and Kalayo. The Imperials took seats to Radig's left. He nodded at them but otherwise offered no greeting. They had not seen much of Radig since their arrival in Jezero. He was spearheading the efforts to prepare Jezero's defenses for the battle ahead and was usually gone long into the evenings. Once again, Darian wondered if Radig would have done things the same way if he could travel back in time. Would he decide to just leave them in that prison in Muog, waiting for Odpor to murder them one by one? It would have made his own life far more straightforward, that was for sure.

Iskra arrived a few minutes later, his face every bit as grim as Radig's. Whatever the reason for this council, it was nothing good for them. Iskra took his seat, saying nothing as a few more dwarves filed into the room. Darian scrutinized the elderly dwarf, trying to take a measure of him. Despite being an old man, Iskra had always seemed so vibrant, so full of life. Tonight he just looked defeated, slumped in his chair, his eyes on the table. Whatever news he had received was grim enough to deflate the eternally optimistic dwarven leader.

"My friends, I am afraid the news is not good, though I doubt this will come as a shock to any of you," he said when it seemed there would be no more arrivals. "Reports from Muog indicate Odpor is finally making his move against us. At most, we have five days until his attack force reaches us. Estimates place their numbers at close to five thousand strong."

The dwarves in the room erupted as one, each trying to shout to make themselves heard above the others. Iskra allowed them to carry on for a minute, maybe too dejected to try to make himself heard above the mighty din. It was Radig who ended it, rising and roaring for silence before sinking back into his chair.

"I take no pleasure from being the one to deliver this news. We still have a long way to go to get all of our civilians out of Jezero. We need to double our efforts while at the same time ensuring we are prepared to mount the most complete defense possible," said Iskra once silence had been restored.

"Why bother defending Jezero at all? We cannot hold it—not if Odpor is determined enough to slaughter us. At best, we might be able to muster two thousand dwarves to fight, and that is an optimistic estimate," a dwarf opposite Darian said. "We should all flee now."

"Because we need to buy time to ensure Odpor's forces do not pursue those who are fleeing already. If we abandon Jezero, their army will pursue us, and we cannot hope to outpace them with so many elderly and children in our company. We need to put up enough of a fight to convince them they have stamped out the Resistance. Besides, if we can hurt his forces here, we may improve our chances of taking control of Muog," replied Iskra. "If we try to flee as one, with all of our children and elderly, they will run us down and slaughter us before we can reach safety. Better if we fight from a position of strength."

Before he could speak further, another roar of protests rose up, drowning out whatever additional thoughts he may have had. Darian had never been involved in a dwarven gathering of this magnitude; he wondered if they always played out like this. Iskra sat patiently, letting each man and woman speak their mind. Darian was sure such a thing would never happen in an Imperial war council. Anyone trying to talk over a higher-ranking officer would be reprimanded immediately, if not taken out and flogged for his insolence.

"Enough!" Radig roared, once again putting an end to the cacophony of arguments. "The more time we waste here, bickering among ourselves, the better Odpor's position will be. We need a plan, and we need one now. This argument helps nobody except our enemies. We cannot change what is coming our way. We need to find a way to be ready for it."

"Thank you, Radig," Iskra said, asserting himself once more. "Radig is right. We need a plan by the end of the night—not just to survive the attack ahead, but also to put an end to this war. Simply surviving is not enough this time, my friends; we have to make our move. If we do not, Odpor will hunt us down one by one until we are all dead. This is likely to be the last time so many Resistance leaders will be in the same place at the same time. How do we survive the attack on Jezero and then bring the fight to Muog?"

"Do you really think you have enough resources that overthrowing Odpor in Muog is plausible?" asked Captain Dunstan.

"I do not think there will ever be a better opportunity for us," Iskra said, and Darian noted that he had cleverly avoided answering the question outright. "I will not sit here and pretend to be overwhelmed by confidence. But I am unwilling to sit by and allow more dwarves to die in this senseless war for Odpor's pride and delusions of grandeur. He has always been a volatile leader, but this is different. If he is bold enough to dispatch an attack force against one of his own cities, his mental state is declining rapidly. He is becoming too unpredictable to leave in power. We have to try while we still can."

Most of the dwarves around the table were nodding in agreement, though a few still appeared uncertain. Darian was confident he knew the reason for their lack of conviction. It was one thing to say you were willing to lay down your life for a cause when that act seemed far-off and unlikely ever to happen. Most of these dwarves had been living relatively quaint lives here in Jezero. Now, the time when that choice might have to be made was drawing uncomfortably close. When the time came, would they all make the courageous choice? Were they willing to die to see Odpor defeated? Examining them now, Darian Tor was not so sure.

"How would you go about eliminating Odpor?" Darnold Dans asked.

"Yes, Radig, how would we go about doing that? If only we had a man well-placed and close enough to Odpor to do something," said a red-bearded dwarf, glaring at Radig from across the room. Radig opened his mouth to retort, but Iskra waved him down.

"That is not helpful. Radig has always acted in a way he felt was best for the Resistance. Nobody in this room should have any doubt about that. Please, my friends, we must focus. Arguing among ourselves is only weakening our position."

It took a moment for it all to click in Darian's head, but it made perfect sense. Radig had been in a position close to Odpor before blowing his cover to free the Imperial soldiers. It would make sense that he was in that position in the hopes of being able to kill Odpor at the right moment. He had sacrificed not only his own safety but maybe even the future hopes of the Resistance in the name of freeing them. Darian felt his gratitude for the risk Radig had taken grow tenfold.

"It is all well and good to say that, Iskra, but our position has never looked more precarious to me," the red-bearded dwarf muttered, though he did not challenge the old dwarf further on the matter. Radig was still glaring daggers at the dwarf, but he did not say a word.

"If Radig had not come to Jezero when he did, we would not know of the alliance between Odpor and this General Sylvester. I am afraid matters are even worse than we originally feared. Our few remaining sources in Muog report that Imperial Supreme General Cadmus Twilcox has been killed and that Sylvester is likely to take his place."

"But Sylvester has no intention of actually working with Odpor. I think we're all agreed on that. Why not sit back and allow them to destroy each other?" Berj Jenson asked.

"Because Sylvester will not be content with merely killing Odpor and his hard-line loyalists. Do you think your army will bother to distinguish between dwarves who support Odpor and those who do not? Thousands of innocents would die in such a struggle," Radig said. "Odpor would invest no resources in defending them either. Every able-bodied soldier in that city will be forced to defend him and him alone. I am not willing to see civilians die because they are caught in the middle of two power-hungry lunatics."

That did indeed jive with the little Darian had experienced of Odpor. Civilian casualties would not matter any more to him in Muog than they would in Jezero. He thought of only one person when making decisions: himself. If Odpor thought the deaths of thousands of innocent men, women, and children would enable him to hold on to his power, he would make that decision without a second thought.

"So, in other words, whatever action we do take against Odpor, we need to be able to act quickly and with stealth," Kalayo said, speaking up for the first time.

"I think similar action will need to be taken against General Sylvester," Captain Dunstan said. "I do not believe he intends to leave the people of Muog alone, no matter what happens with Odpor. He has his power now, but that's not enough. He will be looking to prove himself in the eyes of the Emperor. He wants to prove his brilliance, and he will do so by putting an end to this war quickly, no matter what that entails. He will move against Muog, and when he does, he will be merciless. There will be no winner. In the end, thousands of dwarves and Imperials will end up dead, regardless of the outcome."

"So, hypothetically, if we are going to succeed, the best thing for us to do would be to eliminate Odpor and General Sylvester at roughly the same time," Iskra said, deep in thought, no longer looking at his hands in dejection. "This would send both forces into disarray. There may be an opportunity to arrive at a truce."

It all sounded good in theory to Darian, but executing such an operation was an entirely different matter than sitting around this table discussing it. While he was more than willing to go after General Sylvester, getting close to him, especially once he had been promoted to Supreme General, was not going to be an easy feat. To do it with such precise timing may well be impossible.

"Maybe we could be of assistance in eliminating General Sylvester," Captain Dunstan suggested, much to Darian's surprise. Dunstan had been supportive of his men and had been very trusting of everything they had told him. But to openly suggest assassinating an Imperial general? That was a different level of commitment. Darian felt a sudden swell of appreciation for the captain.

"Do you think you will be able to get close to him?" Radig asked. "He was plotting to have these men killed, and I cannot imagine he will be overly trusting of you if you turn up out of nowhere. As I recall, you did not exactly have permission to come after them, Captain Dunstan."

"He won't trust any of us, but he will also want to find out what we may or may not know. He will want to know if we are a threat and if we shared anything with Odpor, or vice versa. That could be our opportunity to get close to him," Max Preston said.

It was possible, but Darian was not overly confident. How could they know Sylvester would not have them seized under suspicion of treason immediately upon their return to the encampment? He was a shrewd man, one who had climbed to the top of the Imperial Army through manipulation and backstabbing. He had not done that by being an overly trusting man or by taking unnecessary chances. Arresting them would put him in an awkward position with the ordinary soldiers, but would that risk be enough to protect them?

"I think we are thinking too far ahead of ourselves," Kalayo said. "We have far more immediate concerns. How are we going to defend Jezero from Odpor's forces?"

"First, we will triple the current rate of evacuations. Anybody who is not fit to fight needs to be out of Jezero in the next five days; that is all there is to it," Iskra said, seemingly gaining more confidence as the meeting went on.

"So, we are just going to concede Jezero?" asked the combative red-bearded dwarf.

"I did not say that," Iskra said, his voice taking on a sharp edge for the first time. "We cannot yield Jezero; we have to defend the city as best we can. If we do not, it will tip our hand to Odpor, and he will grow suspicious of what we intend to do. If he does not believe that we are making a valiant last stand here, he will realize we are planning something else. This is not a time to drive him deeper into his paranoia. And as I said earlier, the more damage we can do to Odpor's forces here, the better."

"What is our move, then?" asked Radig.

"They do not have the means to attack us from the lake. They are not going to wait long enough to build enough boats to ferry their forces into the city. The attack will come by land. We will open the trench and force them to pass through it. When the bulk of their forces are in, we will open the floodgates and drown as many of them as possible. Any survivors who make it to the walls, we will hold at bay with archer fire for as long as we can."

"Sooner or later, they will get inside. Sooner, if I had to guess. The walls here are not as formidable as those in Muog," Kalayo said.

"We do not have to hold them at bay for long; we just need to convince them we are trying our hardest. If we can make it appear as though we are just buying time for the last of our civilians to escape, it will not be overly suspicious for them to find the city deserted once they breach the walls. Our remaining warriors can flee under the guise of being terrified civilians. Odpor's forces will not see them as being fit to pursue," said Iskra.

It wasn't a bad plan, especially considering the challenging circumstances. It was unlikely anyone would supply better, and as the seconds stretched on, it seemed nobody was willing to try. Iskra's eyes moved from one face to another, and he never said a word, as though he was trying to measure each man's thoughts. At that moment, Darian wasn't sure he was confident in what his own feelings were. All he knew was that he wanted to save as many innocent people of Jezero as possible and secure justice for Axel. If this plan was the best chance at doing so, then so be it.

"Very well, it seems we have no better suggestions forthcoming," Iskra said, pausing one last time for anybody to speak their mind. When nobody did, he continued. "Now, we need to figure out the next part of our plan. I am speaking, of course, about removing Odpor and General Sylvester from power."

"Getting our fighters back into Muog is going to be no easy feat," Radig pointed out. "It could take as long as a fortnight to have enough inside the city to make a move against Odpor that has any hope of succeeding. I think we can count on increased security along all of the known paths into the city. We will also have to enter in larger groups to reduce the number of trips. If too many of their guards go missing, it will raise too many suspicions, and he will add to his personal guard."

"We have no idea what we are walking into in the Imperial encampment," said Dunstan. "It may take us some time to find a way close to General Sylvester as well."

"We need a specific date and time to put our plans into motion. If we can throw the command structure in both Muog and the Imperial encampment into turmoil simultaneously, we may just have a chance at ending this war," Iskra said, looking around the table for ideas.

"What about the full moon?" suggested Kalayo. "It just occurred a week ago, which means another will not occur for another four weeks. That gives us time to evacuate Jezero, defend it, yield it, travel to Muog, and find a way to get close to each leader."

"It would allow us three weeks after they reach Jezero. It should be enough time, but is it too much time?" Iskra pondered. "We have to find a way to conceal our forces inside Muog, and our Imperial friends have to find a way to avoid drawing the suspicion of Sylvester once they have returned. Doing so for such a long time will be difficult. Still, I have no better suggestions. Anyone?"

Once again, nobody had a better suggestion to offer. It was not a perfect plan—in fact, it had more holes than Darian could ever recall seeing in any other plan—but it was the best they had to work with. He took comfort from one fact. Whether they succeeded or failed, this would all be over in four weeks. Either he would be able to move on into a future after this senseless war in Qwitzite, or he would go down to darkness knowing he had done everything he could to stop it.

Chapter Eighteen

Alexander Sylvester stared down at the envelope, unable to bring himself to tear it open. It was addressed specifically to him and sealed with the wax star sigil of the Emperor, but he still could not bring himself to believe it to be true. Captain Garrison had delivered the letter nearly ten minutes earlier. After asking Garrison to wait outside while he read it, Sylvester had indulged in a glass of his finest wine, wanting to enjoy the moment fully. But now it was here, and he had never been more terrified. He was confident the letter held the news he had been waiting for, but now that the moment had arrived, he found himself plagued by uncertainty.

Was he truly up for this challenge? It was all he had desired since he had been old enough to want anything. But did wanting something badly enough mean you deserved it? Did it mean you were built to meet the trials and tribulations ahead? He had worked hard, and every decision he had made for the past twenty years had been with this goal in mind. Was it enough? He poured himself another glass of wine and drank it down in one gulp before forcing himself to reach out and lift the letter. His hands trembled as he tore the seal and unfolded the parchment. Taking one last deep breath, he began to read.

Alexander,

I was deeply saddened to hear news of the death of Supreme General Cadmus Twilcox. He served the Empire with courage and grace for decades, and I considered him a close friend for much of that time. I will never forget our first meeting shortly after my coronation. I have heard how you rushed to his defense, and I would like to extend my personal thanks to you for your courageous efforts to save his life. If every man in the Imperial Army possessed even half of your courage, we would never need to fight another war. You are truly an inspiration to every soldier under your command, and I hope you will continue to provide this example for many years to come.

While the wound of Cadmus's death is still fresh, there will be another time to grieve. We are still entrenched in a bitter conflict in Qwitzite, one that needs to end as soon as possible so that the Empire can return to a semblance of normalcy. I understand that your fellow officers have placed you in command of the forces at Muog on an interim basis. I could not possibly agree more with this decision. Therefore, I would like to formally extend to you an official offer of promotion to the level of Supreme General of all Imperial forces.

You will be responsible for the current conflict in Qwitzite and all Imperial military operations going forward. If you accept this offer, I look forward to forging a friendship with you as strong as the one I enjoyed with Cadmus Twilcox for over a decade. I believe fate does not make mistakes, and this moment has brought us together for a reason. Together, we can lead the Empire through this conflict and into a new era of peace and prosperity. Please send your response to my offer immediately; we need to have a new command structure in place as soon as possible.

Assuming you accept, please also send any proposals you have for putting an end to this conflict with the dwarves. My latest reports from Cadmus were none too optimistic about the current situation. My understanding is that Chieftain Odpor will not budge from his current position of secession from the Empire, which, I am sure you understand, I cannot allow under any circumstance. To allow the numerous resources Qwitzite provides to the Empire to slip through our grasp would have catastrophic consequences for the entire Empire.

I look forward to reading your acceptance letter and your proposed strategies for resolving the Qwitzite conflict.

~Archer Vladar III, Emperor

Sylvester read the entire letter three times, still not believing it could be true, even though the words were right there on the paper in front of him. This moment did not feel the way he had expected. He had long anticipated a moment of vindication of all of his years of hard work. Instead, he just felt empty, as though he was realizing for the first time how much more work was ahead of him, even once he had reached the pinnacle. If he did not do an adequate job, he would find his hard-earned prize stolen from him in no time at all. There was always another man of ambition just waiting to seize the first opportunity to gain power. *At least you know this. You aren't a naive, trusting fool like your predecessor,* he reminded himself.

"Captain Garrison, can you come back in here please?" he asked, struggling to keep his voice from shaking.

Garrison entered immediately; he must have been waiting right outside, ever the dutiful servant. He did not speak, but his face betrayed his expectations. He had obviously guessed the contents of the letter Sylvester had received.

"Captain Garrison, this letter is from the Emperor. He has formally extended an offer for me to become the Supreme General of all Imperial forces. I intend to write him a response shortly, accepting his offer."

"Congratulations, sir! There is no other man alive who deserves this honor as much as you do," Garrison replied. "It is long overdue. At last, the Imperial Army will be led by a wise commander, one who is willing to fight for the security and prosperity of the Empire."

The words were right, but the delivery felt off to Sylvester. Was

Garrison having doubts about what they were trying to accomplish?

It's your mind playing tricks on you again, you paranoid fool. There is no more loyal servant than Terrence Garrison. He lacks the mental capacity to be anything else.

It was true: he was being paranoid. Was this how it always felt to be in a position of absolute power? To be plagued by paranoia and mistrust at every turn? Setting aside his misgivings, he decided there was one way he could ensure Garrison's spirits would be high.

"That is not the only piece of good news I have to share, Captain Garrison," he said. "Your hard work these past few months has not gone unnoticed. I am pleased to inform you that I am formally promoting you, effective immediately. From this day forward, you will be known as Major Terrence Garrison of the Imperial Army."

Garrison's eyes widened at the news, his cheeks going red. He was silent for a few seconds before finally managing to sputter out a response.

"Sir, you honor me more than words can ever say. I work not for promotions but merely for the good of the Empire. I would never have thought to achieve even the rank I already hold."

"That is precisely why you deserve this promotion, Major Garrison. A promotion that will come with a significant increase in your pay, I might add," Sylvester said, smiling reassuringly. "You serve not for your own glory but for the good of the Empire. If only there were more men such as yourself. We need them, now more than ever."

Garrison still looked uncertain but at least managed to return the smile. Just like the news of his own promotion, Sylvester found Garrison's reaction to be somewhat underwhelming. Convincing himself that such feelings would fade as he grew used to the feeling of his new power, he realized a lot of work still needed to be done. Garrison was likely trying to appear professional, given the gravity of the moment at hand.

"Major Garrison, please fetch me parchment and quill. I need to draft my response to the Emperor right away. Then please carry word to the other officers in the camp of my promotion and that I will hold a war council tomorrow evening at the usual time. I will also be moving into Twilcox's old tent, so if you could please ensure that the remainder of his things are moved out in a timely matter, I would very much appreciate it."

Garrison retrieved the requested parchment and quill, then saluted before setting off to see to the rest of his duties. Once he was gone, Sylvester could not help but wonder again why Garrison had seemed less enthusiastic than he would have expected but again brushed his worries to the side. He had far more pressing matters to attend to than Terrence Garrison's happiness. Sitting at his desk, he began to write.

Your Excellency,

It is with a solemn sense of responsibility and humility that I accept your most gracious offer. When I joined the Imperial Army at the age of eighteen, I sought only to serve my people in any way possible. To stand here now, all these years later, as Supreme General of all Imperial forces is an honor I never sought nor expected. Still, I feel I can do much to benefit the people of the Empire, and so I thank you most sincerely for the faith you have placed in me.

Replacing a titan of the stature of Cadmus Twilcox is a daunting task, but it is one I hope to pursue with honor. I will do my utmost to fill his shoes in a way that would make him proud. I, too, considered him a dear friend and mentor, and his legacy will live on forever. I assure you I will not rest until I have put an end to this war in his memory.

You asked me to send any strategy proposals, and I am happy to oblige. I do not know if Cadmus informed you of this, but I have been negotiating personally with Chieftain Odpor, attempting to find a route to peace between our two sides. I regret to inform you that after these extensive negotiations, I do not feel such a path exists. Odpor is too proud and stubborn to admit defeat, a trait that seems quite common among his people. I do not believe the dwarves will ever lay aside their desire to secede from the Empire.

However, as you have said, this is something we cannot allow. Qwitzite's numerous resources are too critical to the continued prosperity of the Empire. However, as valuable as the natural resources of Qwitzite are, can we honestly say the same about the residents? It pains me to say this, but if the dwarves are willing to see the remainder of the citizens of the Empire suffer, do the dwarves have a place in the Empire? Thus far, our strategy has been a patient one, which is understandable considering the sensitive nature of this conflict. But I believe if we continue along this path, there will never be peace. Even if Odpor were to perish, I feel most of the dwarves would continue to pursue his rallying cry for secession.

With your permission, I will begin aggressive operations to retake control of Qwitzite in the name of the Empire. To be clear, I am proposing the total and complete extermination of the dwarves. Their values and wishes run contrary to the well-being of the Empire, and we cannot allow this to continue any longer. This is a grim proposal, and it is one I take no pleasure in delivering to you. But I believe in my heart that it is more humane than allowing the Empire to suffer through the impacts a prolonged siege in Qwitzite would bring us. With your leave, I will begin operations at once. We outnumber Odpor's forces by the thousands. Muog's defenses are a difficult challenge to overcome, but I will devise a solution and end this siege in short order—I guarantee it.

Once again, I extend my sincerest thanks for this unbelievable honor you have bestowed upon me. I will live every day of my life seeking to live up to the trust you have placed in me. Long live the Empire.

~Supreme General Alexander Sylvester – Imperial Army

He folded the parchment carefully and sealed it. It would not do for any man other than the Emperor to see the words he had written. While most of the men in this army carried no love for the dwarves, the thought of such a genocide would still likely make many of them uncomfortable. They would come around in the end; they would have no choice. In time, he would make them see the necessity of such horrific actions, just as he had seen it from the start. If they allowed the dwarves to continue this rebellion unpunished, how long until the elves followed suit? Or even the dimwitted ogres? A brutal example had to be made of the dwarves. It was the only answer. Seeing the need for such a sacrifice was one of the burdens of leadership.

Major Garrison returned within a few minutes, and Sylvester handed over the letter. Garrison looked at him quizzically as he accepted it.

"This is to be sent by a carrier bird; it is a matter of great importance. See to it that they use the best bird they have to deliver this directly to the Emperor. It is for his eyes only. I have accepted the promotion and included my strategic proposals. The sooner he receives them, the sooner he can approve them, and the sooner we can get started on ending this war."

"Your plan is still the same, sir? To exterminate the dwarves entirely?" Garrison asked.

"Unfortunately, yes, it is. Nasty business, but there is simply no way around it. If we don't send a message here and now, how long until those pointy-eared elves or blue-skinned ogres decide they should also have their independence? We need to be clear about who is in control of the Empire. The dwarves made the mistake of rebelling first, but if we don't end this madness soon, they won't be the last. You and I have much work ahead of us, my friend. We will need to begin devising a way past those walls of theirs."

"Yes, sir. I will see that this is delivered at once," Garrison replied, snapping a salute before leaving the tent. Sylvester paid him no mind as he left, already plotting the end of the dwarven people in his head.

***

Terrence Garrison hurried through the Imperial encampment, his stomach twisting into knots as he walked. How could he be a part of a plan so vile? But how could he possibly disobey General Sylvester, the man who had done more for him than any other? He had come to see Sylvester as a father in many ways. Sylvester had taught him virtually everything he knew about the workings of the Imperial Army and had elevated him to a rank he had never dreamed of attaining. He owed Sylvester everything he had ever achieved.

Garrison dutifully delivered the letter to the camp postmaster, along with Sylvester's instructions that it should reach Valdovas as soon as possible. After he did so, he retreated to the latrines, where he promptly heaved up his meager lunch. Images of the dwarves he had seen on his trips into Muog were swirling through his head. Not Odpor and his men, but the ordinary people going about their business in the streets. They had not seemed all so different from the men, women, and children you might see in any other city of the Empire. Did they really all need to die to ensure the security of the future of the Empire?

After finally finishing in the latrine, Garrison retired to his tent. As a captain, he was entitled to private quarters, which would soon be growing now that he had been promoted, all of it thanks to General Sylvester. He couldn't go against Sylvester no matter how wrong following his orders made him feel. Burying his head in his hands, Terrence Garrison felt the tears begin to stream down his face. It felt like Sylvester was asking him to take part in actions that would cost him his humanity, but how could he refuse?

Chapter Nineteen

Darian Tor stood on the docks overlooking the crystal clear waters of Lake Isabella, wondering if he had ever seen a more beautiful day. As he looked down into the lake's waters, the reflection of the surrounding hills and buildings peered back at him. It was the first time he had visited the shore since the day they had rescued the schoolchildren from the Odpor loyalists. The scene could not have been more different. Last time, the docks had been full of life, countless merchants, workers, and civilians going about their daily business. He had felt like a stranger, invited into another's home but not truly welcome. Now he had the place all to himself. He felt as much kinship to the dwarves of Jezero as he did to most of his fellow Imperials and felt like he would be perfectly content to stay there forever.

Their desperate mission to evacuate Jezero was nearly complete. By the end of the day, every last dwarf who was not involved in the Resistance would be safely spirited away from the doomed city. Odpor's forces were closing in on Jezero quicker than expected, but for the moment, scouts reported that they seemed hesitant to climb down into the trench surrounding the city. They must've realized what Iskra had planned for them and were likely trying to plot a way around it.

"It is a beautiful sight, is it not?"

The voice startled Darian. He spun around, his hand reaching for the pommel of his sword. To his relief, he found it was only Radig. He had hardly spoken to Radig since they had arrived in Jezero; the dwarf was always away on business for Iskra. Just as he had been at the war council, he was reminded that he would most likely be dead by now if it were not for Radig. As he took a close look at the dwarf, he thought he could see numerous new lines crisscrossing his face. These past few weeks had not been easy on any of them.

"It reminds me a lot of my home in Verizia. I had never thought to find a lake like this in Qwitzite. All I knew about this province before coming here was that it was the home to most of the Empire's gold and mineral mines. Imagine my surprise to see a place like this, surrounded by forests. It feels like paradise to me. It makes you realize how similar our people are despite the distance and differences between us."

"Enjoy it while it is still standing. I imagine Odpor's forces will burn Jezero to the ground regardless of whether or not we concede it. We will rebuild it one day after we have removed that lunatic from power. But it will take years, and it will never truly be the same. I wanted to come down here and take one last look at the lake. By the time it is all rebuilt, I might be long dead and gone," Radig said, gazing out across the water.

"We should be down to the last group for evacuation now, right?" Darian asked.

"Yes, just one group left. They are Resistance dwarves, but they are those who have small children. Some wanted to stay and fight, but Iskra would not hear of it. He has no desire to see orphans made of more dwarven children. As soon as Dunstan and Dans return, we will all escort them out. Then you and your friends can begin making your way back to your encampment before the attack comes."

"You will stay here for the battle?"

"Aye, I will. Kalayo left for Muog this morning, and she will begin the work of finding places to harbor the incoming Resistance dwarves. Odpor knows I am a traitor to him now; it will raise suspicions if I am not seen here trying to thwart his assault. I must be seen. It is for the best. I would never want to concede this beautiful city without the opportunity to draw blood from its attackers."

It felt so strange to Darian, staring out at Lake Isabella's tranquility, knowing the mayhem that was about to descend upon this peaceful place. He was reminded of the way he had felt before setting off on their mission into Muog. It was the calm before the storm, and as little as he wanted the peace to end, he would rather the blow fall already and get it over with.

"What are the two of you conspiring about?" Berj Jenson was coming down the dock with Max Preston at his side.

"We were debating which one of you has the ugliest face we've ever seen," Darian quipped, drawing a rare and surprisingly raucous laugh from the normally stoic Radig.

"I would recommend you take a look down at the reflections in the lake," Berj shot back.

"Captain Dunstan and Darnold should be back soon. Dunstan said to meet them here, said something about supplies for our journey," Preston said.

"I changed the plan on that one but did not have a chance to tell him before they set out. I moved your supplies outside of the city walls. I figured if Odpor's forces attack sooner than expected, you will not want a bunch of gear weighing you down as you flee," said Radig. "You can retrieve the supplies once you are clear of the city."

"Smart thinking, Radig," said Berj, clapping the dwarf on the back as he arrived. "That must be why Iskra trusts you with everything. How did the pair of you get into business together anyway?"

"I was a soldier, and I had just been selected to serve as a member of Odpor's personal guard. It did not take long after that. Being close to the man revealed how unfit he is to lead the dwarves. I stood guard in many of his councils, and Iskra was the only one who made any sense among the sycophants and zealots. It is why Odpor gave Iskra command of Jezero: to keep him out of his hair. He did not kill him, which I have always questioned. Odpor has never been one to shy away from making brutal examples of his opponents. I suppose it was out of respect for his late father, who was Iskra's best friend. Or maybe it was simply because of Iskra's popularity among the common people at a time when Odpor was trying to rally support for his secession plan. Who can say what that madman's reasons are? But I was ideally situated to keep tabs on Odpor, and I offered to do so for Iskra."

"Well, you played your part well," Berj said. "I still haven't forgotten how you helped Krillzoc torture us that night."

Radig's eyes shot down to his feet. It was something they had never discussed openly. The mere mention of the torture they had endured made the brand in Darian's skin tingle. It was true, Radig had been one of Krillzoc's assistants that night, though, in Darian's eyes, the dwarf had more than redeemed himself by rescuing them.

"I have done a lot of things in my life that I am not particularly proud of, Private Jenson," Radig said. "All the while, I convinced myself I was serving the greater good. Sacrifices had to be made. But after watching what Krillzoc did to all of you that night, I knew I could not stand in silence anymore. Odpor is too far gone for anyone to reason with him. So, I decided to take action. I am sorry for what I helped him do to you that night, for whatever that apology is worth to you."

Berj did not comment further, but Darian suspected he was not fully satisfied with Radig's explanation from the look in his eyes. He couldn't blame Berj; what they had endured that night had been nothing short of monstrous. Double agent or not, Radig had played his part in it. Radig had just opened his mouth to say something more when the horn rang out from the south.

"That is the signal. Odpor's forces are advancing!" Radig cried, bolting off to the south.

The three Imperials tore off after him without a second thought. There were still children in Jezero, and they needed time to escape. The battle was not supposed to happen yet. How had Odpor's forces gotten past the trench so quickly? There had been no sound of the floodgates opening; what had happened? All of these questions swirled through Darian's mind as he raced through the city, fighting through the aches and pains that still plagued him from his fall.

Once they reached the city's southern edge, Radig led the way into a tall building, making a beeline for a staircase once they were inside. They climbed and climbed for what felt like forever before emerging through a door and out onto the roof of the building. There were about a dozen dwarven warriors on the roof, armed with longbows, Iskra standing in their midst. The Imperials hurried to the edge of the roof, looking out to the south. There was Odpor's army, row upon row of them, no more than two hundred feet from the wall. Darian could tell at once that they must number several thousand strong.

Iskra was gazing out at the opposing force, his face somber. It was the first time Darian had seen the elderly dwarf armed for battle, dressed from head to toe in some of the most beautiful plate armor Darian had ever seen. He clutched a massive battle-axe in one hand, a weapon so heavy it was amazing the old dwarf could still wield it at his advanced age.

"How did they get past the trench?" Darian asked.

"Krillzoc is a clever man," Iskra said. "They brought two siege towers with them, but these were no ordinary siege towers. They were able to tilt them sideways, allowing the army to use them to cross the trench like a bridge. It must have taken quite an engineer to design those towers on such short notice. I remember plans for such a device once. I assume they were kept in the records office in Muog, and Krillzoc must have found them there."

It was unbelievable; their best line of defense had been passed without a single death among Odpor's forces. Their plans going forward depended on being able to inflict damage to Odpor's ability to defend Muog. How could they possibly make a difference now?

"Well, this is not looking good." Captain Dunstan and Darnold Dans had arrived on the rooftop.

"Captain Dunstan, the last group of evacuees is waiting on the second level of this building. Will you and your men please see them safely out of Jezero before making for your camp?" Iskra asked. "Two buildings to the north, there is an underground tunnel that leads far out of Jezero to the east. That is the best hope you have of getting out of the city unseen, but you will have to move fast. Their army is closing in on us quickly."

"We are happy to do so, but what will you do?" Captain Dunstan asked.

"Defend the city to the best of our ability for long enough to be convincing, then—" Iskra began, but he never finished his sentence.

A blast unlike anything Darian had ever heard shook the earth so violently that he was certain for a moment that the building beneath them would collapse. A great wall of flame had risen in front of them and was racing toward the city walls faster than the eyes could follow. How was such a thing possible? The dwarves had proven themselves to be ingenious, but it was still too much for Darian's mind to comprehend. It must've been an act of sorcery; there was no other logical explanation.

The wall of flames reached the walls within seconds, a wailing sound crying out as it reached the stone. The Imperials watched in amazement and disgust as the stone wall simply began to melt from the heat's intensity. The hundreds of unfortunate dwarves manning the wall never stood a chance; the flames had moved too fast, clearing the distance to the wall in the blink of an eye. Hissing, the fire dissipated within a few seconds, leaving behind nothing but a smoldering ruin where the walls of Jezero and the trees beyond them had once stood.

"Captain Dunstan, please go now!" Iskra cried. "Those children must survive. The Resistance will live to fight again; remember our plan. The night of the full moon!"

"Good luck, Iskra. May fortune smile upon all of us. Let's move, men!" Dunstan cried, drawing his sword and leading the way back into the stairwell.

Darian raced to keep up with his friends, his heart pounding. His injuries from the burning building still plagued him, but he forced the pain from his mind, willing his body to move as quickly as possible. Through the open door above, he could hear the rumbling of thousands of feet surging forward. Odpor's army was not wasting any time. They were coming to stamp out the Resistance once and for all. When the Imperials reached the second floor, the evacuees were already waiting by the stairs, drawn out by the sound of the blasts.

"No time to explain! Move, move, move!" Berj Jenson shouted.

The urgency in his voice was apparently all the convincing they needed. The dwarves formed up behind them, rushing down the final flight of stairs. As they broke out onto the street, the sounds of Odpor's advancing forces greeted them once again, much closer this time. In the time it had taken them to climb down from the roof, the attackers had already reached the edge of the city, and they were now scrambling over the charred crumbled remains of Jezero's outer wall.

"Hurry!" Captain Dunstan cried, leading the way toward the building Iskra had indicated. As one, the Imperials and dwarven evacuees raced after him, hoping it was not too late.

***

The situation looked even worse to Radig, positioned back on the roof. He had never seen anything like the attack Odpor's forces had used to breach the walls quickly. Krillzoc was a clever man, but he had taken them by surprise with the flaming assault. Radig could not imagine how long Odpor's enforcer must have spent poring over the records in Muog, searching for just such an attack.

A smart dwarf must have designed that attack a long time ago, probably as a last resort of self-defense. I wonder if they ever suspected it would be used against their own people.

The enemy forces were pouring into Jezero without resistance now, leaving their siege towers behind and surging forward on foot. The dwarves meant to delay them with archer fire from the walls had died instantly in the blazing attack. A few Resistance dwarves fired down into the rush of enemy soldiers from the roof, but they were not enough to even make a dent in the invading forces. Krillzoc had perfectly countered both of their planned defenses: the flooding of the trench and the archer fire from the walls. They had always known the best they could hope for was a delaying action, but now Jezero seemed poised to fall within the opening minutes of the assault.

He thought for a moment of Kalayo, his beloved wife. Almost the entirety of their lives together had been spent in this conflict. They had fought on, knowing that one day they would see an end to it, a path to a normal life. Watching Odpor's forces flood the streets beneath him, Radig realized such a future would never come to pass. He would die here, and he would never see Kalayo again. He would fight until his very last breath, but he would die nonetheless.

He wondered if Kalayo and the Resistance dwarves who managed to reach Muog would be able to kill Odpor. It was a long shot—it always had been—but there was still hope for her and the future of the dwarves. He hoped that would provide a small measure of comfort when the time came to draw his last breath. That time was drawing close. He tightened his grip on his mace. When they came for him, he would take as many of them with him as he could manage. With any luck, maybe he could even crush Krillzoc's skull before he fell.

"Radig," Iskra called to him. "I want you to get out of here."

Get out of here? Was Iskra out of his mind? Even if he could bring himself to flee, which he couldn't, there was no way out now. Odpor's forces were surrounding the building. They would be making their way up the stairs to finish them off at any moment.

"Iskra, take a look around you. There is no way out of this. I will not dishonor myself by trying to flee in vain," he said.

"There is a way, though only for one of us," Iskra said, bending and reaching into a sack at his feet. He withdrew a folded cloth with several long ropes and narrow wooden poles attached to it. Radig had never seen such a thing and watched in amazement as Iskra began to unfold the strange implement.

"Krillzoc is not the only one with an old trick up his sleeve," Iskra explained. "Attach the harness and ropes to your belt and jump from the side of the building, as far as you can. The cloth will unfurl in the wind and slow your descent. The easterly wind should be strong enough to carry you clear of the enemy forces. It is an ancient secret of our people, long forgotten by most. They say some dwarves used to do this for fun, to experience the feeling of flight. They would launch themselves from mountaintops. I brought it today in case things went wrong, though I could never have imagined just how wrong they would go."

"Iskra, you should be the one to use it," Radig protested. "You are the leader of the Resistance, and you are the one who must survive. Our people need you. I will lead the defense to hold back Krillzoc's men and give you a chance to escape."

"I am an old man, Radig. Even if I survive my fall from this rooftop, I would never be able to make it back to Muog alone. They would find me, and I would die a far more unpleasant death than the one that awaits me here. At least here I can die fighting with my axe in my hands and a smile on my face, surrounded by my brothers and sisters. I was the leader the Resistance needed, but my time is gone. You are the leader they will need if they are to succeed in what lies ahead. You must hurry."

Footsteps were echoing through the doorway behind them now. Odpor's forces had finally entered the building. Time was running out, but still, Radig hesitated. How could he live with himself if he fled now, leaving Iskra and the others on this rooftop to die?

"I will dishonor myself forever if I leave you behind," he tried to explain, fighting back the tears that were forcing their way free.

"Piss on your honor, Radig!" Iskra snapped, much to Radig's surprise. He reached out and began tying the ends of the ropes to Iskra's belt loops as he continued. "Does your honor mean more to you than the future of our people? If it does, I will kill you myself, right here and now, and die disappointed to have been so wrong about you. They need you in Muog if they are to succeed. If you die here, they will fail and die there, and that includes Kalayo. What does your honor say about that, you stubborn fool? Now go! There is a strong easterly wind blowing. It will carry you, hopefully beyond their forces. If they see you in the air, they will shoot at you. May fortune smile upon you if they do, because I do not have any other protection to offer you. Once you hit the ground, you run, and you do not stop running! Go, Radig!"

The elderly dwarf was shouting by the time he reached the end of his monologue, the sound of approaching footsteps growing louder by the second. Radig tore his eyes away from Iskra, who was already turning away from him to meet his attackers, his battle-axe clutched in his hand. The tears flowed freely now; he hastily checked the knots on the ropes around his waist as Iskra had instructed. Would this really work? It sounded too ludicrous to be true, but there was no time to wonder about it now. Iskra had never led him astray before. He sprinted toward the edge of the building, never slowing down. He threw himself off the side and into the void, wondering if he would live long enough to regret this decision.

***

Iskra was not watching as Radig went over the edge; his eyes were focused solely on the doorway to the building below. They were coming for him; he could hear them more clearly with each passing second, even with the hearing loss that had accompanied his passage into old age. There was nowhere for him to run, and even if there were, he knew the time for running had passed. He was an old man, and his life had been a full one, most of it filled with friendship and joy. There was only one thing left for him to do. He could only hope his final act could provide hope for those who needed it, for those who still had an opportunity for a better life.

The face that appeared in the doorway first was a familiar one, as he had suspected would be the case. His warriors gathered in front of him, ready to defend him to their dying breath. Their arrows were spent, all fired into the hordes of enemy forces below. *I should have told them to save one last volley for this piece of scum.* With a simple word, Iskra commanded them aside. Of course, they would die with him; there was no helping that now. Still, he would not allow them to die before him. His life was no more important than theirs. It was a belief that had always separated him from Odpor, and it was the reason Odpor could never inspire the love he so desperately craved from his people.

"It has been a long time, Krillzoc," he said as the other man advanced, dozens of dwarves filing out onto the rooftop behind him.

"It certainly has, Iskra. And this will be the last time, unfortunately for you. Chieftain Odpor has decreed there is no need for a trial in your case. You have been sentenced to death for the crime of treason, and I am here to carry out the sentence. Still, there is no need for you to suffer. If you lay down your weapons and kneel, I promise I will do you the honor of killing you with a single clean blow. I suggest you accept this offer; it is more mercy than a traitor such as yourself deserves," Krillzoc said.

Odpor would love that, wouldn't he? To be able to tell the tale of me kneeling down and meekly accepting my fate. A final act of cowardice. But Iskra had no intention of giving Odpor or his sadistic enforcer that satisfaction. He had no fear of his impending death, but he would fight to delay it for as long as possible nonetheless. Rather than dropping his battle-axe, he tightened his grip on it. He had been a skilled warrior in his youth, though he would have been no match for the odds before him even at his absolute prime. But if Krillzoc thought he would cower in the face of such a prospect, he was sorely mistaken.

"I had a different idea in mind, Krillzoc."

"With all due respect, traitor, I am not much interested in your ideas," Krillzoc shot back, along with a sinister grin. "Save the words of your silver tongue for those who are foolish enough to believe them. Unfortunately, there will not be many of them left alive after today."

"Kill me if you must, but at least have the honor to fight me yourself," Iskra said, raising his tone to ensure every dwarf on the rooftop could hear him. "Do not hide behind your men. Step forward and fight me until one of us can fight no more."

"Do you think I am afraid to fight you, old man?" Krillzoc was openly laughing now.

"If you are not, then come here and prove it!" Iskra shouted for all to hear, stepping forward.

Krillzoc hesitated despite his bravado. Iskra couldn't help but smile in satisfaction. Krillzoc was clearly wondering if his adversary had one final trick up his sleeve. Iskra did not, but he was happy to let Krillzoc wonder. But there was no escape for Krillzoc. Iskra had issued a direct challenge in front of all of Krillzoc's men. If Krillzoc turned away from that, especially from such an elderly foe, he would never have the respect of his men again. Even now, every second he delayed was a black stain on his reputation. Seeming to reach the same conclusion, Krillzoc drew his sword and began to advance once more, calling for his men to stand down.

If I can at least kill you, I can go to my grave happy, thought Iskra.

Krillzoc attacked first, stepping forward and lashing out with a vicious three-strike combination that would have skewered a less experienced fighter. Iskra may have been old, but his reflexes had not yet left him entirely. He evaded the first two strikes and deflected the last, his massive battle-axe sending Krillzoc's sword careening away harmlessly. Iskra counterattacked with an attack powerful enough to cleave a man in two, but Krillzoc was too quick on his feet, stepping away with ease.

Krillzoc came in more aggressively now, seeming to sense that Iskra had no more cards to play. If all the old man had to offer him was an honest fight, there was no reason for Krillzoc not to finish matters quickly. He hacked and hammered with his sword, stringing attacks together at lightning speed. Twice his sword broke past Iskra's defenses but glanced off of the elder's plate armor, careening harmlessly away. Iskra struck back with everything he could muster, struggling to drive his massive axe past Krillzoc's defenses with brute force, knowing the younger dwarf was far too fast for him to outmatch. But Krillzoc was too good, batting away and evading Iskra's attempts with relative ease.

"You are too slow, old man," Krillzoc taunted, growing more confident with each passing second. "Too old, too slow, and too weak. What did you think was going to happen here? Did you really think you stood a chance against me? Did you think the power of your self-belief would be sufficient? Your arrogance is a wonder to behold."

"You fight for your leader, Krillzoc. You fight for one man, a man unworthy of the devotion you have shown him. You do so for nothing more than the desire to fulfill your own ambitions and for the pleasure of the cruelty he allows you to inflict on others. I fight for my people. I fight in the name of every last man, woman, and child in Qwitzite and their right to be free of the tyranny you and Odpor have thrust upon them. And when you fight for something more than yourself, you can achieve amazing things."

Krillzoc started to laugh, his cunning yet simple mind unable to wrap itself around such an idea.

Let's see how hard you are laughing after this, Iskra thought, gathering himself for one final attack. He sprung forward, moving faster than he had in fifteen years, his axe lashing out toward Krillzoc's head. Krillzoc sidestepped the attack, the sneer still etched across his face. The sneer was erased a moment later as Iskra brought his other hand around, clenched in a tight fist. His heavily armored hand collided with the side of Krillzoc's head with sickening force. A collective gasp sounded out from the dwarves behind each fighter.

Krillzoc recovered quickly, though his left eye was already swelling shut, the bone surrounding it likely broken. He brought up his sword, no longer playing games, ready to put an end to Iskra once and for all. Iskra did not raise his axe to defend himself this time. Instead, he opened his hand and let it clatter down to the rooftop. In the end, he would not allow Krillzoc to have the satisfaction of having bested him in combat.

Snarling, Krillzoc stabbed forward, driving his sword through a gap in the plates of Iskra's armor and deep into his chest.

It did not hurt—not like Iskra was expecting. To his surprise, he felt a strange sense of relief washing over him. His work was done, and now he could finally rest. He felt the life fading from him surprisingly fast, though he felt he had the strength to do one last thing. Reaching into his belt, he drew a small dagger and lashed out one last time in the direction of Krillzoc's sneering face. His vision was going black, but he heard a distant cry of pain as the last ounce of life faded from his body. Iskra collapsed to the rooftop, a smile etched across his face as he drew his last breath.

***

The Imperial soldiers raced down the stairs to reach the tunnel Iskra had directed them to use, but the sounds of pursuit were never far behind. Darian Tor forced himself to set aside his aches and pains, focusing on continuing to put one foot in front of the other. Still, the futility of their situation was quickly setting in on him. They would not be able to keep up this pace for long, especially the children, and when they slowed down, they would die.

What was the point in getting through the tunnel if they brought this pursuit with them? But at the same time, Darian knew there were not enough of them to turn and fight. He had only glanced back a few times, but it had been enough to reveal that their pursuers had them vastly outnumbered. They reached the tunnel, finding it was only wide enough for about four people at a time. The Imperials stepped aside, allowing the dwarven evacuees to go ahead of them.

"We aren't going to get much farther like this," Preston gasped, his eyes turning toward the sound of pursuing footsteps on the stairs above.

"We're getting those kids out of here. We told Iskra we would, and we will," Berj Jenson said, drawing his sword. "You all go on, and I'll stay here and hold them back for as long as possible. At least the tunnel is narrow enough that I can buy you a few minutes."

"That's not happening," Captain Dunstan snapped, turning back.

"Yes, it is, Captain Dunstan. There's no time to argue about it. Those people need you, and you all need to get back to camp if we want to have any hope of ending this war. I'm staying right here and making sure those children escape. Any of you who wants to try to stop me will have to kill me. Now get out of here!"

Darian was speechless. Berj Jenson had come to Qwitzite with little in his heart but disdain for the dwarves, yet here he was, ready to lay down his life to save theirs. He couldn't leave Berj behind; they had to stay and fight together, all of them, just like they had promised when they left the training complex in Salvamoan. No sooner had the thought passed through his head than Captain Dunstan was shoving the rest of them ahead. Darian looked over his shoulder one last time to find Berj smiling as they moved away from him, a sword in one hand and a dagger in the other. Then he turned away from them, turning to meet their pursuers, their footsteps thundering closer by the second. Unable to hold back his emotions, Darian cried as he ran.

***

When Odpor's forces reached the bottom of the stairs and entered the tunnel, Private Berj Jenson met them like a wild man, even by his standards. Sergeant Harter Arsch had told him numerous times throughout his training that his reckless fighting style would get him killed one day. He had never expected to meet that death with open arms, but here it was, and he had no intention of backing down from it. He would fight until every last one of the bastards trying to kill those dwarven children were dead or he was.

The dwarves Krillzoc had sent to pursue them were hardened killers, but not one of them had ever encountered a man like Berj Jenson. He slashed out at anyone who came within range of his sword, paying absolutely no regard to his own safety, bellowing taunts and insults at them all the while. He received numerous wounds in return, but it didn't matter. Within moments, he could taste his own blood, but it didn't matter. He lost his dagger, unable to pry it from the eye socket of a fallen foe, but it didn't matter. His vision began to blur, and he was unable to clear it, but it didn't matter. He was ready to die in this tunnel, and nothing they could do to him before that would stop him from fighting.

"Come on, you bastards! Kill me if you can!" he screamed, releasing every primal emotion he held inside his body. "Eat mud, you bunch of sniveling cowards!"

In the end, Berj Jenson didn't know how long he fought. He didn't know how many foes he'd slain, but they were numerous, forcing their comrades to scramble over their bloodied corpses to try to get at him. The weight of his injuries took its toll on him slowly, driving him to his knees, but still, he fought on, slashing upward at his oncoming enemies. At last, he could fight no longer, the numerous injuries overcoming him at last, the sword falling from a hand that had gone limp. He collapsed forward into the darkness, the final thought to dart through his mind that he hoped his sacrifice had bought his friends enough time to escape.

Chapter Twenty

The sun was beginning to fall out of sight on the western horizon as Darian Tor and his fellow Imperial soldiers said their goodbyes to the refugees from Jezero. They had made their way through the tunnel safely thanks to the unbelievable courage and selflessness of Berj Jenson's sacrifice. As soon as they had emerged from the tunnel into the forest east of Jezero, the dwarves had gone to work on collapsing the tunnel behind them to prevent Odpor's forces from following. Darian had initially been livid, screaming in protest, thinking they were trapping Berj below the ground with their enemies. But Captain Dunstan had stepped in to calm him, and Darian had been forced to grapple with the truth. Berj would not be joining them again, tunnel or no tunnel. The fact that Odpor's forces had not caught up to them already was all the proof they needed of that.

They had marched northwest ever since, determined to see the dwarves safely away from the bulk of Odpor's army. They had encountered no resistance in the forest, though as they marched, the unmistakable stench of smoke rose into the air behind them. As Radig had predicted, Odpor wanted Jezero to burn to the ground. They marched on, refusing to look back at the city each of them had fallen in love with as it was destroyed.

They marched in silence, not wanting to betray their position to any enemy forces that may have been nearby, but in truth, they had nothing to say. The loss of Berj had been shocking and sudden, along with everything else that had happened that day. Darian felt numb to it all. For the first time in days, he felt no physical pain, though he suspected this was his body's way of protecting his mind from being overwhelmed by everything that had occurred over the past few hours.

As they said their farewells, each and every dwarf thanked each soldier individually, expressing their sorrow about Berj's death. It was the first time it had been acknowledged out loud since leaving the city, and while it hurt for Berj's friends to hear it, they each maintained their decorum. The dwarves set off to the north, hoping to reach refuge in Dranath near the border with Floresta, and the Imperials continued eastward, hoping no pursuit would come after them or the dwarves Berj had given his life to rescue. Captain Dunstan led them, not explaining their route, and none of them cared enough to ask. As Darian saw things, their route didn't matter. All that mattered was eventually finding their way back into the Imperial encampment. When they did, they could finally begin forming their plan to kill Alexander Sylvester. *And you will die, Sylvester,*Darian promised himself. *For Axel, for Berj, and for every Imperial soldier or dwarf who has suffered for your pride, you will die.*

They continued well into the night, pushing through their exhaustion. They didn't want to keep going, but they all knew it was necessary. There was no way to tell if Odpor had soldiers in these woods, searching for survivors of the attack on Jezero. They needed to put as much distance between themselves and the city as possible.

The first hints of dawn were beginning to creep into sight on the eastern horizon before Captain Dunstan finally brought them to a halt.

"We will rest here for a few hours, gentlemen. Odpor's forces might still be out searching, but we've covered a lot of ground. We need some rest, or we will collapse long before we can make it back to camp. Just try to keep your eyes and ears alert."

Darian collapsed to the ground, not caring about rest but knowing Dunstan was right. Darnold Dans immediately set about searching for some sort of food in the surrounding trees. There had been no time to retrieve the supplies Radig had left for them outside the walls of Jezero. They had been in too much of a hurry to escape the falling city. Tarrying too close to Jezero during the attack would likely have been the end of all of them.

Sitting still for the first time in nearly a day, Darian wondered what had happened to Radig, Iskra, and the rest of the dwarves on that rooftop. Odpor's forces had descended upon the city so fast; was it possible any of them had managed to escape? It seemed unlikely.

"There are a few mulberry trees over here," Darnold said. "It's probably the best we're going to get for now."

Realizing for the first time how famished he was, Darian forced himself back to his feet and walked over to join the others. They ate their fill of the berries and passed around Max Preston's canteen, the only one with any water still in it. They ate and drank in silence, each man lost in his own thoughts. Darian wondered if they were all thinking of their memories of Berj Jenson, the same as him. First Axel, now Berj. It was so bitterly unfair that he couldn't stand the thought of it. Why should they have died while Odpor, Sylvester, and Krillzoc continued to draw breath? It seemed like a lifetime ago that they had been standing on the shore of Lake Isabella, full of hope for the future and a sense of satisfaction at having saved so many dwarves.

"What are we going to do when we get back to camp?" Max Preston asked as they finished eating. "Sylvester is going to be suspicious of us, especially you, Captain Dunstan."

"I've spent much of the past week wondering the same thing," Dunstan said. "Every time I think I've found an answer, I find a flaw in it. Unfortunately, I don't think we're going to have an answer until we arrive and see what type of welcome is waiting for us."

"Why don't we just walk in and shove one sword up Sylvester's rear and another down his throat?" Darian asked, not even certain himself if it was a joke or not.

No one replied right away, Darnold and Preston averting their eyes from him. He felt much the same as he had in the days after Axel's death: angry and in need of vengeance. He had found purpose in helping all of those innocent dwarves escape Jezero, but that purpose was gone now. Any small victory they might have achieved felt hollow in light of the events of the past few hours. Once again, all he wanted was to see those responsible for his friends' deaths answer for their crimes.

Captain Dunstan had not looked away; rather, his eyes stared right into Darian's. He would be suspecting what was going on in Darian's head, of course. Their conversation in Jezero had revealed how attuned Dunstan was to his men's feelings. He might even have been feeling similar emotions.

"Unfortunately, Private Tor, I don't think that is a legitimate option," Dunstan said.

"Maybe not, but I wish it were," Darian muttered, turning his eyes toward the ground, doing his best not to scream out in frustration.

"Do you think anyone from the Resistance escaped?" Darnold asked. "Things on that rooftop did not seem promising. By the time we reached the ground, Odpor's forces were already closing in on that building."

"I think some of them must have; I can't bring myself to believe otherwise. Even if they didn't, Radig said Kalayo had already gone ahead to Muog. She will do her best to kill Odpor, along with whatever Resistance dwarves are left. I think the best thing we can do is proceed as planned unless we discover something that tells us otherwise," Dunstan said.

"So, we try to execute a coordinated time-specific mission without even being certain if the other party is still on board? Or even still alive for that matter?" Preston asked.

"I think killing Sylvester without killing Odpor as well would be a temporary solution at best," Darnold said. "As long as Odpor is determined to secede at all costs, they will keep fighting, and the Emperor will just appoint a new commander to lead the war. Would he be a better man than Sylvester? Probably, but that doesn't mean the war would end anytime soon. We need the dwarves in Muog to want peace for this to work."

He was right, but Darian was still uncertain. So much had gone wrong in the span of a few short hours. His life, ever since he had decided to join the Imperial Army, seemed cursed. How had everything gone so awry? What possible hope was there for them going forward?

"How are you going to explain your absence?" Darnold asked. "You're potentially going to be viewed as a deserter."

"I haven't quite figured that part out yet," Dunstan admitted. "I almost think it might be better if I don't come back into the camp with you. You can tell them I died trying to rescue you or that you have no idea what happened to me at all. I could possibly hide nearby and join you on the night of the attack."

"What if Sylvester has talked to Odpor again? If so, he might have heard about you appearing in the fight when we escaped. I don't think they will fall for that," said Preston.

So the debate raged on until it was time for them to resume their journey south. Questions were asked, with no answers produced. It would take them several days to reach the Imperial encampment. Darian hoped they would be able to think of better alternatives by then. They were too caught up in the whirlwind of everything that had happened to think logically. There was only one thing of which he was sure: come the full moon, all of those who had led them down this path of death and destruction would face justice, no matter the cost. Sylvester, Odpor, Krillzoc, all of them. He would accept nothing less.

If you enjoyed my dad's book, please consider leaving a review! All of the book money goes to my chew toys and treats! Thank you! ~ Teddy

Acknowledgements

I told you the last time out that I didn't expect the wait for this book to be very long. I hope you would agree that I have been a man of my word this time around. I hope you enjoyed reading about this part of Darian's journey as much as I enjoyed writing about it. There is one more installment yet to come in this trilogy, which you can expect to see in the spring or summer of 2025. Then, the Thrawll Saga shall continue onward with another trilogy! What am I working toward with all of these trilogies? I suppose you will have to wait and see, but if you pick up the final book of this set, you may just find a hint or two! As always, there are so many people to thank for helping to bring The Soldier's Anguish to life!

Natalia Leigh of Enchanted Ink Publishing, always my editor extraordinaire! She's always there to point out when I'm repeating myself or slipping into a conflicting POV. You cannot begin to imagine the mess these books would be without her talents! Natalia, I hope to keep you busy for many books to come!

My cover artist and one of my oldest friends, Joseph Gruber. I really love what he is doing with this trilogy, and I think this might be my favorite cover yet! Joe, you manage to top yourself every time, and I can't wait to see what's next! He's also an incredibly talented 3D printing artist, go check out his work at Spagooters 3D!

Mercedes! My bride, my rock, and my other half. One day, maybe I'll figure out how I got so lucky, but for now, I'll just keep rolling with it.

Thank you, my love. Thank you for everything, but above all thank you for being who you are!

Finally, if you're still reading, I really need to thank you! As long as you keep coming back for more of these, I will keep writing them! Your support and readership mean more to me than you will ever know. Until next time!

~Pete Biehl

About the Author

Pete Biehl is a lifelong lover of stories who always felt the pull to create his own. When not sitting in a room by himself and making things up, he enjoys traveling, gaming, and searching for his next read. He is currently hard at work on the next installment of his epic fantasy series *The Thrawll Saga*. He lives in Idaho with his wife, dog, and so many rescued/spoiled cats.